"Dare has a knack for romance and spins an engrossing tale."—*Publishers Weekly*

PRAISE FOR THE NOVELS OF JUSTINE DARE

High Stakes

"It is always an extraordinary treat when a new Justine Dare book is released. You can always bank on Ms. Dare to deliver an outstanding and exciting reading experience."
—*Romantic Times*

"Intensely passionate characters. . . . Fast-moving, suspenseful."
—The Romance Reader

Night Fires

"Intrigue and mystery permeate *Night Fires*. Once again rich characterizations and emotional depth lift Ms. Dare's tales to memorable heights."
—*Romantic Times*

continued . . .

D1400270

Dangerous Games

"*Dangerous Games* is going to win much acclaim for Justine Dare. The lead characters are a wonderful couple and the villain is as deadly a killer to come along in a novel in a very long time. . . . Ms. Dare has dared to raise the quality level [of] rousing romantic intrigue."
—*Midwest Book Review*

"This is a page-turner, with an emotional and sexual intensity that makes it stand out from the crowd."
—Under the Covers

"When it comes to intrigue, passion, and deft character-izations, no one delivers like the incomparable Justine Dare. Stake out your local bookstores today, so you won't miss getting your copy of *Dangerous Games*."
—*Romantic Times*

"A dynamic page-turner!"   —Catherine Coulter

Dangerous Ground

"Dark, mysterious, erotic . . . wonderful."
—Elizabeth Lowell

"Your pulse will pound and your blood will sizzle . . . the very best suspense."   —*Romantic Times*

AVENGING ANGEL

Justine Dare

AN ONYX BOOK

ONYX
Published by New American Library, a division of
Penguin Putnam Inc., 375 Hudson Street,
New York, New York 10014, U.S.A.
Penguin Books Ltd, 80 Strand,
London WC2R 0RL, England
Penguin Books Australia Ltd, Ringwood
Victoria, Australia
Penguin Books Canada Ltd, 10 Alcorn Avenue,
Toronto, Ontario, Canada M4V 3B2
Penguin Books (N.Z.) Ltd, 182–190 Wairau Road,
Auckland 10, New Zealand

Penguin Books Ltd, Registered Offices:
Harmondsworth, Middlesex, England

First published by Onyx, an imprint of New American Library,
a division of Penguin Putnam Inc.

First Printing, December 2002
10 9 8 7 6 5 4 3 2 1

 REGISTERED TRADEMARK—MARCA REGISTRADA

Printed in the United States of America

PUBLISHER'S NOTE
This is a work of fiction. Names, characters, places, and incidents either are
the product of the author's imagination or are used fictitiously, and any
resemblance to actual persons, living or dead, business establishments,
events, or locales is entirely coincidental.

ACKNOWLEDGMENTS

There are people who come into your life and make a difference, people who are so very special for so many different reasons. People who are always there, or people who are in the right place at the time when you need them the most. Some say they are only doing their job, yet they do it in the best possible way, and in that alone make a difference. Some begin as strangers doing a job, but end up as precious friends.

As someone who desperately needed some of those kinds of people in her life recently, I want to thank them all. Not just the doctors, who usually get their thanks firsthand, but the frontline people, the people in the trenches, the ones who make the day-to-day differences. There are more than I could ever list here, but to begin:

Pamela, ICU nurse extraordinaire, and one of those most precious friends who was there when we needed her. Again and again and again.

The North Kitsap Fire paramedics, who have twice come through for us like the heroes they are.

The ER and Neurosurgery staff at Harborview Medical Center, Seattle.

Eric, visiting ICU nurse extraordinaire; it's a great gig and you play it well.

Alicia, Neuro ward nurse, who personified caring.

Josie, rehab nurse in name, guardian angel in fact. Neither of us would have made it without you.

The entire staff of Martha and Mary, Poulsbo.

Anne, Diane and S.K., therapists par excellence, helping us make those first steps back into life.

The entire staff of Harrison Silverdale Rehab.

And most especially Dr. Susan Shlifer, that rare and treasured kind of family physician, the kind with a passion for her patients and her work that gives you hope and peace.

> *Our eternal and heartfelt thanks to all of you.*
> *We still have a very long way to go, but when we*
> *make it, it will be thanks to all of you.*

PROLOGUE

"Never again." The voice was low and harsh, the words fierce. "You will never hurt a woman again."

"What the hell are you talk—"

The blade glinted as it moved closer to the man's throat, and the angry flow of words stopped with a gasp. Silence, broken only by harsh breathing, descended, the kind of silence only the night can bring. The man's feet scraped on the asphalt of the deserted parking lot. The light from the pole towering above was yellow, casting a sulpherous sort of glow. The silence made him even more aware that there was no one around, not even another parked vehicle awaiting its owner, no hope of help. He was in the middle of civilization, yet as alone as if it were wilderness. Except for the apparition that had loomed up out of nowhere, as if it had materialized out of the shadows.

"You know what I'm talking about. You've escaped justice too many times. You will not escape again."

"Look, whoever you are, I never—"

"Your lies will do you no good now. You've lied to the police, to the court, and probably to yourself. But now you will face the truth."

A shudder went through the man. He was beginning to believe.

"Look, she drove me to it—"

The blade drew blood. It trickled down the man's neck.

"That is the biggest lie of all, the lie of making it your victim's fault. They are innocent, *you* are the guilty one. It is *you* who is rotten to the very core. And it is you who will, at last, pay the price."

Pressure, unrelenting, impossible to resist, began on the arms trapped behind him. Pain shot through him, and tears filled his eyes. It kept on, and he had no choice but to fall to his knees. The rough texture of the asphalt dug into soft flesh.

"That's where you belong," the voice said. "On your knees, begging for forgiveness. Beg it from your God, because you won't get it from me."

"But I never meant to really hurt—"

"Another lie. You knew what you were doing. The pitiful, small man you are has to feel bigger by exerting power over those smaller or weaker. How does it feel to have the tables turned? To be the weak, helpless one, your life in another's hands?"

The man croaked out a sound that might or might not have been a word.

"You have another lie to tell?"

"No . . . I . . . I'll never . . . I promise . . ."

"You promise you'll never beat your wife again?"

"Yes, I—"

"And how many times have you made that promise before?"

"But this time I mean it, I—"

"As you meant it when she came back to you, against all advice, and within minutes you slapped her?"

The man went very still. "How could you know that? Who *are* you?"

The laugh that came from above his head was triumphant, joyous, and terrifying. "All you need to know is that I am your final judgment come to life."

The man thrashed again, trying to escape the steely hold. There was desperation in him now. Hands grabbed at the blade, a futile effort. Blood ran down helpless fingers.

The sound that escaped the man now was a whimper. "Please—"

"Are you afraid? You should be. By rights, you should live a very long time in fear, as those you damaged were forced to. But I can't indulge in that much balancing of the scales, so you get off much too easily."

His hands were suddenly released, the blade lifted. "My God," he whispered, sagging in relief. He brought his hands in front of him, easing the ache in his shoulders. He rubbed at his wrists, shakingly thankful that it was over at last.

He had misinterpreted the words, as intended. He thought he was going to live.

"My God," he said again, and as a moment passed with no response from his captor, his mind flicked to the woman who had caused all this. Had she hired this crazed avenger? She must have, how else would he know those details? If she thought he'd let her get away with—

"How quickly you forget." The harsh whisper struck a chill through him; it was as if this dark phantom had read his mind. "You go ahead and pray to your God. You will have to tell your lies to him now. He is waiting. See if he believes you."

"Wait!"

"Pray to him. Now. It's the only thing left to you." The knife was at his throat once more. "Pray! Your hands in front of you, like the good boy you never were."

He went rigid again, panicking now. "No, don't, please!"

"You want more time? I'll give it to you. I want you to think of your wife, the last time you battered her into unconsciousness. Think of the last time you kicked her so hard you broke her ribs. Think of what the decent world considers you, trash not worth sweeping up off the street. Do you have any idea how revolting the rest of the world finds you?"

He struggled again, flailing wildly.

Laughter, strong and relentless, rang out in the darkness. "Had a little accident, did you? Wet your pants like the bully you are? What a perfect ending. And the perfect way for God to send you straight to hell."

He shuddered. "No, please, you can't do this!"

"Give me one good reason. One reason that will make up for what you did to the ones you were supposed to protect."

"It wasn't my fault!"

The blade edged forward. Blood flowed.

"The last cry of the trapped coward. But now you're going to do what you should have all along."

"I'll do anything, I swear—"

"Not anything. One thing. What any real man would do for his family."

"I'll do it, I promise!"

"Yes, you will."

"Tell me, just tell me what to do!"

That laugh again, triumphant now. "Why, you'll die to protect them, of course."

The blade flashed, bit, slashed. Blood gushed. Then pumped. The gurgling sound was grim, final. Severed vocal chords were useless. The man flopped like a landed fish. Then slumped, dying, released at last from the steely grip. His killer knelt beside him and reached for the trophy, the symbol taken from them all, stripping it from the dead man's wrist before rising and looking down at the prayerful corpse.

"Vengeance may be the Lord's, but payback is mine."

CHAPTER 1

The newspapers were calling him "The Avenger." The women at Rachel's House were calling him an angel.

Deep down inside, beneath her natural repugnance for violence, Regan Keller was experiencing a sense of satisfied retribution she wasn't sure she was proud of. Just as she wasn't sure she was proud of the fact that what mattered to her most was that the killer not be one of her women.

"Good morning!"

The cheerful hail from their neighbor, Mr. Pilson, seemed jarring after her grim thoughts. The thin, wiry man was unfailingly chipper, to the point of being annoying. But he was so good about having Rachel's House as his next-door neighbor, always willing to lend a hand, that she didn't want to be rude.

"Good morning, Mr. Pilson. How are you?"

"I'm fine, just fine. Good news this morning, isn't it?"

She blinked. "What?"

"Another piece of slime cleaned off our streets."

A little stunned at their bespectacled neighbor's rather cold-blooded observation, she was glad to be saved from trying to answer when his telephone rang and he retreated into his tidy little house. In a way his reaction was comforting, but it was also unsettling.

She picked up the newspaper, still warm from the California morning sun, and looked at the picture on the front page.

The victimizer becomes the victim. . . .

She'd have to tell Dawn. The coroner's deputy who had called this morning—as an ex-wife Dawn didn't rate a personal visit—had offered to tell her, but Regan had said she would do it. She didn't want the already unsteady woman to hear it that way, from a stranger over the telephone.

Nor did she want her to just see it in the newspaper, which the deputy had warned her already had the news. When she'd agreed to be the director of Rachel's House, she'd agreed to all that came with it, including dealing with fragile psyches. And Dawn's was definitely fragile.

Regan wasn't sure what this news would do. Most people on the outside would assume it would be good news; with her abuser dead, her hell was finally over. But most people hadn't been in Dawn's shoes, with her world ordered, controlled, and consumed by her husband. Convinced that it was love. That that's what love was.

But if she'd stayed with Art any longer, Regan knew Dawn would likely be dead.

Now *he* was dead. And there was no denying the pattern that had formed.

"Regan?"

She nearly jumped. She turned to look toward the kitchen doorway, where Marita Bowers, who had been at Rachel's House the longest, was standing. Once a strikingly beautiful woman, her loveliness was now marred by the crooked line of her nose, broken once too often by her brutal ex.

"Yes, Marita?"

"Dinner at six, or should we plan for seven, give time for Amber to get here?"

Regan knew Marita was being optimistic. The chances of Amber Winn returning to the shelter that had given her a brief respite from her boyfriend's abuse were slim to none. Regan had learned to judge such things over the years. That Amber might be unable to come back was something Regan knew she didn't have to bring up. These women had lived Amber's life; they knew too well how fragile it was.

So all she had to decide was if it was better for them to maintain the fiction for a while, or face the truth now: after twenty-four hours Amber wouldn't be coming back.

When in doubt, go with the truth, she told herself.

"Six," Regan said. Marita hesitated, then nodded. She turned toward the kitchen, then stopped and looked back. Her gaze flicked from Regan to the newspaper she held, then back.

"Another one?"

Of all the women at Rachel's House, Marita was the most stable. She had come a long way since her

arrival several months ago. She was, Regan
thought, the least likely to fall apart. Or fall back,
back into the life she'd escaped.

"Yes," she said.

"Number three."

Regan nodded. A third brutal murder that everyone, despite the caution of the police, knew was
connected to the previous two. They had to be connected. Every victim had been male, and according
to the news story, the only common thread between
them was that each had at some time been charged
with domestic abuse.

There was another factor they had in common,
something Regan doubted the reporters knew. But
she knew. She knew, and it put her in a very difficult place.

She suppressed a shiver. So much was at stake
here. There was too much invested in Rachel's
House, in too many ways, to make a hasty decision,
to do what her instinct said and call the police immediately. So, she thought, perhaps she should
start by calling the person who had made the
largest investment. Rachel's House wouldn't exist,
after all, without the money behind it, and the person whose dream it had been. And if that dream
was now threatened, it only seemed fair to—

"Not mine, I suppose. I'm not that lucky," Marita
said, looking at the newspaper with a grimace.

Regan understood the woman's biting sarcasm
completely, but didn't answer. She couldn't tell
anyone before she told Dawn, not even Marita,
who had become her unofficial assistant.

Marita had left behind one of the most brutal

men Regan had ever come across. She'd only seen
Daryl Bowers once, when she'd gone to court with
Marita for moral support, but she knew his heart
and his twisted mind by what he had done to his
wife. The memory of the woman's face, battered
and swollen, the cast upon an arm broken for a
third time in a year, would stay with Regan for the
rest of her life.

She hadn't understood then. She'd simply been
so angry, not just at Daryl but at Marita for going
back to the man. It had been a major turning point
for her to understand that Marita, like many
women who stayed with batterers, honestly believed she deserved no better.

But Marita was going to make it, Regan thought
with grim determination. She would not accept any
other alternative.

"Girl," Marita said, "you've got that look on
your face again."

Regan blinked. "What look?"

"That 'don't cross me' look. That 'I don't care
what you say I'm going to make it happen' look."

Regan didn't think she should admit her
thoughts had been aimed at Marita herself. And in
reality, Regan knew that Marita's battle was her
own to fight. All she could do was make sure she
had the time and space—and the safety—in which
to do it.

"I envy you that," Marita said, her voice very
soft. "And what you've got inside that lets you
look that way and mean it."

Marita retreated to the kitchen, leaving Regan
feeling a bit like a spoiled child. Her life had held

tragedy, but it had been a festival compared to Marita's. Until the day she had come home to her apartment and found her best friend's dead eyes staring at her from the bloody mess that had once been her face.

Rachel, for whom this place had been named.

Rachel and Regan, sisters by choice.

Even now, eight years later, Regan's stomach churned and a cold sweat broke out on her skin. She stood up, overcome by the need to move. She walked to the window and looked out, not really seeing.

She lowered her gaze to the fresh bouquet of flowers Mitch Howe had clipped from their own garden and brought inside, as he did every morning. The gardener was a treasure left them by the previous owner of Rachel's House. He'd worked there for years now, and had taken the change from a private residence to a woman's shelter completely in stride. He'd even been willing to share his twenty years of gardening experience with the residents. It gave them something else to think about, something to care for that wasn't any kind of a threat to them. For some, the gardening lessons were the first step along the long road back to a normal life.

Regan glanced at her watch. Mindy should be back by now from the part-time job the Rachel's House Next Step program had found for her. Regan went into the living room, a big space with a sofa and an unusual number of chairs, placed there for the frequent free-for-all talk sessions. One corner held the well-used computer; E-mail was often the only safe way for the women of Rachel's House to communicate with their families. Each of them had a mailbox, set up to receive mail only from selected senders, and outgoing mail was untraceable, protected by an expensive firewall.

Next to the front door was a clipboard with the current residents' code names—a security measure Regan herself had instigated—and a sign-in and -out space. Mindy had signed out at seven-thirty this morning, but hadn't signed back in yet.

Regan's stomach knotted. She verified the time. In less than five minutes, Mindy would be half an hour overdue. That was the deadline for being late without calling and verifying you were all right.

Regan walked quickly toward her office, already thinking of the encrypted computer file where she kept the records of the women's various employers, including the phone number for each. She dreaded calling, in part because it called more attention to the person trying so desperately to live a normal life, but mostly because there was always too big a chance the worst had happened.

There was another possibility, though, she thought. Quickly she looked up the number in Mindy's file and called. After several rings, a man answered. Regan could hear talk and metallic sounds in the background, and guessed he was in the garage where his truck was housed.

"Marty? This is Regan Keller."

"Hi," Mindy's brother replied. "How are— Is something wrong with Mindy?"

"No," she said quickly. "She's just a little late, and I thought she might have come by to see you."

"No," he said, and Regan heard anger building in his voice already. "Damn it, if she's with that bastard again—"

"There's no reason to think that, Marty," Regan assured him.

"He lays a hand on her again, I swear I'll kill him!"

Regan felt a chill sweep her. She told herself Mindy's brother was just angry, and rightfully so. Still, something in his voice made her wonder just how angry he was. Angry enough to kill? To have already killed?

"Maybe I'll go find him right now, and make him pay for what he's done. The courts never will."

"Marty, no, you can't do that."

"I will," he raged. "Nobody gets away with treating my sister like that. I'll hurt him worse than he ever thought of hurting her."

"Marty, calm down. You won't do Mindy any good by getting yourself arrested again."

"I don't give a damn about that. He deserves to die, and if I have to—"

She heard a noise at the door. "Marty, wait."

Regan looked over her shoulder, and with relief saw the petite, fragile-looking blonde come into the room.

"Marty? It's all right, she's here now. I'm sorry to have bothered you."

"She's all right?" Marty sounded only slightly less furious.

"She's fine," Regan assured him. "I'll have her call you later, okay?"

As she hung up, she wasn't sure he was much

calmer, but she had to deal with Mindy. The girl paused in the entry, fumbling with purse, sunglasses, and keys. She turned and took a shopping bag from Mitch, who had apparently stopped his hedge trimming and held it for her while she opened the door. Then the girl spotted Regan and grimaced.

"Yeah, yeah, I know, I cut it close."

"I'm just glad you're all right. I bothered your brother, and I was about to call your work."

"God, don't do that. Nobody but my boss knows, y'know, and if you start checking up on me all the time . . ."

"It's the rule, Mindy," Regan reminded her patiently.

The girl made a face. "Yeah, well, it's a pain, always checking in, having you on me if I'm a little bit late. How's that any different from what I left?"

Regan said nothing, just looked at Mindy steadily, letting her words hang in the silence. The young woman, barely out of her teens, wasn't doing well with house regulations. Not because she wasn't used to rules—her boyfriend ran or had run her life on an iron schedule—but because she hadn't quite given up on the idea that he might really change this time. That was always the hardest fantasy to give up.

Regan wondered if maybe they'd pushed her too fast, if she wasn't ready for the next step in Rachel's House. Perhaps she should still be in a full shelter.

After a moment, the girl lowered her eyes. "I'm sorry. I didn't mean that."

"I know you didn't."

"I just . . . it seems so . . . I mean I know it's so I'm safe but . . . the reason I was late? I saw Joel."

Regan stiffened. "You what?"

"I didn't talk to him, or anything. But he was driving by when I left work."

Coincidence? Regan doubted it. "Did you call the police?"

The girl cringed. "No. I couldn't, Regan, I just couldn't. So I went back in and left out the back door. He never saw me." Tears welled up in her eyes. "But it was so hard. If I hadn't known it would just about kill my brother, I'd have gone to him. Joel swears it'll be different if I just give him another chance."

"Another chance to put you in the hospital?" Mindy's hand shot up to her temple, where Regan knew the headaches she still got were centered. "Is that what you want? You want Marty to have to come visit you in the hospital again? Maybe get so angry that he gets into trouble again?"

Her brother had already been arrested. After the incident that had put her in the hospital, he'd cornered Mindy's boyfriend and threatened him with a torque wrench.

"Especially now," Regan added, "when the police are looking for somebody with a reason to kill abusers?"

Tears began to brim in Mindy's wide, baby blue eyes. "No," she said. "But . . ."

"I know it's hard," Regan said. "So hard to believe the man you love will never change. But you've already given him half your hearing in one ear. How many more body parts are you willing to sacrifice in the hope that he'll keep the promise this time?"

"But you don't know him, he can be so sweet—"

"He *has* to be sweet, Mindy. That's what makes it work for him. He has to be charming, sweet, and contrite, and do it believably. Maybe he even believes it himself. Until the next time. And there will be a next time. There always is."

But Regan knew Mindy still hadn't given up hope, and until she did, she was in danger of going back to Joel Koslow.

Regan watched the girl gather her things and trudge upstairs. Regan went over and pulled the front door closed, sighing wearily. She couldn't put it off any longer, she had to tell Dawn. And she had no idea how the woman would react. Relief or hysteria, it could go either way. Or perhaps both, when she learned her violence-prone husband had paid the ultimate price, just like the two men before him.

She hadn't been surprised when she'd read about the first murder, a few weeks ago. Cal Norman had been a cold, vicious man who had never given up trying to find his ex-wife. Just two weeks before he'd been killed, he'd taken Rosa's family hostage, trying to get them to tell him where she was. Eventually he'd found her, and her death had been violent, bloody, and horrifying.

When the second murder had happened, her first reaction had been relief. Marcia had left the shelter and gone back to Rod just days before, and he had already begun the endless cycle of abuse again. But before he could seriously hurt her again, he was dead.

Her second thought had been that the police would be showing up soon. But they hadn't, which had puzzled her.

And now Dawn's husband.

It couldn't be coincidence. Regan had sensed that even before this killing. Deep in her gut, in that same place that told her to watch out for that guy across the street, or that the noise in the night hadn't been just the wind. That place so many women were taught to ignore. That thing called, too often belittlingly, women's intuition, that warned you when you were in trouble, even if you didn't think you had a single concrete fact to back it up.

She had to tell Dawn the news, and then she had to make that phone call to their benefactor, their prime supporter. It was only fair. After that she had to prepare herself, and the residents of Rachel's House. Because she knew it was only a matter of time.

Soon, the police were going to be knocking on their door.

Alex Court spotted Grimm the moment he stepped into the terminal. He knew what was coming. His mother's long-time aide-de-camp was never far from her side. He eyed the tall, cadaverous-looking man as he approached. As a kid he'd always thought of Grimm as his mother's version of Lurch, from the Addams family, complete with appropriate name. He had nearly been caught countless times imitating the man's lumbering gait and deep, spooky voice behind his back. And to this day he made Alex feel, even at six-one, short.

Alex dispensed with the formalities, as he knew Grimm preferred. "Where is she?"

"She is waiting in the VIP lounge," the rusty-hinge voice said, gesturing Alex toward the concourse walkway. "She leaves for New York in half an hour."

"Wants to make sure I don't have time to argue, doesn't she?" He tried not to look like he was having to push to keep up with Grimm's long strides.

"Mrs. Court does not like wasting time."

"And arguing with her is definitely a waste of time," Alex said.

"Precisely."

"I don't suppose you have any idea what this is all about?"

"I do."

"What, then?"

"That's for Mrs. Court to explain."

He should have known better, Alex thought. Getting more than a sentence at a time out of the taciturn Grimm had been a lifetime challenge that had rarely been met by anyone except his mother. The only time he recalled it happening was the day his father died.

"What if I hadn't already been on my way home?"

"Then she would have summoned you."

Alex got the message. And he knew the man was right. His mother wouldn't have ordered this hasty meeting if it hadn't been urgent. But he was tired after flying across the Pacific Ocean.

"I just flew nearly nine thousand miles, a lot of it in a puddle-jumper plane. I spent three hours in the

airport in Seoul, and my brain still thinks it's tomorrow morning. Cut me some slack."

"It's a short step from slack to slacker," Grimm
intoned imperiously.

Alex groaned. "Where *do* you come up with
those things?"

Grimm made a nasal, grunting sound that indicated he was through with the exchange. Alex let it
go, knowing better than to try to pry out anything
more. Grimm had worked for his mother for as
long as he could remember, and when he was done
talking, he was done talking.

A blast of air-conditioned air hit the back of his
neck as they walked into the airline's VIP lounge.
He didn't mind; the jungle he'd left had been in the
mid-nineties, coupled with the added joy of ninety-
five percent humidity. He couldn't wait to get out
into southern California's drier air.

His mother was on the telephone, deep in conversation with, Grimm told him grudgingly, someone from Aurora Technologies, the troubled
software company CourtCorp had a controlling interest in. She glanced at him, but made no more acknowledgment than to look at her watch. But to his
surprise, she ended the conversation abruptly and
hung up.

"Sit down, Alexander. We don't have much
time."

"Nice to see you, too, Mom," he said as he
stretched his legs out gratefully. She was her usual
perfectly attired self, in a navy suit that showed off
the trim figure she worked hard to keep. The short
businesslike haircut made her look younger than

her sixty-two years despite the pure white of her hair. It suited her, as did the discreet display of gold at her throat and ears. "Will I be going to New York with you?"

"No. The problem is here."

"And the problem is?"

"Murder."

Alex's grin faded as he stared at his mother. "What?"

Lillian Court grimaced. "You heard me."

Alex straightened, shifted to the edge of the seat, and leaned forward. "Who got murdered? Someone from CourtCorp? When? By who?"

"Three people, no, within the last seven weeks, and that's why you're here."

It only took him a split second to work out the four answers, and when he did his brows furrowed. Not at the idea that his mother would send him out after a murderer, but why they were getting involved at all.

Outside, he heard the muffled announcement that her plane had arrived at the gate. Grimm walked away without a word.

"The police don't generally care for civilians tromping through the middle of their investigations," he said, his tone neutral.

"I trust you to handle that appropriately. And you won't be in the middle, not really."

Alex studied his mother for a moment. She was a master at hiding her emotions when necessary, but he was her son and he could see that she was deeply troubled.

"What is it?" he asked. "If it's not our people, why is this your personal concern?"

She took a thick manila file folder out of her briefcase, the battered, distinctive, initialed case that had been his father's. In the beginning she carried it, she had told him, as a subtle reminder to those who might underestimate her that the power that had once been Edward Court's was now hers. Now, when no one in their right mind would doubt her authority, she carried it simply because she was used to it.

She handed the folder to him. "Those are the clippings on the murders, plus everything Research was able to access. You will find that the . . . victims all had two things in common."

Alex didn't miss the change in his mother's voice on the word "victims." He tapped the folder with a forefinger. "Save me some time."

"They were all abusers. Each one of them put a wife, girlfriend, or their own child in the hospital. Some repeatedly."

"And somebody's paying them back?"

"So it seems."

"What do the cops say?"

"Officially?"

Alex's mouth quirked up at one corner. "Unofficially. I assume officially is in the file and I'll get to it."

"The murders were all committed within a fairly small area, and each body was found in a very public location."

"Meaning they were supposed to be found?"

"One assumes."

"They're up to three bodies, the official standard, so any feds involved?"

"Not yet. They're not even officially agreeing the killings are linked, despite the similarity of method."

"So they haven't got a solid suspect yet?"

"No. Chief Raines says the killer is very good, and very careful."

Alex knew his mother was on good terms with the local police chief. She had been instrumental in helping the city put together the deal that had drawn the man to Vista Shores from Arizona.

"By the way, Chief Raines also said he's considering forming a task force, calling in help from the county and other agencies."

"Not a bad idea. This is a bit much for our quiet little town to handle, and it could help stall off the demand for him to call in federal help."

"He hasn't decided yet, but I thought you should know."

Alex nodded. "You said they had two things in common."

"Yes. I got a call this morning from Regan Keller, the director at Rachel's House."

Rachel's House was, Alex knew, the battered women's shelter his mother funded. She provided the operating budget, ran interference with bureaucrats if necessary, and took a close personal interest in the entire operation.

"And?"

"Each of the murdered men's victims are or have been residents there."

Alex's brows rose, and he drew back slightly. "Do the police know?"

"They should by now. I told Regan to call them."

"Good. They'd find out eventually, and it would look pretty bad if she had withheld that information."

His mother nodded. "That's what I told her. She already knew she was going to have to call them, but she wanted to talk to me first. I appreciated that."

"Looks like you were right about her."

"Yes. She's smart, and competent."

"And she's dedicated to your cause," Alex pointed out.

"It's her cause, too. But most important, she doesn't panic in an emergency. Now, the police will no doubt want all the Rachel's House records. I want you to see that one of our lawyers handles that process. I don't want to stand in the way of the investigation, but I won't have those women endangered unnecessarily."

Alex nodded just as Grimm returned from the gate to announce they would begin boarding momentarily. Alex suspected this had all been perfectly timed.

"So, what am I supposed to do that the police aren't doing?" he asked.

"The police are focused on finding the killer."

"I would hope so."

"I want you to be at Rachel's House."

Alex blinked. "What?"

"I want you to be there as much as possible with-

out raising suspicion. I want everyone there protected."

Alex hesitated. Rachel's House was his mother's
most passionate cause, so he chose his words carefully.

"Am I missing something? It seems for once it's
not the women who need protecting here. Not," he
added quickly, "that I'm saying guys like that deserve protection."

"Protected from everything," she amended.

He got it then. "You mean keep them from being
intimidated by any overzealous investigators?"

"Chief Raines assures me his best people are on
it, but I want to be sure those women don't have to
face this ordeal alone. I've arranged for you to take
the place of a workman they're already expecting."

"Mrs. Court?" Grimm asked, stiffly formal as always. "They are finished preboarding, and are
boarding first class now."

She stood up, nodding. "Alexander is just leaving." She looked back at her son. "Gerard"—his
mother was the only one who called the re-
doubtable Grimm by his first name—"will give you
any details that aren't in the file. I want regular reports. I'll be at the Marvilles' flat when I get to London."

Alex sighed and gave in. It would be nice to be
home for a while.

"When will you be back?"

"Ten days."

He got to his feet, wished his mother a safe trip,
and headed for the door. Then she called his name.
He stopped, looking back at her.

"Be careful," she said. She seemed to hesitate, so odd in his decisive mother that he took a step back toward her. She waved him off.

"Just don't forget there's a killer out there."

She knew the moment she heard him that it was going to happen again. His voice had that edge, that biting, angry tone that told her he was looking for someone to take his anger out on. And that someone was always her.

She wondered what it was this time. Instinctively she reviewed her own actions since she'd last seen him, searching for anything she could have done that would have set him off. She couldn't think of anything, but then, she rarely knew what would hit him wrong until it was too late.

Perhaps someone at the office had given him some sass, or the parking valet hadn't treated his precious new car with the proper respect. Worse yet, perhaps the mail carrier had bent the corners on his precious golf magazine.

The string of invective that he poured over her doused any tiny hope she had left. She knew the way things would go now. Knew it too well. When the curses finally slowed, the beating would begin. And only after that would she find out what she'd done. And by then she wouldn't care.

"You stupid, fat bitch, you knew I'd find out. I always find out. You know you're not smart enough to hide anything from me."

She stayed silent, knowing that even trying to speak in her defense—although she still had no idea what the charge was—would only antagonize him faster. Pointing out she was not fat, but thin to the point of emaciation because she couldn't keep food down, would have the same result.

Getting to her feet would likely get her killed.

She waited. Seated. Head bowed. She knew the drill.

He came to a halt before her. So close all she could see were his knees, clad in the expensive silk blend fabric of his suit.

"I told you what would happen the next time you tried anything, didn't I?"

She held her breath, trying to decide if now was the time to begin the inevitable process. But she couldn't do it. She'd been too long out of the habit of making decisions.

"Didn't I?"

He was towering over her now. He was so much bigger than she, so much stronger. And like in any part of the animal world, the biggest and strongest always won. Any nature show could tell you that.

Out of the corner of one eye she saw his hands flexing, fingers curling. Soon they would be fists. She saw the glint of light on the huge, showy diamond ring he wore. Could almost feel already the tearing of her flesh as the cold, impervious stone ripped through her skin.

"You didn't really think you could get away with it, did you? *You?*"

She felt herself begin to shut down. Preparing. Not bracing, for it did no good. Not even trying to figure out what she'd done this time. She'd given up on that long ago.

"Do you really think he wouldn't tell me? Don't you know you can't hide from me?"

She knew that. Too well. She'd tried so hard, wishing she could simply disappear, even if it meant she could never return. Surely just . . . ending would be better than this.

"Where did you get the money?"

Money? She had none. Ever. He saw to that.

"Did you steal it?"

She recoiled. *As if she'd have the nerve to steal.*

"You forgot who runs this house, didn't you? You forgot who you answer to."

"I could never forget."

It was tiny, pitiful, certainly not worth what happened next. She knew it would be the trigger the moment she whispered the words under her breath, but they escaped anyway.

She saw him move in the instant before pain flashed in her head. She felt her body lift, but didn't try to catch herself before she hit the floor; it would only enrage him further. She tasted blood, her familiar companion. Not the worst blow she'd felt in her life with this man she'd once loved, and who had once sworn to love and honor her, but far from the lightest, if there was such a thing.

"Get up."

She couldn't move.

"I said get up! Get up and explain to me how you dared do this."

She knew she would pay for it, but she simply couldn't move. And in the next moment she saw his leg move. She cried out before his foot even made contact, knowing the fierceness of the pain to

come. It exploded in her chest as his foot connected. She felt the fire spread, knew he'd at least
cracked a rib this time.

"I was stupid," she croaked out, taking a wild
stab at any words that would placate him. "Please,
I'm sorry, so sorry, I'll never do it again." Her
pleading was simply fuel to his fire.

"You're damned right you won't, you stupid
bitch."

He reached down, grabbed her arm, and yanked
her to her feet. She screamed as agony seared her
side. He slapped her, the other side of her face this
time. Then the first again. She felt her lip split, and
realized with bitter irony that she was silently tally-
ing how long she would have to hide indoors this
time.

Push him, she told herself. *Make him madder, mad
enough to put an end to this forever. Do it.*

She couldn't. She didn't have the courage. She
was vaguely surprised she'd even had the nerve to
think it.

"—know you are never to do that. I decide what
William gets, I decide when, and I give it to him."

*William? This was about their son? Something she'd
done for their son?*

But she hadn't, she knew better, she— Dear God.
The crayons? It couldn't be. Could it? The child had
wailed for them, in the grocery store, and to quiet
him—the last thing she'd needed was for *him* to
hear about a scene in a public place. So she'd put
them in the cart, with barely a thought for the fact
they hadn't been on the list he always prepared for
her. It was for his son, so he wouldn't get mad.

Or so she'd thought.

She had to ask. She knew better, but she had to ask, had to know if her life had truly deteriorated to this. Stealing from him, when all she'd done was buy their son the simplest of toys? But then she remembered what he considered stealing; anything that involved her making a decision on her own, even if it was to spend less than a dollar on something he hadn't approved.

"The crayons? You can't be talking about the crayons?"

At her disbelief, his anger erupted. He hit her again, and again, and again. She knew this was going to be the worst of all, wondered if perhaps he would truly kill her this time. And for the first time in a very long time, she cared. She didn't want him to kill her, not now, because she was feeling something she hadn't felt in so very long . . . anger.

It was the smallest of flickers, a tiny flame deep inside that place where she buried all thought of unfairness, but it was there, and it warmed her.

CHAPTER 2

Detective Lynne Garrison finished transcribing her notes, then sat back in her chair, tapping her lips with her forefinger. Regan Keller hadn't sounded happy during the call Lynne had just finished documenting for her report. The woman had frankly confessed she was torn, and Lynne had understood. Regan wanted to protect her residents, but her father had been a cop.

They would have discovered the connection to Rachel's House eventually, but they'd just been saved time that was precious in a case like this one. Up until now, they'd been reduced to trying to track down every person who had ever threatened an abuser, and there were so many of those it could take them until Thanksgiving.

"You ready, Garrison?"

Ben Durwin's words were laden with sarcasm and abrasiveness. At fifty-three, he was the crankiest man under seventy she'd ever known. Lynne was thankful they were only assigned together temporarily for this case.

Of course, being assigned to a serial killer investigation when she was supposed to handle sex crimes and domestic violence was a trial by fire in itself. But that's what happened in a small department that didn't have a dedicated homicide detective. Everybody had to pitch in.

"In a minute," she said. She walked off without further comment, ignoring his grumbling as she headed for Captain Greer's office. The door was open, so she paused in the doorway.

"Captain? Got a minute?"

The detective division commander looked up, a smile creasing his dark face. "Lynne, good. I was about to come looking for you. This came in." He handed her a file.

The moment she opened to the first page, she knew what it was. She didn't need to look at the boldly scrawled signature to confirm it. There was only one homicide expert from the sheriff's office who could also provide them with a profile on their serial killer. It was almost inevitable that Drew would get involved.

"Good," was all she said. "I'll make sure Ben reads it, whether he believes in them or not."

Greer smiled, and Lynne wondered if he was relieved that she hadn't reacted. If he was, he didn't say so, only asked, "What did you need?"

"Do you remember a cop here named Keller, from a ways back?"

John Greer laid down the pen he'd been holding. "Patrick Keller?"

"I'm not sure. Daughter named Regan?"

Greer nodded. "God, yes. Pat Keller. Damn fine

cop, and a better man. He was killed, line of duty, must be fifteen, twenty years ago now. Boy, time flies." He frowned. "His kid's not in trouble, is she?"

Lynne thought better of pointing out that Regan Keller was hardly a kid anymore. "No. She called me about the case. She's running a battered women's shelter now."

Greer looked thoughtful, then nodded. "That wouldn't surprise me. I remember Pat talking about how she was always bringing home injured animals. And after he bought it that way . . ."

Lynne lifted a brow at him.

"It was a four-fifteen family," he said. "A chronic disturbance, one we'd been to a dozen times. We'd arrest the guy, but the woman kept dropping the charges and taking him back. This was back when the victim had to prosecute."

Lynne frowned. "He bought it on a domestic violence call?"

"He was first on the scene, and never had a chance. The guy came out firing. Pat took him out with a shot to the head, but it was too late. By then he was hit."

Lynne shuddered. It was every cop's nightmare. You rolled on so many family disturbances that turned into nothing, you couldn't help but let down after a while. You couldn't psych up for the worst every time. But it only took once. One time when you weren't ready, and the worst really did happen. Then your friends were listening to taps, "Amazing Grace" on those mournful pipes, and a motorcade of cops was saying good-bye to another member of the family.

"There's something else," Captain Greer said, brows furrowed, "something about a friend of hers being murdered by a boyfriend, too, while she was in college. I can't remember any more details."

"Well, that'd be enough to give you a cause," Lynne said.

Greer nodded. "It's probably her way of coping. If you talk to her again, tell her hello. God, I remember her and my boy playing in our pool, seems like just the other day. In fact, what's the name of the place?"

"It's Rachel's House . . ."

"Sometime today, Garrison! We've got people to see!" Ben yelled across the detective division office, then stalked out the door toward the parking lot.

"He getting on your nerves?" Greer asked when Lynne winced.

"Only when I bring them."

Greer grinned. "You know, he's not really a sexist, he hates everybody. Until you earn his respect."

"I may not live that long," Lynne said dryly.

Greer laughed, and waved her out of the office. She headed toward the door Durwin had used.

"Hey, honey, want me to knock the old geezer on his butt for you?"

Lynne turned to look at Nick Kelso, auto-theft detective extraordinaire. Tall, blond, good-looking, Nick was the division charmer and knew it. He considered himself gallant as well, always offering to slay dragons—or anything else that bothered them—for just about any woman he met.

"No, thanks, Mr. White Knight. I'm saving the pleasure for myself."

Lynne wondered how the world could produce two such different men, grumpy Ben and charming Nick.

What I should be wondering about is how the world can produce men who batter the people they supposedly love, she thought as she trotted down the outside stairs to the secured lot where the department vehicles were parked.

She knew it was her job to find who was killing those men. She would do her job, as she always did. It was just that this time, some of her enthusiasm was missing.

"I know . . . you think . . . I'm crazy, especially after last week, but . . . I . . ."

"I know," Regan said, her voice quiet, soothing as Dawn hiccuped between her sobs. The petite brunette was usually lovely, but weeping had reddened her hazel eyes. "It's all right to cry. You still loved him, a little bit."

"I know it's stupid, but . . . he could be so sweet."

"Yes, he could." *They all could*, Regan added silently.

But right now all Dawn needed was comforting. "It's natural to feel this way. You spent nearly six years with him, since you were twenty. He was a big part of your life, even if sometimes a bad part."

There was a gentle knock at the door to Dawn's room. Dawn shuddered, and pushed bangs that were too long back out of her eyes. She sniffled, wiped her eyes, and seemed to try to pull herself together.

"Dawn?" The voice from the other side of the door was tentative but familiar.

"Mitch," Regan said. "Shall I let him in?"

Dawn nodded, wiping her eyes again. Regan rose and opened the door. She was met by a sweet scent and a huge spray of flowers, arranged in a jar with the gardener's usual artful touch. He was nice-looking in a quiet way, of average height, but strong and fit from his work. He was also deeply tanned from his work outside, with mouse brown hair that took on a golden glint in the summer sun.

"I just thought these might help," he said.

"Thank you," Dawn whispered.

Mitch set the jar down carefully on the dresser. Then he looked at the weeping woman. "It will be all right," he said.

Dawn nodded, and gulped. "I— I know, Mitch."

Regan smiled at him, and squeezed his arm in silent thanks. He smiled back at her, gave Dawn another concerned glance, then left, easing the door shut as he went.

Regan looked back at Dawn, who was staring at the bright, cheerful bouquet.

"Do you want me to stay, or would you rather be alone?"

"Alone, I think."

But when she reached for the doorknob, Dawn stopped her. "Regan?" She turned back. Dawn hesitated. She bit her lip, then asked, "Was it really . . . that killer?"

"That's what they think."

Another moment passed. Then, in a very low voice, "It's hard to know how to feel."

"Free," Regan suggested. "But that doesn't mean you can't be sad, too. Any death deserves that much. And to you, this wasn't just any death."

For just a moment Dawn met her gaze. "You really do understand. But you've never been there."

"Someone very dear to me was." Regan pulled open the door, then added pointedly, "And she wasn't as lucky as you. We had to bury her."

Regan closed the door quietly behind her, leaving the distraught Dawn to her thoughts. She really did understand. She knew how it worked, that a woman in even the worst kind of relationship could be so desperate to salvage it she would sacrifice anything. Her health, her life, sometimes even the lives of her own children.

She sighed as she headed back downstairs. So many nights she had sat up with Rachel, listening and trying to be supportive as she talked about how Carl could be such a nice guy, and how sure she was he would be again, as soon as he worked out what was bothering him. When all the while Regan had been silently screaming, "Wake up! He's not going to change. This is who he is, who he'll always be!"

But the one time she had said it aloud, Rachel had gotten furious with her, and it had taken a long time to mend the rift. They had mended it, but three months later, Rachel was dead. Brutally murdered by the man she'd always defended.

So this time the bad guy paid, Regan thought as she

opened her office door. She felt that same sense of grim satisfaction that had bothered her before.

"She talked to him again, you know."

Regan snapped out of her reverie. Mitch was plucking fading petals off the arrangement on the credenza behind her desk. He made sure fresh flowers were always added every day, so in effect Regan had a never-dying bouquet. It was a touch of beauty in what could be a grim house at those times when the occupants lost sight of where they were going in the horror of where they'd been.

"She what?"

"I heard her. On the phone with him. Just yesterday."

Regan went still. "Who called who?" Not giving out this phone number was one of the strictest rules of Rachel's House, right after not letting anyone pick you up or drop you off. And if you took a bus, it had to be at least one stop beyond the closest one. Regan hammered on those rules constantly, and on the fact that a violation didn't endanger just you, but everyone here.

"I didn't hear it ring, so I think she must have called him," Mitch answered.

"When?"

"Yesterday. She was planning to meet him again."

Regan's brows furrowed. Voluntary contact with your abuser was cause for serious reevaluation of resident status. Rachel's House was the next step beyond a safe house. While it still protected women the same way, it was for those who had made the break and were ready to move on, to rebuild their lives. They tried to accurately guess when a woman was ready to make the break, but sometimes they were wrong.

The women were taught skills if they had none, prepared for job hunting if they did. They acquired experience, often in a Court company; Mrs. Court's involvement and generosity was on all levels. And Regan hated to see it go to waste when she misjudged someone.

"You're sure she was going to meet him?" Regan asked. She hated to think Dawn would risk it, knowing she was up for review because of the last contact.

"From what I heard, there was no doubt." Mitch's brown eyes were wide and troubled. "Why do they do it? Why do they go back?"

Regan let out a weary sigh. "I could give you all the standard reasons, no confidence, financial dependence, self-esteem so low they're convinced they deserve the abuse—"

"But you give them all that here. You give them a way out, and they still go back to those mutants."

Regan gave him a flicker of a smile. The name Mitch always used for the abusers was appropriate, she thought. "Some just can't break the pattern," she said. "But some make it, and that takes more courage than most of us will ever have. And you help them find it, Mitch, with the time you spend with them, and"—she gestured at the flowers—"in making this place a little brighter."

For a moment the gardener just looked at her. Then he smiled warmly, and Regan smiled back.

"I've got this cleaned up now," Mitch said, gesturing at the arrangement. "My mother always says you should keep them nice or throw them away."

"It's lovely, Mitch. You be sure and take your mom some, with our love."

His eyes grew even warmer, as if the bad things had been forgotten. "I will. She'll like that."

The man took his plucked petals and left the office. Less than a minute later he was back, looking flustered. "There's a strange man outside."

Regan tensed immediately. Her first thought was always that one of the women's exes had found them.

"Is it the police?" she asked.

Mitch blinked. "The police? No, no, I don't think so. He says he's here about the roof."

"Ah." Regan relaxed. "The roofer. I've been expecting him." She'd warned the residents he'd be coming today, but hadn't thought to tell Mitch when he'd arrived this morning.

Regan headed for the front door, pausing when she heard a low whistle to her right. She glanced over and saw that Mindy had come back downstairs and was peeking out through the miniblinds. The slats were always kept at an angle on the street side, to prevent anyone from being able to see in from outside. They were on a cul-de-sac with only one entrance, but that didn't mean they could be careless.

"Mindy?"

Caught, the girl giggled. She glanced around as if to be sure no one else was there before saying,

"Boy, he's enough to make you put a hole in the roof yourself!"

Regan grinned in spite of herself. She knew Mindy's comment was the kind of thing that likely would have gotten her punched if she'd said it near her boyfriend.

"Don't forget. I told Marty you'd call him, let him know you're all right."

"He can wait a minute," Mindy said.

Despite her offhand tone, Regan knew Mindy adored her big brother. It had been Marty who had talked her into getting away from Joel, Marty who had convinced her she deserved better. From what Mindy had told her, Marty had been more of a father to her than their brutal biological father.

When Regan got to the door, she was glad Mindy had prepared her. If she'd opened the door to this man without warning, she probably would have gaped. As it was she did stare for an instant before recovering. She had to agree with Mindy's assessment. He might not be knockout gorgeous, but thick, dark hair, killer blue eyes, and a scar that tilted one brow upward made him very attractive. Even the worn condition of his jeans, T-shirt, and running shoes didn't detract from the appeal.

"Hi," he said, "I'm Alex Edwards. The roofer."

"And?" She'd learned never to assume anyone was who they said they were.

"Sorry if I shook anybody up. Mrs. Court told me I should be careful."

Regan relaxed a little, but not completely. It was hardly a secret that Lillian Court was involved with Rachel's House.

"Did she tell you anything else?"

The smile became a grin. "Yeah. That I should tell you—you are Regan, aren't you?" At her nod he went on. "She said I should tell you September fifteenth, lunch at the Shores Grill."

She did let down then. She and Lillian had worked out that code—the place they had met to plan Rachel's House—long ago, when Regan had realized how hands-on the woman intended to be. It had become clear they would need some way to verify she had actually sent a person to take care of this problem or that, so they had worked out this password system. They changed the dates regularly, just in case.

"Come in," Regan said. "I'll get you the report we had done that shows the problem areas."

He stepped inside. He was taller than she'd realized, when he'd been standing one step down. He glanced around and Regan wondered if he was surprised at the relatively new furnishings and fresh paint. But then again, if Lillian had sent him, he had to know there was solid money behind them. And she and Lillian had agreed that nice surroundings were essential to the residents.

"Is all that really necessary?" he asked as she closed the door behind him. "That password thing?"

"Do you know what this is, Mr. Edwards?"

"Alex, please. Yes, she told me, but—"

"We don't expect you to understand, just observe the rules."

He blinked. Figures, Regan thought. Eyelashes a

mile long. The distribution of assets was really
messed up in this world.

"Sorry," he said, sounding stung, and she realized what she had sounded like.

"No, I'm sorry," she said. "We're just wary
around here."

"I guess you have to be, but . . ."

"A couple of years ago, at our old shelter, the ex-
husband of one of our residents managed to get his
eight-year-old son off his school playground. He
dropped him off out in front with orders to call for
his mother while he hid. When she came outside,
he blew her away with a shotgun from the bushes."

Alex went still. All traces of amusement vanished. "He used his own child as bait?"

Her mouth twisted downward. "You find that
surprising, from a man who would murder a
child's mother right in front of him?"

Regan watched him grow pale. If he was going
to be working here, she had to make the point of
how crucial it was that he tell no one.

"The little boy was still there?" His voice was
barely above a whisper.

"His mother was still holding his hand."

He looked queasy. He swallowed hard.

Point made, Regan thought.

He'd read the file. He'd flinched then. But the
dry, detached wording of Grimm's report on the incident, which left out the more gruesome details,
had only made him react intellectually. Regan
Keller's stark recounting made him sick.

"I'm sorry," he said, meaning it. "I didn't mean to sound like I wasn't taking you seriously."

She studied him. He held her gaze, sensing it was important just now. Not that it was painful; she had a fascinating, if not beautiful face. Her eyes would normally be a warm hazel, he guessed, but at this moment, they were cool and assessing.

After a long moment she nodded. "We're overly cautious," she admitted. "But I had to be sure you knew how important it was that you tell no one who or where we are."

She gestured him toward an open door that he could see led to an office. "How did he find out? The guy who . . . with the shotgun? Did the child tell him?"

"No. Somebody sold us out to him."

He stopped dead. "What?"

"The police found out it was a delivery guy who had brought out a new appliance for us."

"And he *sold* the location of the shelter?"

"Yes." She stepped into the office ahead of him. "We were worth a thousand dollars."

"Not much for a life," Alex muttered.

"Two lives. Jamie, the boy, will never be the same. He's ten now, and still has nightmares. And other social problems."

She walked to her desk. As she opened a drawer and pulled out a folder, he took the chance to look around the office. Unlike the main room they'd come through, it was furnished more for utility than decor, but there were touches that drew the eye: profusion of flowers in a bright blue vase atop a credenza, a bulletin board full of notes and color photos of children and women who were apparently the success stories of the shelter.

"Here's the inspector's report," she said, handing him several stapled pages.

He took it from her, noting there were no rings on either of her hands. No jewelry at all, in fact— her utilitarian watch hardly counted as such—and he wondered if she had soured on men altogether after working here for so long.

"You do understand I'll need to know your hours of coming and going, and that you can't show up unexpectedly."

He nodded. Grimm had briefed him on the rather unique requirements. "And no coming in the house unannounced. You have to be let in."

"I will be careful," he promised. "I know you must be more on edge than usual around here these days."

She stiffened. "Why would you say that?"

"Well, with those murders . . ." His voice trailed away.

"I'd appreciate it if you didn't bring that up to anyone here," she said, her voice flat and emotionless. "Is there anything else?"

His first instinct was to back off, to let her be. This was odd enough to him that he took note of it. "A sore subject? Have the police been putting the pressure on?"

Her head came up then. "On us? No, why would they?"

He shrugged, as if it were merely casual conversation. "Motive's usually where they start, isn't it?

And I'd guess your people, and their families, have as much as anyone."

Suspicion flickered in her eyes, and he knew he'd come close to the line. He backed off. "Just wondering if I should be expecting the cops to drop by while I'm here."

The suspicion changed to wariness. "Is that a problem for you if they do?"

Alex winced inwardly; he didn't usually get in trouble this early on. Something had thrown him off stride. He countered with the truth. "No. Mrs. Court would make sure of that."

"You could have lied to her."

His mouth quirked. "I'm not stupid."

"She . . . trusts you?"

"I've done several jobs for her over the years."

Quit while you're ahead, he told himself. He held up the inspection papers. "I'll go take a look, and see what materials I'm going to need."

"Do you need money?"

"No. Mrs. Court set up an account, said this wasn't in your budget."

"No, it's not," Regan said. "If not for her, it wouldn't be getting done this year at all, let alone before the rainy season, such as it is here. But I wasn't sure how she wanted to work it."

"It's taken care of. I'll go get started."

She nodded. "Do you need anything else? I have to run over to the office for the afternoon."

"Office?" Wasn't this her office?

"We have an administrative office off-site, for business, and a center for donations and information."

So nobody knew where they were. What a way to live, he thought. "Oh. But you live here, with the other women?"

She nodded. "They need to have me here, to know they can count on me at a moment's notice." She opened the center drawer again, took out a business card, and handed it to him. "If you have any questions or problems, the main office number and my cell numbers are on there."

He nodded and stuffed the card into his back pocket.

"I'll go get started," he said again, and when he got out of the room he was surprised at the relief he felt.

It must be because this was so important to his mother. It put an extra fillip of pressure on that he didn't usually feel when working on something. Satisfied he'd figured that out, he headed back out to his truck for a ladder.

She wasn't comfortable leaving him there, Regan thought as she took a random, roundabout route to the off-site office. But she trusted Lillian implicitly. She would make sure of anyone she sent here.

She made a stop at the post office to drop off some bills, then started out again in the opposite direction from the office. It was more important to take a circuitous route on the way back to the shelter, but since she generally went to the office at least three days a week—although she tried to vary the days to avoid predictability—it made her feel better to do the roundabout both ways.

When she finally arrived, she was greeted by the

young volunteer and Mrs. Tanaka, the administrator, but since a woman and child were sitting in the lobby, no one said anything about who she was. If asked, they knew to say she was just another volunteer.

She was deep into one of the files she'd been left, trying to absorb from the dry, dispassionate reports whether the woman whose sad story was told there would be a good match for Rachel's House, when she heard a stir up front. It wasn't an alarmed stir, the kind she heard when some angry ex-husband or boyfriend showed up demanding to know where the woman who had dared to leave him was, so she finished the sentence she'd been reading before she looked up.

She might not have guessed about the woman, but she'd have known the man was a cop in an instant. In fact, she thought she did know him. She must have met him on one case or another. She couldn't remember specifically, but had the uneasy feeling the experience hadn't been pleasant.

"Regan?" Danielle, the high school volunteer, sounded concerned.

She closed the file folder and out of habit locked it in her desk drawer, then got to her feet. "Come on back," she said. "We can use the private office."

"I'm Detective Garrison," the tall blonde with laugh lines around her green eyes said, extending her hand. She was a healthy, athletic-looking woman, but still feminine, Regan thought as she shook hands with her. Her grip was firm but not out to prove anything. "And this is Detective Durwin."

"I believe we've met," Regan said neutrally as the paunchy, partially balding man came in and pulled the door shut behind him.

"Yeah, we did." He took a seat without waiting to be asked. "The Rodriguez case, couple years ago. Whatever happened to her?"

"She's one of our successes, I'm glad to say." She took the seat behind the desk, and the woman detective took the remaining chair. "She took the computer training we got her and landed a good job out of the area. She and her son are doing very well."

"Hmm."

He didn't say anything else, but Regan suddenly remembered why she hadn't liked this man. He showed no sympathy for the battered woman. She might as well have been another criminal.

"I want to thank you for your call," Detective Garrison said.

"We would have found out anyway," the man put in.

Regan didn't think she was wrong in guessing that the glance the woman gave the other detective was irritated.

"Does anyone come to mind who might be doing this?" the female detective asked. "Anybody who's made threats, or has never quite calmed down?"

Marty Baker and his fury jumped into her mind, but she hesitated, fearing she would get him in trouble.

"If you know something, you'd better tell us," Durwin said.

That decided Regan. "You have the list of family members?"

"Yes," Detective Garrison said. "We've talked to some of them already."

"I have no names to add to that," she said. Detective Garrison flicked a glance at her partner, as if she knew Regan's sudden coolness was his fault.

"Was there something else?" Regan asked.

"Your residents at Rachel's House," Garrison said. "I assume you are aware of where they are most of the time?"

Regan nodded. "We try not to make it like a prison, since most of them have just escaped from that kind of situation. But for their own safety, we do keep fairly close track of them, yes."

"A written record?"

"They sign in and out. So we know if anyone hasn't returned when they were supposed to."

"Which is rarely good news in your case, I imagine," the woman said, and Regan thought the sympathy in her voice sounded genuine. The detective wore a plain gold band on her left hand, and Regan wondered what it was like to be a man married to a cop.

"No," Regan agreed, "it's not often good news. Batterers don't give up easily."

"I know. But we'll need you to tell us where each of them was at these times," the woman said, handing her a piece of paper with three dates and range of hours listed. The times of the murders, she thought, and tried not to shudder.

"I'll have to check at the shelter. I don't have those pages here," she explained.

"What about the other files, the case histories on the women?" Durwin asked. "The files that show where the men are?"

"They're also at the shelter. Once they're a resident, they're kept on-site. It makes the women feel better."

"Why, do they like to read them?"

Regan stifled the urge to call the man an unpleasant name. The blond woman looked beyond irritated now, she looked embarrassed. And that enabled Regan to rein in her anger.

"The files are locked up, so no one can read them. That's what they like, Detective Durwin. Horrifying as it is in this day and age, there are still some dinosaurs out there clinging to the idea that abuse is somehow the woman's fault."

Durwin didn't react, but Regan guessed he'd been at this long enough to hide whatever he was thinking.

"Who has access to those files?" he asked.

"I do, at Rachel's House. And when they come through here, our administrator, Mrs. Tanaka."

The woman nodded. "If you could get that info to us as soon as you can, please?"

"You don't really think one of the residents is the killer, do you?" Regan asked.

"Female serial killers in the traditional sense, like in these cases, are extremely rare," Garrison acknowledged.

"There are always exceptions," Durwin said flatly.

Garrison went on as if he hadn't spoken. "Women tend to be the Black Widow or Angel of

Death sort of killer, killing spouses for money or people they think already doomed anyway."

"These women are victims," Regan pointed out. "And most of them are too terrorized themselves to even think about hurting anyone else."

"I underst—"

"Which brings us to the other thing we need," Durwin said, interrupting his partner without apology.

"Of course," Regan said with exaggerated politeness. "And that is?"

"The whereabouts at those times of the most likely suspect, the one who would be best able to find the victims, the one who is not afraid."

Regan blinked. "What?"

"You, Miss Keller. Where were you at the time of the murders?"

Regan was once more nose deep in paperwork, trying to rid herself of the nasty feeling Detective Durwin had left her with. She realized when she found herself reading the same paragraph for the fourth time that she wasn't having much luck.

She tossed the page down on her desk and rubbed her eyes. She realized they were just doing their job, looking at everyone, and that the more murders that piled up, the harder they pushed, hoping something—or someone—would break. She realized all of that, but it didn't make her feel much better. Her dad might have been killed a long time ago, but she'd never forgotten what he'd taught the little girl she'd been, that the police were the good guys. And she—

"Regan!"

The call from the front of the office snapped her out of her reverie. Danielle's voice held an unmistakable note of unease. Regan stood up quickly to look out her office window. Her heart jumped as she saw the short, stocky man with the slicked-back hair. Daryl Bowers. Standing there with another man she didn't recognize. Marita's soon-to-be ex-husband wore an expression Regan had seen far too often. She wasn't surprised; the divorce was in the final stages, and he had to be getting desperate by now.

Regan picked up the receiver of the cordless phone she'd added to the office just for such situations. She checked for a dial tone first—a lesson she'd learned after one irate boyfriend had cut the phone lines before he'd come in to demand they give him back his punching bag—then turned it off again and dialed 911, knowing it would dial itself the moment she hit the call button. Then she stepped out of her office.

"—know where she is, and you're going to tell me, you little bitch."

Danielle was standing her ground, but Regan could see the girl was frightened.

"Don't mind him, honey," she said as she came up behind her. "Mr. Bowers has a problem being civil."

"You're the one with the problem! I'm not leaving here until I talk to my wife." He glared at Danielle. The teenager, apparently feeling stronger with Regan's presence, answered calmly.

"I told you, I don't know where Rachel's House is."

"Bullshit."

Spittle flew from the man's mouth, and Regan pondered the wisdom of blatantly wiping her face. Deciding against it, she handed the girl the phone instead.

"It's set to dial 911," she told her. "Use it if he so much as reaches over that counter."

The man swore again. And for the first time the older, taller man spoke. "Let me handle this, Daryl. Take a walk."

Regan looked at the other man, but she never let Daryl Bowers out of her peripheral vision. She saw him open his mouth to protest. Then shut it again, glance at the man beside him, and turn and walk away.

Any man who could make Daryl Bowers do anything was someone to watch. Carefully, Regan added to herself as the man spoke again.

"Now, you listen to me, girlie," he began, in the condescending tone of a superior lecturing a flunkey, but Regan cut him off.

"I don't listen to anyone who calls me by an antiquated, sexist diminutive," she said, as patronizing as he had been condescending, "but I'm sure we can do better, can't we, Mr. . . . ?"

"Why, you—" He stopped, seemingly flummoxed, and unsure whether to respond angrily to her comment or provide her with the standard fill-in for her unfinished sentence. "The only thing you need to know is that I am Marita's father. And I

have every right to know where she is. I wish to
speak with her."

"She's not indicated any desire to see you."

"I don't care what she wants! She's my daughter,
and I demand you tell me where she is!"

Marita had never mentioned her father also
being abusive, but it didn't take a psychic to figure
that one out. "Did you know," Regan said conver-
sationally, "how likely it is that a girl whose father
was abusive will marry a man who is also abusive?"

He swore then, a string even more creative than
Bowers' had been. Those extra years of practice,
she supposed. He slapped his hands down on the
counter and leaned toward her.

"You bitches really stick together, don't you?"

"And men like you only know one way, don't
you?"

He swore again, harshly and at length.

"Regan? Should I call?" Danielle asked, clutching
the phone in white-knuckled fingers.

"Not yet. I'm sure the . . . gentleman will be leaving immediately."

Regan saw the man's hands curl into fists on the
counter. This particular breed of leopard rarely
changed its spots. Even if they were liver spots, she
thought wryly.

Although perhaps she couldn't assume that this
old predator wasn't still dangerous.

CHAPTER 3

It was disconcerting, Alex thought. He had never before realized how accustomed he'd become to women reacting to him in a positive way. These women kept hurrying away from him as if he carried some virus. In a sadly twisted way, he supposed he did. For these women, the Y chromosome was dangerous. And sometimes fatal.

He could only hope it would get better. Maybe once they got used to him, they'd relax a little. Otherwise this was going to be a very long job.

Of course, it was liable to be long, anyway. He was in good shape, but he wasn't used to this kind of physical labor for eight hours a day. He hadn't worked like this since he'd spent his summers as a teenager laboring on various CourtCorp developments, his father's idea of learning the company from the ground up.

"Back to work," he told himself aloud. As he began to move again, he felt protests from various muscle groups he hadn't heard from in a long while. Grimm had set him up with a small apartment nearby, as part of his cover, but an hour or two in the hot tub at the family house might be in his plans for tonight. Especially if he wanted to be able to move tomorrow.

He went back to ripping off the old shake shingles, a fire hazard and then some here in southern California. The skip sheeting beneath looked in pretty good shape, considering the condition of the roof. He had this section almost cleared, then he'd have to lay the plywood so he could walk on it safely to get to the rest of the roof.

"Hello?"

Alex glanced downward, surprised to hear a male voice. The man who'd called out looked vaguely familiar, with his thinning hair, black horn-rimmed glasses, and tall, wiry frame.

"Hi," Alex returned casually.

"I'm Gene Pilson, from next door," the man said. "I kind of look out for things here. You're the roofer?"

Alex thought that was self-explanatory, but merely nodded.

"Going to be here long?"

"As long as it takes," Alex said. "This roof needs a lot of attention."

"Hmm. Well, I'll be around," Pilson said, and Alex wondered if that had been merely information or a warning.

He glanced at his watch; he'd already put in a full day. He didn't want to leave before Regan returned, until he knew she was safely back for the day, but he wasn't sure how long he could hang around without looking suspicious. He'd give it

another half hour, he decided, until he had those
shingles cleared. He worked slowly, at the same
time watching the street for the green Honda coupe
he'd seen her leave in.

Once one of the women stepped outside, the one
called Marita, he thought. He remembered the
slight bend in her nose, clearly from a bad break.
When she saw him, instead of darting away as the
others did, she merely stared at him. There was no
mistaking the suspicion in her eyes. He supposed
she didn't trust men in general. After a moment she
went back inside and he returned to his work, and
his watching.

From his vantage point on the ridgeline he spotted the car as she turned the corner. He picked up
his pace, spreading a tarp over the roof area he'd
cleared, then headed down the ladder.

When he reached the ground, he looked toward
the street. The green coupe was nowhere in sight.
He knew it hadn't gone by so, puzzled, he walked
toward the sidewalk until he could see down the
street. He spotted it parked down three houses.
There was no sign of Regan.

Frowning, he headed back toward the house. He
was up on the porch, reaching for the door handle
to go in, when he suddenly remembered and
backed up hastily. Just as he did so, the front door
swung open.

"I didn't expect you to still be here." Regan's
voice was tense, as if his presence bothered her as
much as it bothered the residents of Rachel's
House.

"I wanted to finish the section I was working on," he said.

"Oh."

"Something wrong? I remembered not to go in," he pointed out.

Her forehead creased for a moment. "What? Oh. No, you're fine, it was . . . something else."

"Problem?"

She frowned. "You could say that."

"Bad day?" She hesitated. "I'm not one of them," he said softly.

She blinked, then flushed as his meaning hit home. "It becomes a reflex after a while."

"I can understand why. When you're around frightened or wary people all the time, it can rub off."

"They have reason to be."

He raised his hands at the tension in her voice. "I didn't say they didn't. Just that it's hard to live on that kind of edge all the time."

She let out a long breath. "I'm sorry," she said, sinking down onto the porch bench. "It *has* been a bad day."

Alex leaned against the porch railing. "Something go wrong?"

"Only if you consider practically being accused of being a serial killer by the police something going wrong."

He frowned. The cops had a suspect? Then the literal sense of her words hit him. "You?" he asked, astonished. "They accused you?"

She flicked him a look he couldn't quite put a name to. "Well, only one of them, really," she said.

"Aren't female serial killers as rare as honest politicians?"

"I suppose he didn't really accuse me, but he was pretty snarly about asking if I had alibis for the nights of the murders."

"Oh." Alex hesitated. He knew that was standard procedure, but he didn't want her mad at him again.

"I know, I know," she said as if she'd read his thoughts. "He had to ask."

"But he didn't have to be obnoxious about it."

"No, he didn't. And he got worse when I told him only the female detective could come here to talk to our residents. And that I had a lawyer who was ready to back us up on that."

He knew, of course, that she had access to the CourtCorp attorney his mother had assigned, but asked anyway, because it seemed like he should. "You have a lawyer already?"

"Thanks to our main patron. Which further irritated Detective Durwin." She grimaced. "I get the feeling he doesn't have a lot of empathy for what these women have been through."

"Then what the heck's he doing on the case?" Alex muttered, already thinking his mother was going to want to know about this.

"I suppose he was assigned," Regan said, looking at him quizzically. "It's not like Vista Shores has a huge department to choose from."

He opened his mouth to tell her if things weren't resolved soon they would have an entire task force to choose from, then snapped it shut. He'd forgotten her history, but the fact that she'd once been closely connected to the police department came back to him in a rush now. Along with the fact that it wasn't public knowledge yet that a task force was being considered.

"Er, yeah," he said lamely. "Still, seems like he should lose the attitude."

She smiled a bit. "I think his partner thought so, too. I'll bet she chewed on him a bit after they left. And I guess it doesn't matter how he feels. The killer's not threatening the women, at least not yet."

"It better stay that way." When he saw his tone had caught her attention, he shrugged. "I hate bullies. Even when they're cops. Maybe especially. They're supposed to be the good guys."

That earned him another smile. "I don't blame him, really. I am one of the only ones with access to the records that include the men's whereabouts, and I can't say I don't have reason to despise men like that."

"We all have reason to despise men like that," Alex said while wondering when she would realize she'd just let slip to him what wasn't general knowledge, the direct connection to Rachel's House. He didn't want her to stop talking now, so he said quickly, "But I read about the murders in the paper. I can't quite see you slashing throats."

Her eyes went oddly flat. "Don't think I wouldn't if it was the only way to stop one of them."

He tried to keep his tone neutral. "That sounds . . . personally fervent."

"Men like that," she said, her voice tight, "have cost me my father and my best friend. Yes, I'm fervent, and yes, it's personal to me."

If she had sounded like that when she'd been talking to the police, he wasn't surprised they were looking at her; there had been a world of anger and vehemence in that declaration. And suddenly he could picture it, this woman taking vengeance like some female warrior out of legend, and the image rattled him.

Regan glanced over her shoulder, and he spoke quickly, before he lost her.

"Your father and your best friend?" He knew the story from the file his mother had given him, but he wanted to hear it from her. If for no other reason than when she knew he knew, he could quit worrying about slipping up himself.

She looked back at him. "He was a cop. He tried to stop one of *them* from murdering his wife. He got murdered instead."

Her mouth twisted into a grimace that made him wince as if he'd felt the pain himself.

"And your friend?"

"Rachel. Rachel Carreras. The best friend I ever had, the sister I never had."

"Had?" he asked.

"She made the fatal mistake of falling for one of them. I never understood why. I still don't."

From the doorway came a soft call. "Regan?"

They both turned. Alex recognized the young blonde he'd thought he'd seen peeking through the curtains at him a couple of times today.

"Yes, Mindy?" Regan said.

"I think you'd better come in. Dawn's on the phone with her father, and it's getting ugly."

Regan responded quickly. Alex decided it was

time to take another step into her confidence and followed her inside.

"—always hated him! Half the times he hit me, it was because of you!"

Alex saw Regan wince at what the petite brunette said. He'd read enough to know that excuses were the hallmark of an abuser. He just hadn't realized how thoroughly the victim sometimes bought into it as well.

"Can't you even have a little respect, when he's barely cold?" The woman paused, listening, while she wiped already reddened eyes. "Oh, yeah, I forgot, your respect has to be earned, isn't that what you always say? Well, I hope you're happy now! I hate you, and I don't ever want to see you again!"

She slammed down the receiver on the wall phone, stood glaring at it through her tears, and only then seemed to realize she had an audience.

"Can you believe him?" she exclaimed. "He wants me to come home, now that Art is . . . oh, God."

A new flood of tears poured from her. Mindy ran to put a comforting arm around her. Beside him, Alex saw Regan take a deep breath before she started toward the two women. He himself was feeling confused. This was obviously the woman connected to the most recent victim, but Alex didn't understand this. She'd had to run from him, hide from his brutality, yet she sounded as devastated by his death as any normal married woman.

"Come on, Dawn," Regan said quietly. "Why don't you go back upstairs and rest for a while?"

"I should never have called him," the woman

said bitterly. "But I thought he'd understand, at least feel bad. But no, not my father. He always hated Art."

I'd hate the man who battered my daughter, too, Alex thought.

"Don't say any more right now," Regan told her. "You're upset, you've been through the wringer. Get some rest. You don't have to do anything or go anywhere right now."

Her calm, soothing tones seemed to have an effect, and Alex watched as Regan led the distraught woman to the stairs.

"Hi. I'm Mindy."

Alex turned to the petite blonde. "I'm Alex," he said. Normally he would have held out a hand, but he wasn't sure that was a good idea here.

"You're working on the roof," she said.

"Yes." He wasn't certain if her words were statement or question.

"Is it going to take long?"

"With just me working, a while," he said. "Sorry," he added, figuring she'd wanted to know how long they were going to have to put up with him.

"No, it's okay, I just wondered. I'm sure Regan wouldn't have told us you were okay if you weren't."

"I'm no threat to any of you," he promised. "Please don't be nervous."

"I'm not. You're a nice change in the scenery around here."

Alex blinked. Was she flirting with him? "Thanks. I think."

Mindy sighed. "God, that's what landed me here. I can't stop flirting, and my boyfriend—ex-boyfriend—hates it."

"Hates it enough to hit you?"

She nodded glumly. "But really, he's not all bad. Honest, he's not. He just doesn't like me talking to other men."

"Like who?"

"Like anybody."

"Even your family?"

"Well, sometimes. But really, he can be so sweet, when he wants to be."

"I don't get it. That's like saying, 'I love him, he's just got this one little quirk, he beats the hell out of me.' No amount of sweet makes up for brutality."

She looked startled. Then, abruptly, angry. "What do you know about it?"

She abruptly turned and ran toward what he guessed was the kitchen, leaving Alex feeling rocky.

When he turned and saw Regan at the bottom of the stairs, watching him, he felt even rockier. He wondered how much she'd heard.

As Regan walked toward him, he held up his hands against the chewing out he was certain was coming. "I know, I should have kept my mouth shut, it's none of my business."

She came to a halt in front of him. "No. I'm glad you did."

"You are?"

She nodded. "It's good for them to hear that, from a totally independent source. Especially a man. They need to know there are men out there who find it as repulsive as any woman does."

"I do. I just don't understand why they stand for it."

"I know." Regan studied him for a moment. "Sometimes it irritates me when someone has no concept of what these women are going through. But then I remember I was that way once. Like all the others who say, 'Why don't they just leave?'"

And in that moment, Alex was no longer working for CourtCorp, or here only because his mother had sent him. For right now, he was just a guy trying to figure out something that had always puzzled him.

"I know most of the accepted reasons," he said. And he did. He'd read every page of the literature his mother had provided. "They think they deserve it, they're convinced it's really their fault, they think it's only temporary, that he'll change, that they have no resources of their own, I know all that. Up here," he said, tapping his temple. "But my gut still doesn't get it."

"Neither does mine."

It was the perfect plan, she thought. He would be out of her life, and she and William would be free. It was so much simpler, really. She knew herself well enough to know she would never have the nerve to leave. She simply couldn't face life knowing he'd be after her, chasing her, knowing he'd kill her if he caught her.

Besides, if she did leave, she would lose her son. She hadn't known that when she'd married him.

She'd signed that prenuptial agreement he'd put in front of her without a protest, after his declaration that it was the only way he could be sure she loved him and not his money. Innocent, naïve child that she'd been then, she'd never realized that in doing so she'd signed away her own child's future. She'd be worse than penniless if she left. Her loving husband had not only made sure she would leave empty-handed, he'd made sure she had no skills or the confidence to seek any kind of employment.

But if she stayed, he would kill her. She no longer had any doubt of that. One day he would go too far and it would be over. She didn't care so much for herself, but she'd been reading, magazines from the doctor's office mostly, and she knew the truth now. Knew her son would be raised to be just like him, thinking women deserved no better than this. Oddly, while she cared little about herself anymore, she didn't want that for her son. Didn't want some terrified woman to someday hate him the way she hated his father.

"Well?"

Snapped back to the present by the growled inquiry, she focused on the man opposite her. She'd risked everything to sneak out and meet this dark, frightening man here in this seedy café. It had taken her days to organize, and she'd nearly changed her mind countless times.

But the last time her husband had beaten her, he'd avoided her face. And somehow that knowledge, that he'd purposely avoided damaging any part of her her that might show at his company banquet next week, that he was that much in control when he battered her, had been the spark she needed to keep the newborn flame of her anger burning.

"Do it. As we agreed. And as soon as possible."

"You're sure? You really want him dead?"

She looked into the cool, assessing eyes of the man she had found on the Internet. She wondered for a moment if he was trying to get her to say it because this was a setup, if maybe he was an undercover cop. But then she realized it didn't matter. Not really. If he was a cop, he'd arrest her, and she'd go to jail. And going to jail would be a blessed relief. Nothing that could happen to her there could be any worse than the hell she lived in every day.

"I want him tortured for eight years, as he's tortured me, but I'll settle for dead," she said firmly.

"It'll cost you," the man warned, running a finger over his upper lip.

She reached into her purse and pulled out a small pouch. Something else fell to the table, and she grabbed it before it could roll to the floor as she told him, "What you can get for that should cover it."

He undid the drawstring and peered inside. He looked at her doubtfully. "I don't know."

"It's all real. And very high quality."

"Yeah, but I'd have to fence it. This kind of stuff, jewelry, it's tough."

"There's enough there to make it worth it," she promised, trying to hide her desperation. If he turned her down, where would she turn?

He looked at her for a moment, in a way that

made her feel like she was a butterfly about to be pinned by a cruel little boy.

"Throw that in," he said, gesturing at her left hand, "and you've got a deal."

She stared down at the gaudy diamond on her ring finger. She had never liked it, but had let herself be convinced it was proof of his great love. If only she'd known then it was merely another trapping of the life he'd carefully designed for himself. The powerful job, the luxurious mansion, the expensive cars, the silk suits, the gold and diamond jewelry, and the beautiful wife, complete with ball and chain disguised as a four-carat diamond. She was no more, and considerably less than some of the rest.

But she didn't dare take it off. He'd notice. And no explanation she could come up with would satisfy him.

"You can have it," she told the killer. "But not until it's done. After that, I'll be glad to be rid of it."

He studied her a moment, as if assessing whether she could be trusted to keep that promise. She wondered what he'd seen when he nodded.

"Deal," he said succinctly. "Just remember I'll know who and where you are. You try and cheat me, and I'll hunt you down."

She looked at the crayon she held, the one she had tucked into her purse as a constant reminder. "If you get this done, you won't have to," she promised him.

"Consider him dead."

I'll dance on his grave, she promised herself.

CHAPTER 4

After arriving this morning to conduct interviews with the residents of Rachel's House, Detective Garrison insisted they be done in the comfortably furnished living room rather than across Regan's more official-seeming desk. "I don't want them to feel this is an interrogation," Lynne said. "This is tough enough on them already."

"Thank you for understanding that," Regan said. "Most people think they should be delighted their abusers are dead."

"I suppose. Personally, I can't imagine a more tangled mess of emotions, especially when you've not had time to establish yourself on your own yet."

"Exactly." Regan hesitated. "They don't know yet. The connection to here, I mean. The current residents didn't know Rosa or Marcia. I wasn't sure if you would want me to tell them. And I didn't want them in the position of worrying if they should warn the men who abused them."

"I appreciate that. And they don't need to worry, we'll handle that once we have the records."

Regan frowned. On advice of the CourtCorp lawyer, Rachel's House had asked for a legal order to turn over the records that revealed the history of the residents. "It's not that we don't want to cooperate—"

Lynne stopped her with a wave of her hand. "No, I understand. And I'd just as soon go by the book every step of the way on this anyway. You'll get your court order, Ms. Keller."

"Thank you. And Regan, please."

Lynne nodded. "All right, Regan. Once we do start calling the men concerned, it will probably come out anyway. But these talks might be easier on them if they don't know yet."

Regan studied the woman for a moment, wondering if she was hoping to find out something if the women didn't know of the connection between the victims and Rachel's House. She didn't like the idea, but she supposed it was the detective's job.

"I've been thinking," she began.

"Yes?" the woman asked when she stopped.

"About the killings, I mean. I've been thinking about this for a while, that they're safe here, at Rachel's House, but they still have to go out into the world."

"I understand. They have to get jobs so they can support themselves when they leave, they may have to go to court—"

"Exactly. That was what got me thinking, and I realized that the first murder happened right after Rosa was killed."

"I remember noticing that. And?"

"The second one happened right after Marcia's

husband got out of jail for trying to run her off the road her first day at a new job, right after she went back to him."

Detective Garrison nodded. "Your point?"

"You probably aren't aware of it, but Dawn saw Art last week. And I just found out she was planning to see him again today. She's not supposed to, but it isn't easy to keep to that sometimes. Anyway, last week he hit her. She came back with his handprint still showing on her cheek. We all saw it."

"No, I wasn't aware." The blonde looked thoughtful. "A pattern," she said slowly, and Regan nodded.

"It seemed like it to me. Three women connected to Rachel's House are hurt yet again by their abusers, and those three particular men end up dead shortly after."

"Which means we don't have just a serial killer, but a vigilante running loose."

Regan shook her head. "I just noticed the pattern, that's all. I have no idea what it means." She grimaced. "Except that it makes Rachel's House even more entangled in this mess."

Detective Garrison smiled at her. "I'm going to do my best to get you un-entangled."

"There's one more thing," she said. "We had a woman leave, yesterday. Amber Winn. She went back to her boyfriend, and I've heard he's already abusing her again."

"You've heard? From her?"

"No. She's probably too embarrassed to call Rachel's House, because she thinks she's failed us by going back. That's a typical response. They don't think about the fact that we're all holding our breath, thinking she's dead." Regan suppressed a shiver. "But Mrs. Tanaka saw her, with her old boyfriend."

"You think he might be a target?"

"I wondered," Regan said.

"Do you have the boyfriend's name?" the detective asked.

"I can find out."

"Do, please."

Regan nodded, then turned to the matter at hand. "I've sort of let them assume you're here because of Dawn's ex," she said.

Lynne nodded. "Fine. I'll work with that in mind."

"Shall we get started? They're dreading this, and I'd like to get through it quickly. Besides, our roofer's at the hardware store, and this is likely the only quiet we'll get till tonight."

"Of course. You have only six residents at the moment?"

"Until we get a woman and child coming in this afternoon."

"I didn't think you took children," Lynne said.

"Normally, we don't. There's generally a focus in this field on the children, and women alone can sometimes fall through the cracks, so we chose to specialize. And we don't usually take women who are freshly out of their situation, we focus more on those who are beyond the crisis stage. But the other shelters are full at the moment, and we're certainly not going to turn away an emergency case like this."

Lynne nodded, then looked down at her list of names. "Let's start with Marita Bowers."

Regan hesitated. "If you're thinking she's a suspect, because of what happened with her husband, you're wrong. She's come further than anybody here. She's put it behind her, and she'll be leaving soon, starting a new life."

"But she did try to kill him," Lynne said.

"She never denied that. But it was only after he'd nearly killed her three times. You should see her hospital records—"

"I have. I know how bad it was for her. And I interviewed her father just yesterday, so I know she grew up in hell, too."

"I didn't know you'd talked to him."

"We thought he might be a suspect."

Regan gave a short, sharp laugh. "He'd be more likely to help you hunt him down, out of fear for himself."

"So I gathered. Look, I'm not saying Marita wasn't totally justified in fighting back. But I do have to consider her actions in this investigation."

Regan let out a held breath. The memory of that morning came back to her, Marita looking at the newspaper headline about murder number three.

Not mine, I suppose. I'm not that lucky.

Marita had said it, with that sort of bitter edge that marked the language of many survivors, but Regan couldn't believe she would do it. She just couldn't.

"I'll go get her," Regan said abruptly.

She found Marita stirring the same cup of coffee she'd been stirring when Regan had gone to answer the door.

"I'm the first victim?" Marita asked, a touch of bitterness in her voice.

"So it seems. But it may not be that bad," Regan told her. "I don't think she's out to get any of us."

"You trust her?" Marita asked.

"I don't distrust her," Regan said, knowing the woman would understand the fine line.

Still, Marita eyed the detective warily as she took a seat on the couch. And when Regan turned to go, Marita protested.

"Can't she stay?"

"I'm afraid not," Lynne said. "I'm sorry. I'll try to make this as painless as possible."

"Sure."

Marita's jaw was set mutinously, and Regan lingered, uncertain.

"I'll need to ask you about the assault on your husband."

"I figured as much."

"In detail."

Marita's mouth tightened. "I figured that, too."

Regan smothered a sigh and left the room.

As he settled the ladder into place against the eave of Rachel's House, Alex watched the attractive blond woman on the edge of his vision.

"She came while you were gone. She's a cop, another detective. The one who talked to me said so."

He turned his head to look at Mitch Howe, the gardener. Regan had briefly introduced them, but although he was friendly enough, Alex had a feeling the man didn't quite trust him. He couldn't blame him for that, he supposed. Strangers were suspect, especially now. Look at the way even the meek Mr. Pilson had charged over.

"Guess they have to talk to everybody," he said noncommittally, although he'd already guessed who she was. He'd known from his mother that one of the lead detectives was female, and that she would be handling most of the contacts with Rachel's House, for the sake of the residents.

"She's pretty, for a cop," Mitch said.

Alex nodded. The blonde looked tough and fit, but there was a warmth about her, a softness in her eyes that suggested she still had feelings beneath the disciplined, businesslike exterior. He wondered if she could hang on to that, after working a long and bloody case like this one.

"You think they'll catch this guy?" Mitch asked.

Alex shrugged. "I don't know. I know they're working hard on it."

"He seems awfully smart. They keep saying he doesn't leave any clues."

"If he was sloppy, they'd have caught him by now," he agreed.

"I'd hate to be one of those guys he's after. They must be looking over their shoulders all the time."

"Which doesn't bother me overmuch," Alex said. "And thinking of them afraid for a change doesn't, either."

Mitch grinned then, and seemed to relax. "You work for the Court people?" he asked.

"I've done a lot of things for them over the years, yes."

"Must be nice, to be that rich."

"They pay me well enough," Alex said.

He was used to the comments, even when they were made to his face as Alex Court. It no longer bothered him. He was secure in the knowledge that his family had worked long and hard to get to where they were. They also put a great deal of their wealth back into the community. There were programs in operation all over the country thanks to CourtCorp, programs to help anybody who wanted a hand up instead of a handout.

"Come to think of it," Mitch said, "they pay me well enough, too. I mean, Rachel's House writes the check, but I know the money comes from the Courts."

"You earn it, from what I can see," Alex said. The man put in long hours three days a week, and Regan had said he often stopped by to do a little extra work on other days.

"Thanks. I think it's important things be as nice as I can make them here. It was so ugly for most of them, where they came from."

"I guess everybody does their bit in their own way," Alex said.

"Everybody who cares," Mitch said. "But nobody does as much as Regan."

No, nobody does, Alex thought. But he hadn't known her long enough to know that, not in Mitch's view. "She seems to work pretty hard," he said instead.

"Not just that. She cares. Really cares. She's special."

Alex couldn't argue with that, either. And he went back to work wondering just how big a thing the gardener had for the redhead. And why he didn't much like the idea.

"Take me, use me, I'm yours."

Lynne Garrison looked up at Detective Nick

Kelso and grinned. "There was a time when that would have made my little heart flutter, Nicky."

The big blond looked at his watch. "Drat. I'm fifteen minutes too late?"

"More like fifteen years," Lynne said with a laugh. She meant it, though. When she'd been fourteen, a man like Nick would have been her ideal. She'd even had a bit of a thing for him when they'd gone through the law enforcement driving school together a few years ago. Being sent from the same department, they'd tended to stick together, had even flirted a little, but when school was over so was the flirtation. She'd wondered if the reason was that she'd beaten him soundly for best final score in the class, but if it truly bothered him he'd never let it show.

And now he was just a tad too handsome—and charming—for her taste. He played the field too widely as well, although she supposed she could understand it after he'd been unceremoniously dumped—as in packing up and decamping in the middle of the night—by the woman he'd been engaged to.

"Just my luck," he said with a dramatic sigh. "But, use me anyway."

"What do you mean?"

"I've been assigned to your case until it's cleared."

Lynne blinked. "You have?"

"Told you my luck was rotten."

"What about Ben?"

"Oh, you've still got him, too. The chief told the captain he wanted to be sure we had equal representation already in place if it comes to a task force.

You know how he hates the sheriff's office or the feds taking over."

"Are you calling our chief a control freak?" Lynne asked with an arched brow, knowing Chief Raines was far from it.

"Do I look suicidal?" Lynne laughed, and Nick's grin widened as he added, "Really, I think Greer just didn't want you quitting on him because you had to work with Durwin every day."

"Reason enough," Lynne said with exaggerated grimness.

"So, want to bring me up to speed?"

In fact, she was glad of the help—and the buffer between her and Durwin—so Lynne quickly gave him the rundown on where the investigation stood.

"He's quick, he's clean, and he's clever," she said as she finished.

"They usually are, or they get caught by now."

She nodded and, when he asked, gave him the files on each murder. She watched as he glanced through each. He paused on the grim crime-scene photographs, but a faint tightening of his mouth and his forehead were the only sign of reaction to the bloody images.

Nick Kelso's armor was pretty thick, Lynne thought. As thick as hers, even though she'd been at it five years longer. Nick had been a late bloomer when it came to law enforcement, joining up at age twenty-five. Although he had a fondness for late nights with the boys, and rumor had it even more fondness for the attractive powers of the badge for a certain type of female, he'd worked hard to live up to the expectations of having graduated second in a large academy class.

After a few minutes, he handed the files back to her. "I'll go over them in depth later."

"Good. Then maybe you can tell me if we're dealing with a real serial killer, or a vigilante run amok."

"Or both," Nick suggested. "What's the latest?"

"I finished up the interviews at Rachel's House this afternoon."

"Anything? Wasn't there one woman there with a record for battery on her husband?"

"Ex-husband, yes. The case fell apart when the guy refused to testify."

"Figures. No guy wants to admit a woman can really hurt him. But they don't dare fight back, or they're the ones who end up in jail."

Even if she didn't have the male ego that made the first part true, Lynne couldn't argue with the last part. "Too bad. The statistics might be a little more accurate if more men would report being battered."

"Not likely," Nick said. "Anything else turn up at the shelter?"

"I did a little pushing, prodding, and may have shaken something loose. I got a call from the ex-wife of the last victim a little while ago."

"Oh?"

"She says she knows who probably killed him." Nick sat up straighter. "She was pretty upset, so I don't know how good it will be."

"So you're heading back there?"

"No. She doesn't want to talk there. We're meeting at Smugglers."

Nick nodded; the popular restaurant was only a couple of miles away. "Let's go, then."

Lynne hesitated. "I don't know, Nick. She's a victim, and you're a man and—"

"Thanks for noticing that, darlin'," he drawled. "Look, I know how to handle these women, okay? She'll love me, I promise you."

Beneath her irritation at that "these women" phrase, something flickered in Lynne's memory. Something from when Nick had been in patrol, and most of the guys on the street had agreed he was the one you wanted to back you up on a domestic violence call. *It's amazing, how the women respond to him. They're spitting mad one second, purring the next, when Nick's around,* someone had said.

Sometimes you had to use whatever tools you had at hand, she thought. "Okay," she said. "But if she starts to get nervous, you bail."

"Sure. But she won't."

They were down in her assigned plain unit, pulling out of the secured department lot, before he spoke again.

"Have you notified potential victims yet?"

It was on her list, but not exactly at the top. "I think the news headlines have been doing that quite nicely with all that 'Avenger' stuff."

Nick snorted. "Yeah, how to egg on a nut case. Give 'em a catchy name in big print, feed the ego. But they've got to be warned, now that we know the connection to that shelter."

She braked to a stop at a red light, glancing over at him. "We've requested a court order. We should have it soon."

Nick stared at her. "A court order? What the hell for?"

"The records from Rachel's House, so we can track down the abusers who might be on whatever list this guy is working from."

Anger flickered in Nick's eyes. "You mean they're refusing to hand them over? People are being murdered here, Garrison."

"And several of those women were almost murdered themselves," she pointed out as the light changed and she turned her attention back to driving. "They have a right to be careful."

"What have they got to hide, anyway?" Nick still sounded annoyed.

"Their whereabouts, for one thing. The more people who see those files, the more likely it is for something to leak."

"We're dealing with a serial killer, for God's sake. That takes precedence over anything else."

She couldn't really argue with that, although she would have appreciated a bit more sensitivity to the plight of the women of Rachel's House. "I think we'll get the order," she assured him.

"You *think*?"

She gave a half shrug. "When you're dealing with a powerhouse like the Court Corporation, you never know."

The light turned green. As she accelerated, she could almost hear his frown. "What have they got to do with it?"

"You didn't know? They're the main benefactor of the shelter. It's a personal project of Mrs. Court's."

"Oh, great." Disgust echoed in Nick's voice. "Just

what we need, a bunch of high-priced lawyers to wade through. Damn, I didn't want this assignment anyway."

"We'll just have to be careful to go by the book with this one. We should anyway, as high-profile as this is getting."

"I know, I know, the media's already having a field day."

"And they'll be really in a frenzy if the connection to the shelter comes out."

"You mean when," Nick said. "You'd think if they wanted to really keep it quiet, they'd have just handed over the files. Now there'll be a court record."

He had a point there, one she couldn't argue with. But she understood why they'd made the choice they had. She supposed no man could really understand the kind of constant fear these women lived with.

The minute they walked into the restaurant, Lynne spotted her. She'd never met the woman, but she knew her instantly, even before she noticed the purple sweater she'd said she'd be wearing. There was just something about the way she huddled in the booth, eyes straight ahead, as if afraid to make eye contact with anyone, that made something knot up in Lynne's chest.

"Dawn?" Lynne asked as they reached her, although she knew she was right.

The woman looked up then. Those eyes were the kind Lynne had seen so often, tear-reddened, frightened, wary, and ancient. She hated seeing those eyes.

Dawn froze, the fear in her hazel eyes intensifying when she saw Nick.

"This is Detective Kelso," Lynne said. Before she could go on, Nick took charge smoothly. He sat down on the opposite side of the table, and gave the woman a smile Lynne was sure had soothed many a female heart.

"If I make you nervous," he said gently, "I'll leave. But I really want to catch this guy, so if you don't mind, I'd like to stay."

"I . . . guess that's all right."

"Thank you, Dawn," he said, with all the charm Lynne had seen him exert on occasion. It didn't fail him now. The woman actually gave him a fleeting smile.

Lynne sat down beside Nick, guessing the woman would feel trapped if she sat beside her, cornering her in the booth seat.

"You said on the phone you know who killed your ex-husband," she began.

Dawn nodded, stifling a sob.

"Who?"

Dawn sniffed. Stared at the table. Ran a finger through a patch of spilled salt. Lynne waited. Nick followed her lead and sat silently.

At last the woman looked up.

"My father," she said.

CHAPTER 5

"What else did you expect them to do?"

Alex could hear Regan's voice from the driveway. Something was obviously wrong. He dropped his tool belt back in the bed of the truck and headed for the porch.

"Dawn, you told them your father was the killer! Did you think they'd just slap him on the wrist?"

Uh-oh. This didn't sound good at all, Alex thought as he reached the door and found it, unusually, standing open. He hesitated in the doorway. He could hear a woman crying, heard other voices, muted, in the background.

"I didn't say he'd done them all, just Art! I didn't know they'd put him in handcuffs, and take him to jail," the crying woman wailed. "I didn't want that. I was just so angry at him."

"I don't think you were angry at him at all," Regan said, her voice almost soothing now. She seemed to grow calmer as the woman got more upset, and he wondered if she had it down to such a fine balance that she knew exactly how hard she could push before she was pushing too hard and they'd break.

"I think," Regan went on, "that you were angry at life, at yourself, at Art, and it just all came out when your father said he was glad Art was dead."

The woman said something too distorted by her crying for Alex to understand.

"Do you really think he killed Art?" Regan asked.

"No, no, he never would. I just wanted to hurt him back," Dawn whined between sobs.

Sounds like you got that done, Alex thought.

"So what are you going to do about it?" Regan said, almost sternly now.

"I . . ." Another round of sniffling, then, "I have to call the police, don't I?"

"I would think so."

"They'll let him go, won't they? God, Regan, it's my father!"

"He was your father when you called them. And he's done nothing but try and help you see the truth."

Alex frowned. It seemed she was being a little tough on the woman. She was already crying her heart out.

"I'll call right now," the woman said.

"Good," Regan answered. "And when you do, Dawn, think about this. Think about how you've made it a little bit harder for every woman here to get believed."

Understanding struck Alex. This was why she was being hard on the woman. He'd never thought of that, that any false report from an abused woman, like the boy who cried wolf, made it harder on the genuine victims. No wonder Regan had chewed her out.

The crying stopped. Alex risked a peek through the door, saw the woman staring at Regan as if she'd just been hit with a bucket of ice water.

"I'll call them right now," she said, looking first stunned, then appalled.

For a moment he just stood there, marveling at Regan, at how she seemed to know exactly what to do no matter the situation. Some of it was learned, he was sure, maybe she'd even been trained, but a lot of it was pure gut instinct.

"You do that," Regan said. "And I'll go see Detective Garrison myself to see if I can help smooth this over."

"Should I go?" the woman asked.

Regan shook her head. "I think you'd best stay away from the police and your father until things settle down a little."

Again, good instincts, Alex thought. Then, as Regan headed toward the open door, he realized if he didn't move, he was going to get caught eavesdropping. He backed up and down the porch steps swiftly, then, as Regan stepped outside, paused with one foot on the bottom step as if he'd just arrived.

"Good morning," he said.

"It's morning," Regan agreed as she pulled the front door shut behind her.

"Oops. But not a good one, I gather?"

"Not exactly." She tugged her keys out of the brown leather satchel that seemed to serve her as both briefcase and purse.

"Problems again?"

"Still."

She was waiting at the top of the steps, and he realized she was waiting for him to move. That struck him as odd. Why didn't she just keep coming and assume he'd get out of her way? Then he decided he was picking at minutiae to avoid thinking about how great she looked this morning, in that bright yellow summer sweater that set off her red hair. He stepped aside and she started down the steps.

She was clearly heading out, probably to the police station. An idea struck him, and before he thought it through, he'd said it. "The police again?"

She stopped in her tracks. "What?"

He tried a nonchalant shrug. "They were the problem yesterday, so I just wondered."

She seemed to relax. Something niggled at the edge of his mind, but she spoke before he could pin it down. "Oh. Yes, only they aren't really the problem this time. We are."

"We?"

"Rachel's House. We've caused them some trouble, and I want to be sure it's straightened out." Her mouth twisted. "Great way to break in the new domestic-violence detective."

"I imagine you need a good relationship with him," he said, although he already knew Detective Garrison was a woman.

"Her," Regan corrected, but without the heat he'd almost expected. "And yes, we do. Especially now, since she's also working the serial killer case."

He tried to think of what the average citizen would ask. "Isn't there a homicide detective?"

"Not a full-time one. He does . . . crimes against

persons, I think they call it now. But because of the connection, they brought her in. And I need to get over there to see her," Regan added, selecting what had to be her car key from the ring and starting toward the walkway that led to the back of the house.

"You always park so far away?"

She stopped again. "I don't park in front of the house. Sometimes I don't even park on this street. I often come here from the off-site office, and I can't be sure I'll lose anyone who might follow me."

Alex gave a slow shake of his head. "What a way to live."

"What a way to *have* to live," she countered, and was gone.

Alex watched her go, pondering what had been bothering him just now. Regan Keller was as much a prisoner as any woman of Rachel's House. That she was here by choice didn't change the fact that she was as wary and suspicious as any of them, perhaps even more because she saw herself as their protector.

He wondered if she had any life at all outside of this place.

"So, one of your women has wasted several hours of our time," Ben Durwin began.

"He had an alibi we verified first thing this morning, in about fifteen minutes," Lynne Garrison said wearily. Durwin ignored her and started back in on Regan Keller.

"I guess we're back to our prime suspect."

Lynne's forehead furrowed. As far as she knew they didn't have a prime suspect. They'd talked to everybody connected to Rachel's House, from the residents to the gardener to the mail carrier on that route, with little result. They'd talked to family members, and had turned up one real and a couple of possible suspects there, but no one she'd call prime yet.

"I'm glad you have one," Regan said.

"Are you?" Durwin almost sneered. "Since it's you?"

"Really?"

Lynne Garrison looked up at the note that had come into Regan Keller's voice when Durwin mouthed off yet again. She knew the man didn't really suspect Regan as the killer, but thought she knew something, and was pushing hard, hoping she'd break.

"I think you know more than you're saying," Durwin said. "Only you and the administrator have complete access to the records that provide the current location of those men. Are you saying that little old grandmother who's not even five feet tall is the killer?"

"Mrs. Tanaka wouldn't hurt anybody," Regan said sharply.

"But you, on the other hand, are angry enough to kill, or help somebody kill, aren't you? I've got right here the text of a speech you gave when that shelter of yours opened, where you made your opinions on men like our victims quite clear."

"Now, hold on here," Nick Kelso put in, his tone placating. "Let's not get off on the wrong foot here. After all, Miss Keller came in to explain and apologize for the trouble that false accusation caused us."

"Before you go all chivalrous on us, Kelso, did you know her father was a cop, and that when she was a kid she used to take target practice on the police firing range?"

The redhead winced, and Durwin pounced on it. "That make you nervous, us knowing that, Miss Keller?"

"For God's sake, Ben," Lynne snapped, "her father was a cop killed in the line of duty. Have a little respect. Besides, whether she can put six in the ten ring doesn't matter much when we're dealing with a killer who slashes throats."

For once Durwin subsided, even looked a little ashamed.

Regan Keller turned to face Lynne. "Thank you." Without a glance at the two men, she went on. "It's true I have access to the records. It's true I despise what men like your so-called victims do, so I guess I do have motive. What I don't have"—she turned to glare at Durwin—"is the stomach for it. If there's anything that working at Rachel's House has taught me, it's that I hate violence."

"So you don't believe in vengeance?" Nick asked, sounding merely curious.

"I believe in the kind of retribution my father believed in. He used to say we were still very much an eye for an eye society, but now the police and the courts get your eye for you. Which is the way it should work. Through the system."

"Nice speech," Durwin muttered.

Lynne had had about enough of Durwin for one morning. She stood up. "Let me see you out," she said to Regan, not waiting for any protest from either of the two men.

She led the way to the door. "You parked out

front?" At the redhead's nod, she continued down the hall toward the public entrance. "I do want to thank you for helping clear that up, about Mr. Gibbs."

"I felt I had to. Things like what Dawn did just make it harder for everyone."

"Yes, they do. I wish more people understood that."

"Once this is all over, I'd like to talk to you about Rachel's House."

"You were on my list, before this got dropped on me," Lynne told her. "I'd planned to contact you. It's important to me as the domestic-violence detective to know all the options I can give victims I come across."

Regan smiled, and Lynne couldn't doubt the warmth and sincerity of it.

Lynne hesitated. She knew that while it was unlikely their killer was a woman, it wasn't impossible that Regan had something to do with the murder. Female accomplices were not uncommon. She hoped not. She liked Regan Keller, admired what she was doing, and her dedication to a tragic, heartbreaking cause.

But had that dedication pushed her over the edge?

"I could, by the way," Regan said.

Lynne blinked. "Could what?"

"Put six in the ten ring."

Lynne laughed. "Do you own a gun?"

"Yes. One of my father's that I kept."

"You don't carry it?"

"No. It's locked up, in my room at the shelter. Has been ever since we moved into this location.

None of the residents know it's there, but I do. Just in case."

Lynne nodded. She'd read about the case of the young mother being shotgunned to death in front of the original Rachel's House, which had precipitated the move.

Lynne walked with Regan out to the parking lot, where they stopped next to a green Honda that was at least a decade old. Odd, she thought. With the Court Corporation behind them, she would have thought the director of Rachel's House would get paid well enough to afford a newer car.

"Thanks for sending over those sign-in logs, by the way," she said as Regan unlocked the car.

"You're welcome."

"Keep them signing in and out," Lynne recommended. "And do it yourself, too."

"To keep Detective Durwin off my back?"

"Mainly," Lynne admitted.

This time Regan's gaze was more pointed. "You think it will happen again, don't you?"

Lynne let out a long sigh. "Yes. I think he'll kill again."

And again, she thought. *Until we stop him.*

Alex tacked down the last corner of the tarp, slid the hammer into the loop on his tool belt, and headed for the ladder. Once down, he stretched wearily. The next time the guy at the gym talked about a full-body workout, he was going to sign him up for a few days of roofing.

He walked up onto the porch. Regan had come back a couple of hours ago. He'd resisted the urge to go down right then and see how things had gone with the police. He didn't want to blow his cover by appearing too curious. But now he was going to have to try to find out. He knocked on the door.

He stretched again, arching his aching back. As he did so he noticed the base of the porch light was askew, one of the screws holding it to the wall clearly loose.

Regan pulled the door open. His head came down abruptly.

"Something wrong?" she asked, gesturing toward where he'd been looking.

"Your porch light's coming loose."

"I noticed that the other day. I've been meaning to fix it."

He shrugged. "I've got a screwdriver right here. I'll do it now."

"You don't need to. You've put in enough work for one day."

"It'll only take a minute. I just wanted to tell you I'm done for the day and off the roof, so if you hear anything up there, it's not me."

Her eyes narrowed as she looked at him, as if she were searching for some sign he was joking. "Thank you for letting me know."

"It hit me today that you'd need to," he said as he pulled out a flat-bladed screwdriver. She smiled at him, a warmer smile than he'd ever seen from her before. "Does that mean you've decided I'm trainable?" he asked.

"You have potential," she admitted.

"Thanks," he said, to his surprise meaning it. "By the way, I met your guardian angel."

Regan gasped. "What?"

He stopped in the act of reaching toward the lamp, realizing she'd thought he meant the killer the papers had been calling the Avenger. "I meant Mr. Pilson."

"Oh." Regan relaxed, and smiled. "Isn't he sweet? He's always bringing over little gifts for everyone, not extravagant, just very thoughtful. He's the perfect neighbor for us, to help the women realize not all men are like the ones they've escaped."

"Lucky break. I can imagine some people wouldn't be happy with a shelter of any kind next door."

She nodded. "Our old neighbors weren't. So we're glad to have Mr. Pilson. The women voted him welcome to visit within a couple of weeks of moving in here."

Better than he was doing, Alex thought wryly.

He reached up to the base of the lamp, which had slid sideways when the loose screw lost its grip. His fingers brushed something that crinkled like paper behind the metal plate.

"Somebody must have tried to wedge this before," he said as he fished it out. "I may need to get a different . . ."

His voice trailed off as he stared at the carefully folded wad of paper that had slipped into his hand. He knew, had known the instant he'd seen how the paper was so carefully folded. He'd seen it often enough to recognize it. But hoping he could be wrong, he began to carefully open the little bindle.

"What is it?" Regan asked.

Alex let out a compressed breath as he got to the center and saw the white powder he'd expected.

He dipped a little finger into it and lifted it to his tongue. The salty, bitter taste was slight but unmistakable.

"Alex?"

"Cocaine," he said bluntly.

CHAPTER 6

Lynne headed back to the detective division, and got there just as Nick was hanging up the phone. The Rachel's House files were in front of him. Nick had groused about having to deal with a high-powered Court Corporation lawyer to get the court order, but Lynne had thought their requests regarding the security of the files quite reasonable.

"Finish your calls?" she asked.

"Everybody I could reach. I've got a few left I'll try later, after the workday."

"Nick Kelso, volunteering for overtime?"

He shrugged off her teasing. "This is important. Besides, since they stuck me on this thing, I'll pull my weight."

"You always do," Lynne said. And meant it. Nick might be a flirt and a charmer, but he wasn't a slacker on the job. "If you're done with those, let's lock them up."

Nick rolled his eyes. "Yeah, like somebody's going to steal them out of the police station."

But he complied, returning the files to the locked cabinet beside Lynne's desk.

"How are they taking it, the men you've called?"

"About like you might expect. Some of them are pretty alarmed."

"Enough to take precautions, I hope."

"I think so. It's the ones who are just mad I'm worried about."

"Mad?" Now there was a reaction she didn't understand.

"Sure. They feel like those women have caused them enough trouble already, they want to leave it behind, and then this."

"'Those women'?" Lynne's tone was icy, although she knew Nick was only quoting the men he'd talked to.

"Hey, I'm just saying that's how they feel." He shook his head. "You try to tell them, they just can't go around losing control so much that women file reports on them, but it just doesn't get through."

"If it could get through, chances are they wouldn't be hitting women and children in the first place."

And she was ready to hit something herself, Lynne thought.

Kelso seemed to sense it, because he got to his feet. "I've got an interview to do downstairs."

He hadn't mentioned bringing anybody in, so she asked, "Who?"

"Marty Baker."

Lynne blinked. "Mindy Baker's brother?"

"Yeah," he said. "He's a good one," he added as he left.

Lynne sat thinking, recalling her interview with

Mindy. It would be devastating to the girl if her brother was the killer. They were closer than most siblings, survivors bound together by a family history of abuse.

After a moment she got to her feet and headed downstairs; she wanted to watch this.

By the time she got there, Kelso had Marty Baker seated at a table, and was on the other side, on his feet and leaning forward. Already working him hard, Lynne thought as she peered through the one-way glass.

"—give it up, Baker," Kelso was saying. "You've got motive, you had opportunity, and we're going to nail you."

"That's bull and you know it." Mindy's brother was red-faced, clearly angry, and Lynne wondered what Kelso had already said to him.

"I know you did it, Baker." Kelso leaned in then, hands flat on the table, pushing himself into Baker's space. "You might as well make it easy on yourself, because if I have to take you down hard, I promise you'll regret it."

"I didn't do it. Why would I kill some total stranger?"

"I figure you're working your way up to your real target," Kelso said flatly. "Figure you're trying to make it look like some serial killer is on the loose."

"That's really stupid. You could never prove that."

"Watch me. You're going down, all the way, Baker. You'll be an old man when you get out, if you ever do. And your sister will be all used up."

Lynne winced. Kelso was just pushing hard, she told herself. He was using whatever approach he thought would work to solve these murders. But she still didn't like hearing a victim, any victim, further attacked in the course of an investigation.

"You're a loser, Baker, a blue-collar slug who doesn't have a chance. You can't afford the kind of lawyer it'd take to save your ass. So talk to me now, and maybe I can get you some kind of deal."

"Deal? Why the hell do I need a deal? I didn't kill anybody."

Kelso leaned in even closer. He was getting into this, Lynne thought as she saw a vein pulsing at his temple. If she hadn't known he was putting on a show, she would have wondered seriously about him. The young blond man who looked so much like his sister drew back slightly.

"The hell you didn't. You figure because your tramp of a sister got slapped around a little that gives you the right to start murdering innocent men?"

Lynne stiffened as Marty Baker lunged at Kelso across the table. "You son of a bitch!"

Baker was big and strong, but Kelso was a powerhouse. He absorbed the rush without a wobble, and slammed Baker down hard on the table.

"Obviously you've got the temper, too. And when you lose it, you get physical."

Marty repeated his last words, only this time it was muffled since he was facedown on the table in the interrogation room. Kelso leaned over him, his voice going low and menacing. "So, that's your answer? Fine. It'll look good in my report when I tell my boss I've got our killer."

"Go to hell," Marty said, but the rage was gone, replaced by more than a touch of fear.

Lynne turned away then, walking out of the observation room. She headed for the soda machine in the lunchroom, thinking every step of the way. Marty Baker was obviously a very angry young man, and with that temper, he could obviously be easily provoked.

She bought her soda, then stood there sipping at it, thinking, wondering if Kelso was onto something. Wondering if he might have put a crack in this case by driving Baker to snap.

And trying not to dwell on the slurs about Mindy he'd used to do it.

Just as she got back to her desk, her phone was ringing. Nick was already there, and picked it up. Irritation flickered, but she told herself he was closer to it than she was, it was only natural, since they were working the same case. Besides, she didn't get personal phone calls here anyway.

"Yeah . . . yeah . . . when?" Nick was saying. "Who's there? Okay, got it."

She knew before he hung up what he was going to say by the grimness of his expression.

"Another one?"

He nodded. "Number four."

Lynne sighed, her mouth tightening. "That makes no sense. It's too soon after the last one. There was a month between the first two, and three weeks before number three."

"He's a serial killer. Who knows what triggers him," Nick pointed out.

She couldn't argue that, but she knew it wasn't typical for such a quick jump, it was usually more gradual.

Not, she thought as she grabbed her jacket, that that made one bit of difference to the victims.

Regan rested her head in her hands. Alex wouldn't be surprised if she had a powerful headache. He certainly would, if he'd been through what she had.

He watched her as she sat at her desk. How could any cop possibly suspect this woman of murder? True, she was dedicated in her protection of the women of Rachel's House, but murder? No way.

Of course, he had very little to base that on. She had no alibi for any of the murders. And he had only a gut feeling, plus the knowledge that female serial killers, very rare in the first place, almost never followed the same pattern as males.

Well, those two things and the fact he could no longer deny, that Regan Keller interested him. Interested him in a way no woman ever had before.

Ironic, he thought as he watched her rub her eyes. His mother hadn't wanted him to get involved, but he hadn't been able to resist doing a little probing. What he'd found had moved Regan from the category of merely an attractive woman to an intriguing one.

But the attraction he ruefully admitted to aside, there were plenty of other suspects, from what he'd heard. And the pool just seemed to be getting bigger.

And now this, he thought, looking at the bindle of cocaine that lay on her desk.

When at last she lifted her head, when he saw the exhaustion in her eyes, he felt a sudden need to lift the burden from her, or at least distract her from it. He said the first thing that came to him.

"I meant to ask how it went with the detective who was here."

She looked startled for a moment, but then answered. "Fine. I mean, she was very good about it. I'm glad she'll be the new domestic-violence investigator when this is over."

"She didn't harass anybody?"

"No, not really. She pushed a little, but no more than I would have expected."

"I forgot, you'd probably know, wouldn't you? With your dad being a cop, I mean."

"If you mean, do I see the police side of things, yes, I do." Her mouth twisted. "Except when it's one of those bullies you mentioned."

"Is that what the problem was that you had to go see them about?"

"No." She rubbed at her temples. "That was a misguided attempt at retaliation by one of the residents. One of the more difficult residents."

"Difficult?" As in difficult enough to be a suspect? From what he'd heard it didn't sound like Dawn had the nerve, but you just never knew. . . .

"She's having—that is she was having—a tough time making a clean break. She kept thinking if she was just more patient, or more understanding, things would change. Even though her ex slapped her within five minutes, the last time she went to see him."

"And this is the man she wanted to go back to?"

"She was afraid, Alex. This is exactly what the problem is. She stays, he may kill her. She leaves, he may kill her family."

Alex shook his head. He was trying to understand, he really was, but this ugliness seemed almost beyond comprehension.

"Besides," Regan said, "in a lot of cases, the very act of leaving is what triggers the partner into violence. Everybody says get a restraining order, but I can tell you about dozens of cases where that order is the trigger. Did you know one study shows that over ninety percent of the women killed after leaving a batterer are killed within the first year?"

"No." He couldn't think of another thing to say.

Regan let her head loll back on her shoulders. Finally she grimaced and said, "Sorry. I seem to lug that soapbox around with me everywhere."

"It must get heavy, twenty-four hours a day. Don't you ever want to put it down, at least for a while? Get a life of your own?"

"This is my life," she said. The instant the words were out, an odd expression came over her face. For a moment she just sat there. "This *is* my life," she whispered, an undertone of pained realization in her voice. "My entire life."

"Regan—"

"I didn't really realize that until this moment. My aunt tried to tell me, even Marita tried to tell me.

She said I was letting myself become as much a prisoner as they were."

"Maybe it's harder to see when it's by choice."

She shook her head, clearly more in revelation than in negation of his statement. "Amazing. I spend half my time trying to get others to open their eyes, and here I am, blind to the obvious."

"So go to dinner with me tonight."

Not for the first time around Regan it was out before he thought, a problem he'd never had before he'd come here. He might wish he'd never said it, but now that he had, he wasn't about to take it back.

"What?"

"Do something about that life you don't have. Dinner. Tonight."

She was staring at him so blankly that a less secure man might have taken it personally. But he was confident enough to realize what her reaction really meant. He leaned forward, resting his hands on the edge of her desk.

"How long has it been since you were on a date, Regan?" he asked.

She snapped out of her haze. "Too long," she said with a rueful smile, "if I can't even recognize someone asking me."

"Now that you have, shall I ask again?"

"No."

Alex felt such a fierce letdown it shocked him. "Oh. Well," was all he could manage to say.

"I just meant you don't have to ask again," Regan said with an almost shy smile. "I'd love to."

"Oh! Okay," Alex said inanely, wondering why a simple smile seemed to have wiped his mind clean.

"But first," she said reluctantly, "I have to deal with that." She gestured to the folded paper on her desk with an expression of distaste.

"What do you want to do about it?" he asked, almost glad she'd changed the subject.

She gave him a sideways sort of look. "You found it."

"But on your property."

"You mean Court Corporation property. They hold the deed."

Which made it in essence his property, Alex thought. Now there was an entanglement.

"Any idea whose it might be?" he asked.

She rubbed her hands up and down her face again, as if the pain were worsening. "There's only one current resident with a drug history, but that only means she got caught. It's not unusual for a woman in an abusive relationship to resort to drugs to cope."

"What would happen to her if you found out?"

"She'd be gone," Regan said grimly. "It's one of the most nonnegotiable rules, no drugs or alcohol."

"So, do you want to find out?"

"Honestly? I don't know. I know my answer should be 'Of course,' but . . ."

"How about 'not right now' for an answer?" he suggested softly.

For a moment she just looked at him, but then she smiled. "That works."

"Good. Forget about it, for now."

"But what do I do with it? I can't just leave it

here, and I'm certainly not going to carry it
around."

"Lock it up somewhere."

She nodded. "All right." She got up, picked up
the bindle as if it were contaminated, walked to the
file cabinet, and pulled open the top drawer.
"There's lots of room, since the police have most of
my files. I just hope they don't come back with a
court order for the whole cabinet while this is in
there."

"I'm sure your lawyer can head them off if they
try."

She brightened at that. "He does seem rather
proficient."

"I imagine CourtCorp wouldn't stand for anything else."

"CourtCorp?"

Oops. Not a term that really fit his current per-
sona.

"Yeah," he managed to say with a grin. "I read
somewhere that's what they call it."

To his relief she just smiled back at him as she
dropped the folded paper into the drawer and shut
it, then pushed the locking button at the top. And
the effect that smile had on him made him wonder
just how stupid he was being, getting more deeply
involved with Regan Keller.

Lynne was already sure, but she kept her mouth
shut. Nick wouldn't be much help, since he'd not
been to the previous murder scenes, but Ben would
see the clue, she was certain. For all his bad temper,
he was a good cop with a lot of experience.

The scene was just as bloody as the previous ones. Even though Vista Shores rarely had murders, she'd seen enough blood in her nine years on the job, and it never ceased to amaze her how it seemed to expand. The smallest spill looked huge and ominous. A pool like this looked horrifying, even seeping into the dirt as it did here. And it had clearly horrified the young couple in jogging gear who had found the body. They were looking shell-shocked as they stood to one side, giving information to Nick.

The victim was a big man, soft around the midriff, in an expensive-looking suit. He lay on his back, his arms flung outward haphazardly, his legs bent awkwardly, as if he'd been simply dumped here already unconscious or dead. The gaping wound at his throat looked even more grotesque above the neatly knotted tie. Bits of white she knew were cartilage showed amid the sliced flesh. The metallic smell of blood still lingered, although the edges of the puddle were drying out.

Lynne blinked as the flash on the crime-scene investigator's camera went off once more. His partner, who normally worked another shift but who had been called in to help with this, was working on the sketch of the crime scene, while another officer tied off more crime-scene tape. Then would come the painstaking work of gathering anything at the scene that could possibly be evidence.

It was a daunting task, in this public area of brush and dirt. The only advantage they had was that it appeared from the blood that the murder had taken place on the spot. Many times in brushy outdoor areas like this they were dealing with a body that had been dumped, which made crime-scene investigation exhausting, time-consuming, and all too often pointless. And the dirt might provide them with a footprint, somewhere.

Durwin had pulled on his gloves and proceeded methodically through his search grid, moving carefully, with plastic boots on his feet to avoid contaminating the scene, doing a visual search only first. He called out things he wanted checked as he went, and Lynne made careful notes to be turned over to CSI when they took over after finishing their photos.

Lynne had deferred to Durwin as the senior investigator on the scene, and when he handed her the man's wallet, which appeared untouched, she retreated to handle the second task he'd tacitly assigned her, that of inventorying and booking the victim's property.

The photograph on the driver's license appeared to match the dead man, and the address was in an upscale area in the hills above where they were standing. Lynne pulled out her cell phone and began the routine records and ID check, asking records to call her back with the local record when they had it, before they began the wider search. The name wasn't familiar to her from the Rachel's House records.

She then inventoried the contents of the wallet. Six hundred dollars in cash; robbery obviously wasn't involved. Several platinum credit cards, a bank ATM card, a dry-cleaning receipt that appeared to be for the very suit he was wearing. She wrote down the name, address, and number of the dry cleaners. Three business cards from different executives with advertising agencies were the last items, and she made the same notes from those before she added them to the evidence bag.

Nothing personal, she noticed. No photos of family, no photos at all. No mementos, no notes, nothing more personal than that dry-cleaners receipt.

By the time she was done her phone rang, just as Durwin straightened up and came toward her. He waited until she was through jotting down the information the records clerk was rattling off, then handed her a very expensive-looking watch and two heavy gold rings, one with a large, solitaire-cut diamond.

"Watch on left wrist, diamond ring on the left pinky, the other on right ring finger."

Lynne filled out the property slip, then dropped the times in a fresh bag.

"Bucks up, this guy," Durwin said.

"So it seems. The address on the license is in Vista Heights. And records says he's clean, except for a couple of speeding tickets and one incident of road rage."

"He the suspect or the victim?"

"According to the record, it was mutual."

"You got them checking the address history for call outs?"

She nodded. "They're running it."

"Name ring any bells?"

"No. It's not anywhere in the records for Rachel's House."

"Could be the wife or girlfriend's using a different name," he said, his voice oddly neutral.

"Still, his real name should be in the files."

"You got an opinion on this, Garrison?"

She looked at the man, for once ignoring the grumpy exterior and instead focusing on the wealth of knowledge and experience he'd gained in his twenty-two years as a cop. She was less than a year into detectives, stuck in what she knew they called the ghetto of sex crimes and domestic violence, assigned to this case only because of the batterer connection between the victims. If she was smart, she'd keep her mouth shut. If she was right, Durwin should see it, too.

But she hadn't got to where she was by playing dumb. It was already tough enough for a woman in this job. She wasn't going to back off from something that was crystal clear to her, just because she was afraid to be wrong. She wasn't wrong. She'd have to be stupid to miss what was so obvious, and she was not stupid.

"Yes," she said, "I do."

Durwin gave an exasperated grunt. "And what is that opinion, Detective Garrison?"

She met his "I dare you" gaze steadily. And said it.

"It's not the same killer."

CHAPTER 7

Regan laughed again, and ruefully acknowledged it had been a very long time since she'd really relaxed. Dinner had been delicious, and she couldn't deny she found looking across a table at Alex Edwards as appealing as the decadent chocolate dessert they were sharing.

"Well, how was I to know that's what the gesture meant there?" Alex said with a grin.

"You've traveled a lot," she said.

"I've been here and there. You?"

She shook her head. "I've lived in Vista Shores my whole life. I've never really been anywhere, except for trips to the Midwest to visit family when I was a kid." She gave a halfhearted laugh. "Sounds pretty pitiful, doesn't it?"

"Only if you want to travel and aren't doing it."

"I'd like to. There are so many places I'd love to see, but I can't be gone that long."

"Nobody seemed upset about you going out to dinner tonight."

Regan almost blushed remembering the teasing

she'd taken from Mindy, Laura, and the others. They had not been upset but delighted that she had a date. That the date was with Alex the roofer only added spice. So much spice that Regan blurted out the first thing in her mind.

"So how did a nice guy like you escape getting married?"

She nearly groaned aloud when the words came out, but he answered easily.

"I think she was the one who escaped," he said with a crooked smile. "It was close, but after a three-year engagement she decided I wasn't serious enough."

Regan swirled the last of her wine in her glass. "Was she right?"

"Probably," he admitted. "What about you?"

She shrugged. "Never any time."

"By accident or intentionally?"

She drew back slightly. "What?"

He took the last swallow of his wine before he answered. "I just wondered if maybe working and living at Rachel's House made you as wary of men as the residents are. Couldn't blame you if it did."

She thought about that. "I suppose I am more wary than most. I don't think about it all the time, like they must, but I do catch myself being surprised when a man really cares about what's happening to these women, or sometimes even when a man is simply nice."

He set down his empty glass, and looked at her so intently she felt pinned by his gaze. "In that case, I hope I've surprised you twice."

"You have," she said, giving him his due. *More than twice*, she added to herself. *A lot more.*

Feeling flustered, she asked the question that had been bothering her since this afternoon.

"How did you know that was cocaine?"

He shrugged. "I've come across it here and there. Had to fire a guy who was using once."

"Oh."

That simply, her suspiciousness faded. And she wondered if it were true that she was becoming more and more like the women of Rachel's House every day, always wary, distrustful, and seeing every man as a threat of some kind.

"I had an idea about that, though," Alex said. "If you decide you want to know whose it is, we could put it back, and install a video camera."

"To spy?" she said, not liking the sound of that.

He shrugged. "I suppose, if you want to call it that. But it would be a good idea to have a camera anyway, just in case the wrong person shows up on your doorstep. In fact, I'm surprised you don't already have one."

"Mrs. Court wanted them, but we've been trying to keep the lowest possible profile in the neighborhood, and having cameras all over the outside didn't seem the best idea to me, until now." She thought again of the cocaine tucked away in her file drawer. "Cameras for security are one thing, but . . . I just don't like the idea of spying on my people. So many of them had to live with that, with their abusers."

He looked troubled. "It's up to you. But if it's

going to happen anyway, it wouldn't take much to set up the cameras now."

"I'll think about it."

"It also might make your people feel a little safer. Might make somebody who's trying to get to them think twice, too, knowing they're being videotaped."

She smiled at him. "You after my job?"

He blinked and drew back. "Sorry. Guess I got a little carried away."

"Don't apologize. I—" The ring of her cell phone cut her off. "Excuse me," she said. "I can't really turn it off in case—"

"I know. Go ahead and answer."

She'd expected it to be Marita or one of the others. The voice of Detective Garrison made her breath catch in her throat.

"I'm sorry to bother you, Regan, but I need to ask you a couple of things."

"All right."

"Does the name William Wheeler mean anything to you?"

"No, it doesn't sound familiar."

"Do you know if any Rachel's House resident has ever had a connection to anyone in Vista Heights?"

"I don't recall any, but I'd have to look to be sure."

"I've already checked the files, I just wondered if you'd maybe heard something that wasn't in there."

"No, I haven't. Is . . . has something happened?"

There was a pause, and then, "You'll hear about

it in the morning anyway. We've had another murder."

"Oh, God," Regan whispered.

"But this time there doesn't seem to be a connection to Rachel's House. Not that we can find, anyway. There was a history of disturbance calls to the police by neighbors, but no arrests, no complaints by the wife."

Regan felt a little bewildered. "No connection?"

"Not that we know of. But don't read too much into this, Regan. There's more to it than I can tell you right now. Please keep on as you have been."

"All right."

"Now I've got to go."

For a moment after the detective had disconnected she just sat there, staring at the phone.

"Regan? Are you all right?"

Alex's voice was soft, concerned. She looked up at him. "There's been another killing."

"I gathered."

He reached out and took the phone she was still holding—white-knuckle tight, she realized—from her hand and set it on the table. Then he took her hands in his. Within moments his warmth seemed to chase the chill that had overtaken her. She met his gaze.

"It'll be in the news tomorrow. But she said this time he's not connected to us."

"Is that what that was about?"

She nodded. "I've never heard of this man." Hope speared through her. "Maybe it's not all connected to us after all. Maybe the first three were just coincidence."

"Did the detective say that?"

"No." She reined in her wishful thinking. "She said there was more to it, but she couldn't tell me yet."

"Better keep on as you were, then."

"That's what she said to do."

"I didn't mean to stomp on your optimism," he said.

"No, you're right. I was just hoping." She picked up her phone and dropped it back in her purse. "But I'd better get back. I'll have to tell them there's been another. But at least it's not one of theirs this time."

"Unless there's a connection you don't know about."

"I don't think so. I know about the husbands, and if any of them had had a boyfriend from Vista Heights, I think I would have heard about it."

Alex went still. "Vista Heights?"

She nodded. "That's what she said. Or at least, she wanted to know if anyone at Rachel's House had a connection to anyone from there."

"What was the name she gave you?"

Regan hesitated, then thought that if it was going to be all over TV and the newspapers in the morning, there was no reason not to answer.

"William Wheeler," she said. He went stiller yet. "Alex?"

"Whew," he said, shaking his head sharply.

Her eyes widened at his reaction. "My God, you know him?"

"Yeah. Yeah, I do. Did."

"I'm sorry," she said automatically. "Did you do

work for him?" Vista Heights was the richest community in Vista Shores, and possibly in the entire
county, and it didn't seem probable Alex would
have met him any other way.

He shook his head again. "I did some work near
his house. But why would the killer pick him?"

"Detective Garrison said there had been several
calls to the house for disturbances."

"Maybe," Alex said doubtfully. "But battering? A
guy like Will? I mean, he's a big executive with a
development company, they're really well off,
and—"

Regan's voice turned to ice. "You think abuse is a
blue-collar crime? That it doesn't happen in
wealthy families, or behind closed doors of man-
sions as well as shacks?"

Alex sat back, an expression of disbelief on his
face. He seemed to be having a very hard time with
this, and Regan reined in her instinctive anger.

"I knew a woman once who lived in the same
kind of neighborhood. Wealthy, powerful husband,
great house, great life, the whole scenario. People
used to talk about her style, how she always
dressed with such flair. Her trademark was colorful
scarves around her neck, to go with every outfit.
No one ever realized she wore them to cover the
bruises. She stayed, because she was too embarrassed to leave. She stayed," Regan said flatly,
"until he killed her."

Alex shook his head again, but the disbelief was
gone. He looked as if he were battling to come to
grips with the idea that even a gilded cage could
hold such ugliness.

"A man like that may appear successful," she said, calmer now, "but inside he feels inadequate. And women aren't quite people to him. In those cases sometimes they're merely ornaments, the crowning element in the image of success he wants to present. And when that ornament dares to have a mind of her own, it ruins his self-image."

There was a long silence then. Regan felt as if she'd said too much, and Alex looked like he had enough to deal with right now. At least he was trying, she told herself. And actually, it said a great deal about him, and about how foreign the concept of abuse was to his life, that it was so hard for him to comprehend.

"Let's go back to the cocaine," he finally said. "It's simpler."

"Sad, isn't it, that that's probably true?"

He nodded, looking about as weary of the whole thing as she felt right now. "What do you want to do?"

"Just wait, I think. I really don't want the police involved with that, not on top of everything else. At least, not yet."

She watched him, wondering if he would go along. Before the thought fully formed, he did. "I can understand that."

"Maybe knowing their hiding place was found will stop them. I know," she added at his doubtful look, "it's not likely. So I'll be watching, too. And I'll do some searching inside the house. And maybe the cameras would be a good idea."

"Don't do that searching alone. I'll go with you.

We can say I'm checking for inside damage from the roof."

She sighed. "I suppose."

He pulled over a napkin and wrote something on it. "That's my cell. If you suspect something and I'm not there, call me."

She looked at the number he'd scrawled in a bold, confident hand. Then at his face. "That's a bit above and beyond the call, isn't it?"

"No."

The short, simple answer said so much, yet left out so much. And she wondered late into the night why a simple roofer would bother to get involved.

"Ben, you're certain of this?"

Lynne stayed silent as Durwin addressed the captain. "Yes, sir. We both agree. It's not the same guy."

Lynne was pleased Durwin had included her in front of the captain. In fact, the old guy had been acting a little oddly ever since they'd left the murder scene last night.

"And you're sure because . . . ?" Captain Greer asked.

"No ritual," Durwin said succinctly.

Greer sighed. His normally clear brown eyes were looking bloodshot this morning. "Lynne, would you do me the favor of being a little more specific than your closemouthed partner?"

Lynne hesitated, wondering if she'd be stepping on Durwin's toes if she answered. She glanced at him, and to her surprise he nodded at her.

"Answer the man," he said gruffly.

Hastily, Lynne gathered her thoughts. "As Ben said, the ritual is missing. The first three victims were all found in the same position, facedown, their knees under them, as if they'd been forced to kneel. Their hands had been placed together, as in prayer, as if he'd made them pray for forgiveness. So far we've managed to keep the details of that out of the press."

"I remember that from the reports," Greer said. "Didn't the ME and CSI say they were positioned after death?" At Lynne's nod he asked, "And this victim?"

"Flat on his back, no arrangement at all. As if he was just dropped there. And no defense wounds on his hands like the others, either."

"Anything else?"

"He still had his watch."

That was the clincher for her. She knew most serial killers took trophies from their victims, and in the case of the Avenger watches were apparently his trophy of choice. Perhaps symbolic of his victim's time having run out.

"Maybe he was interrupted this time."

"I don't think so," Durwin put in. "Indications are the man was killed where he was found, which was out of sight in that brush below the bluff. Another reason I think it's not the same suspect. The other three were found in the open, in paved, commercial areas. That's part of the reason clues have been scarce. No branches to snag fibers or hair, no dirt for footprints."

Slowly, Greer nodded. "So you think it's a copycat?"

"Or somebody taking advantage of the situation to get rid of the victim," Durwin said.

"All right," Greer said, accepting their assessment. "I'll assign Kelso to that one as a separate case. You two continue as you were. And take anybody you need to help with the grunt work."

"Any decision on a task force yet, sir?" Lynne asked.

"I don't know, but I have a meeting with the chief this afternoon. This may help him stall for time."

"So he'll go public with the news it's a different killer."

"He'll probably have to." Greer seemed to hesitate. "Are we certain there's no connection to the shelter?"

"You mean, are any of the residents themselves suspects?" Durwin asked. When Greer nodded, Durwin gestured at Lynne. "She's done those interviews."

Lynne was already shaking her head. "I don't think so. There's one with a prior assault charge, but it was dismissed as self-defense. There are no indications strong enough to counter the unlikelihood of a female as the killer. As an accomplice . . . I don't know. It's possible."

Greer sighed. "Conspiracy. Just what we need."

Lynne made sure her voice was even before she spoke this time. "Investigator Garrison's profile indicates it's probably a solo act. He thinks the Avenger aspect would prevent the killer from using anyone at Rachel's House to help him."

"He's got the best gut in the county on this stuff,

so we'll go with that," Greer said. "But keep pushing for any ideas from the shelter people, no matter how far out."

They both nodded and turned to go.

"Lynne, can you spare me another minute?"

"Of course," she said, turning back as Durwin left.

"Close the door, will you?"

Uh-oh, Lynne thought as she did as he asked.

"The chief told me that at the least he'll probably have to accept the sheriff's office offer of their head homicide expert."

Uh-oh indeed, Lynne thought. "Yes, sir."

"You have a problem working with him?"

"Nothing that will interfere," she said, hoping her voice didn't sound as odd to him as it did to her. But working in close step with her ex-husband was an idea that put a strain on more than just her voice.

"Good."

She walked out of her boss' office thinking she'd been lucky when the biggest problem she'd had was working with cranky Ben Durwin.

"It's true, Alexander."

His mother sounded as tired as he felt. He'd called her with the shocking news, and she had immediately set to work ferreting out the truth of the matter, personally calling the police chief and anyone else who had the information she wanted. Finally they had to face the fact that the Court family had been living within a block of a batterer so typical it made them feel blind and stupid to have missed it.

Priscilla Wheeler had been treated repeatedly for telltale injuries: black eyes, broken bones, contusions.

It had taken a while for the police to gather her records, but once they had, the evidence was all there in grim black and white. Different doctors, different hospitals, but put together a horrific pattern.

"Right in our own backyard," his mother said wearily. "And for all my fighting for the cause, I never saw it."

"It's not like you were close to them, Mom."

"But I saw Priscilla on occasion. And never pushed when she would make some obviously false excuse for having missed this or that function." She sighed. "Perhaps we can help her now."

"I met Will more than once, and never suspected a thing," Alex said. "You never expect to find something like this so close to home."

"That's no excuse."

No, his mother had never been one for excuses. And if he knew her, this would fire her to even more intense involvement.

"What would you have done?" he asked, suddenly curious. "If Dad had ever . . . you know."

"I'd like to think I'd have left him alive," his mother replied. Then her tone changed abruptly. "That was facetious, and this is not a joking matter. I cannot imagine your father ever doing such a thing, but I loved him with all my heart, so perhaps I would have given him a second chance. But only one second chance. Unless he struck you in that way. There are no second chances for anyone who hurts my child."

Alex smiled. His mother was still a lioness when it came to her cub, never mind that he was capable of taking care of himself. He doubted that would ever change.

Regan would understand that, he thought. And then, as if she'd read his thought, his mother asked, "How is Regan?"

"Torn, I think. She's upset about another murder, but relieved there's no connection to Rachel's House on this one."

"Which reminds me," Lillian said. "Lewis Raines told me something, in strict confidence."

"Which you're about to betray by telling me?"

"Because I trust you to keep it to yourself," she said pointedly.

"Yes, ma'am," he said in the exaggeratedly dutiful tone that usually made her laugh. She didn't.

"They're reasonably certain William Wheeler was not killed by the same person as the others."

Alex let out a low whistle. "So that's what she meant, that there was more to it."

"Who?"

"Detective Garrison."

"I spoke to her. I liked her."

"Regan does, too."

"You two are getting along all right, then?"

"Me and Regan?" He was startled by the little spurt of warmth he felt just at the sound of their linked names. "Sure. Why wouldn't we?"

He wasn't about to tell his mother that, up until the phone call, the night he'd taken Regan to dinner had been one of the best evenings he'd had in a long time. Mom had been at him to settle down for a long time, but since her idea of that included gluing himself to a desk at CourtCorp, he was in no hurry.

"By the way," she said, "we heard from Jakarta. The leak was who you thought it was, and it's been handled."

Alex let out a breath of relief. "Good. I'm glad. That'll do our manager good, too. He felt pretty bad about that component getting into the wrong hands."

"He said to thank you."

"Yeah, yeah," Alex said. It was his job, after all.

After they'd hung up, Alex leaned back in his chair, rubbed his eyes, and then his right shoulder, which had been telling him lately just what it thought of this new activity he was subjecting it to.

If this kept up, he was going to have to slow down his work or be faced with coming up with an excuse to hang around after the roof was done. He was done with tearing off the old roof, had the new plywood sheathing down, and had started nailing the new asphalt shingles down on one section.

He could drag out the trickier stuff like doing the valleys, ridge vents, and the flashing around the chimney, but eventually he was going to be done. His mother had given no indication that anything had changed in her view. He was to stay put, his mission the same as it had been.

He could get her back. Joel Koslow knew he could. He could make her come back to him, just as he always had. She'd never leave him for good, he knew she wouldn't. She didn't have the brains, for one thing. And that was the way he liked it.

"She's not worth it, Joey. No woman is. I hate seeing you mooning over some worthless bitch."

"Hey, Pop, Mindy was okay, when things were

right. I had her trained, she knew how I liked things."

"You can train another one," his father pointed out.

"Yeah, but I liked this one. I want things back the way they were."

"Easier to get a new one."

"I hate that. It took me a long time to find Mindy. Most women are just above themselves, think they're too good for a guy."

"If you take her back, you'll have to break her for good," the senior Koslow warned.

"She'll do what I say."

"If that was true, she wouldn't be in that place, she'd be where she was supposed to be."

"She'll be back. She knows she's nothing without me. She adores me."

"If she adores you, why'd she report you when all you did was teach her a little lesson?"

"She got talked into it by some whiny bitch cop, I bet. She'd never think of it on her own."

"Women are nothing but trouble, son. I tried to warn you about that one. She's just like those others, seems like she knows how things ought to be, but then they pull this kind of crap."

"She'll be back, Pop. She'll be back, and when she is, I'll straighten things out once and for all. She'll—"

The ringing of his phone cut him off. He picked up the receiver and said hello. He heard the voice that responded and then, slowly, a wide grin spread across his face. He kept the phone to his ear, but punched the mute button and looked at his father.

"I told you she'd be back!"

CHAPTER 8

After a week, Regan began to relax a little as they settled back into their old routine. It was quieter than she could ever remember, and the women of Rachel's House were slowly unwinding. For the moment, every abuser in the city was lying low. Thanks to the Avenger, whoever he might be.

The new video cameras on the exterior of the building probably helped, too. Mrs. Court had accelerated the schedule, because of what was happening, she said. Regan wondered if perhaps Alex had mentioned it to her. He didn't seem at all intimidated by the formidable woman, and it seemed too coincidental coming on the heels of their conversation.

But today, on a lovely, sunny afternoon, it was hard to believe anything could really be wrong. Mindy, Marita, and a couple of the others were out in the yard weeding and trimming, since Mitch had been sick and missed his last two visits. Mr. Pilson was here, helping out and chatting with everyone. The newcomers, Donna Grant and her son, were in the house. Even though they had managed to escape the boy's father, they were still skittish, uncertain. Regan understood that and had told them to stay comfortably inside.

She'd had to have a talk with Donna when she'd heard her telling the child that his father wanted to kill them both, explaining that right now nothing was gained by further terrifying the already frightened little boy. The woman had seemed offended, something most of the women she met didn't have the energy for, but she had retreated quietly to the room they'd been assigned.

"We should send Mitch flowers," Mindy said. "He's always doing them for us."

Regan smiled widely. Mindy had just taken a big step, although she doubted she realized it. But thinking of doing something for someone else was a tiny step out of victimhood, and it gave Regan hope for the girl.

"That's not a bad idea, Blondie," Marita said. "Shall we pick him some?"

"I don't know," Mindy said, looking around. "He's awfully particular about where you take them from. When he was picking some to take his mother the other day, it was like he'd throw the world out of balance if he took the wrong one."

"Mitch," Marita said with a grin, "is particular about everything in his garden."

"And it's beautiful," Mr. Pilson put in. "Anyone for lemonade?" They all chorused a yes, and the man smiled delightedly and trotted through the hedge to his house.

"He's so sweet," Mindy said.

"Yes. He never misses a chance to help, even if it's just to carry groceries in for me," Marita said in agreement.

"He helped me with that file cabinet when it got stuck last week," Regan said. "We definitely got lucky with him for a neighbor."

A sound from above drew their attention. With a sideways glance at Regan, Marita said, "Now, there's a man with some real nice particulars."

Mindy giggled. "And he's showing them off today."

Regan blushed. In the heat, Alex had pulled off his shirt about an hour ago. About the time Mindy had suggested they go out and catch up on the garden chores. Regan hadn't made the connection until the unguarded moment when she'd glanced up and seen him. For the longest time she'd stood there, probably gaping.

"So when are you going out again?" Mindy asked her.

"He hasn't asked," Regan said, turning away before she couldn't blame her high color on the sun any longer.

"He will," Marita told her. "He's just working up to it, that's all."

"I thought you didn't quite trust him," Regan said, remembering when the woman had warned her to be cautious, saying she just had a feeling.

"I just said I thought there's more to him than we're seeing," Marita pointed out. "Not that he's hiding something bad."

"Unless it's 'bad' in a very good way," Mindy said, giggling again.

Mr. Pilson returned with a tray and frosty glasses full of lemonade that he passed around. Regan took a long drink of hers, and thanked the man for thinking of the perfect drink for a hot day. She also admired the tray itself, a black and red lacquered piece that looked oriental to her.

Alex didn't come down off the roof, nor did Mr. Pilson invite him, which was unlike the kindly man. But speaking of Alex, that wasn't the only thing unlikely around here of late. The reaction of the women of Rachel's House, Regan thought as she plucked dead petals off of one of Mitch's prized roses, didn't make sense to her. She would have expected them to warn her off, to tell her not to trust any man. She hoped it was a good sign that they didn't, that it was a sign they realized there were good men out there. Men like Alex.

Because he was a good man. He was obviously a hard worker, and he also tried hard to understand Rachel's House and the occupants. Most men just here to do a job wouldn't bother.

The cordless phone clipped to Regan's belt rang once, then stopped. She frowned, reached for it, hit the talk button, and held it to her ear.

"—right outside, I'll get her."

Irritation shot through her. She'd given Donna a copy of the house rules, which included the residents not answering the business phone, but either she hadn't read them or hadn't understood it was for their own protection. Regan headed for the house at a run.

Donna beat her to the front door. Looking perfectly calm, she smiled at Regan and said, "Phone call for you. A Mrs. Court?"

Okay, maybe the chewing out Donna deserved would have to wait. Or maybe she should just give Donna the benefit of the doubt; she was new at this. "Those rules I gave you when you got here? *Read* them."

Donna frowned, but Regan hastened past her to her office and picked up the phone and uttered a slightly breathless greeting.

"Regan? It's Lillian Court."

"Hello, Lillian." It had been one of the major tasks of her life, learning to call the elegant, imposing Mrs. Court Lillian, but the woman had graciously insisted. "Are you home?"

"Yes, I arrived back last night."

"How was your trip?"

"Productive, I hope."

"I was hoping more for relaxing," Regan said, meaning it. She'd never known anyone who kept up the pace this woman did.

"Thank you for worrying, dear. But it's you we should be worrying about. How are you holding up under all the strain?"

"It's been rough," she admitted.

"I'm sure it has."

"The Court lawyers have been wonderful, though. They've really helped, made us feel like we're not dealing with this all alone."

"Good," Lillian said. "Now, if you don't mind, I'd like to come by this afternoon."

Regan's smile turned to a grimace. She wasn't surprised, but that didn't stop her nerves from tightening up. No matter how kind Lillian had always been to her, the innate power of the woman still made her nervous. She managed to answer steadily enough.

"Fine. I'll make certain I'm here."

"I just want to be sure you're all all right," Lillian reassured her. "And see if there's anything you need. Oh, by the way, did that roofer show up?"

Regan felt herself blush, and was thankful Lillian had asked now rather than in person, when she couldn't have helped but see it. "Alex? Yes, he did. He's doing a great job. Very helpful."

"He's done good work for me before."

"He told me. He seems . . . very nice."

Lillian laughed, and there was a tone to it that Regan thought sounded odd. "He must be on his best behavior, then."

"He's been wonderful," Regan said, feeling oddly compelled to defend him. "He's been great about being careful around the residents. I don't think any of them are wary of him anymore. And he's really making an effort to understand things."

"He has a curious nature, I've noticed," Lillian said, that note Regan had heard in her laughter now in her voice. "I'll see you in about an hour, if that's all right."

"Fine," Regan said again.

When she replaced the receiver, she looked up to see all the women except Donna clustered in the doorway.

"Where do you want us to start?" Marita asked.

"The kitchen," Regan said.

"I'll help," Mindy put in. "I have to leave for

work—thank goodness, she makes me *so* nervous—but I've got about twenty minutes."

Regan smiled at them all, and at her own urge to immediately scrub Rachel's House top to bottom, as if Lillian cared about their housekeeping.

"Let's clean the kitchen, and just tidy up elsewhere."

"Just the big chunks, then," Marita said. "You got it."

"What about that box of stuff in the living room?"

A large carton of domestic items had been delivered that morning, donations from the community left at the off-site center. They hadn't yet had a chance to pick through it and see what was going to be useful. And now it sat in the middle of the living area, so heavy it would take them forever to drag it out of the way. They could empty it, but that would only spread out the clutter.

"Mr. Pilson just left. Maybe he could come back and help move it," Marita said.

"It would break his back," Mindy said, then brightened. "I'll bet Alex could move it. I'll go ask him."

"I'll bet you will," Marita said teasingly. Then her dark eyes narrowed. "No poaching, girl. He's Regan's."

Regan groaned aloud. "Stop it, will you? He took me out to dinner one time, after a rough day. That's it."

"Sure," Mindy said, then laughed and ran toward the door.

That she had been decidedly let down that a

week had passed with no indication Alex wanted a repeat of that evening was not something Regan cared to admit.

"You know," Marita said, "it almost sounds normal around here."

Regan nodded. "It does, doesn't it?"

"It's good to hear laughter again." Marita gave Regan a wide grin. "Even that girl's giggling sounds good."

Regan laughed, but it died in her throat when the front door opened and Alex walked in—shirt back on, Regan saw thankfully—Mindy at his heels.

"Heard you needed some heavy lifting," he said.

"Regan does. We're cleaning the kitchen, before the big cheese arrives," the women chorused, then vanished into the kitchen, leaving Regan and Alex alone.

"What was that all about?" Alex asked.

"Nothing," she said, thinking that if he would just drop it, she could avoid total humiliation. "There's the box."

He looked at her as if he knew exactly what she was thinking. But he didn't say a word, just walked over to the box, and she let out a silent breath of relief.

"Where do you want it?"

"We don't really have anyplace to get it out of sight, so just out of the middle of the floor and against the wall would be fine."

It wasn't a light weight even for him, but he managed it a lot quicker than they would have. "Anything else?" he asked when he was done.

"I don't think so."

He looked around. "What's the big deal? Just because Mrs. Court is coming?"

"She doesn't come here all that often, so we like to make a good impression."

Alex shrugged. "I'd think she cares more about what you're doing than how clean you keep the place doing it."

Regan knew he was right, Lillian had said so in so many words before. She let out a breath. "You're right. I don't think she's the white glove inspection type, if the job's getting done."

"Sounds like you really admire her."

"I do. I've always thought the best part of being wealthy would be to be able to help people who have really gotten a raw deal. She does it."

"What about the con artists, the ones who scam generous people?"

She shrugged. "That's the price you pay. And worth it, if you help those who are honestly trying."

Alex smiled. "No wonder you two get along."

Regan gave him a rather sheepish smile in return. "She just makes me nervous."

"She has that effect on people."

Odd, Regan thought. It took her a moment to figure out exactly what had struck her, then realized it was the same tone in Alex's voice that she'd heard in Lillian Court's when she'd spoken of him.

"Besides," Alex added with a grin, "this place is fine. You ought to see mine."

Don't you dare blush again, Regan ordered herself. She ignored his words and said, rather stiffly, "Thank you for moving the box."

His forehead creased, but only for a moment. "Sure."

After he'd gone she told herself she'd never really expected him to ask her out again, he was just being nice, and went back to her office determined not to think about it anymore.

Joy filled her. It was going to be different this time. She was sure of it. Her life would return to the fairy-tale happiness she'd known when Joel had first fallen in love with her, when he'd been so swept away he'd demanded she not see anyone else after their second date.

She reached out to take his hand as they lounged on two chaises on his apartment balcony. He smiled at her, that lovely, sweet smile that had so charmed her in the beginning.

"I've been thinking," he said. "We should move."

"Move?"

"Yeah." He gestured over his shoulder toward the apartment that had been the site of many an ugly scene between them. "Away from here, so we can start over. Up to the mountains."

She was touched. She'd always loved the mountains, but didn't realize that he'd ever taken notice of the fact. That he would think of this, for her, only proved she was right. Things would be different this time.

"Pop's got a place up near Arrowhead. It's small, just a cabin with one bedroom, but we could add on another."

Her heart leapt. There was only one reason she could think of that they'd need another bedroom:

children. At last, she thought. Her most precious
dream was finally going to come true.

The joy welling up inside her overflowed; it really was going to be all right. Joel had a need to
have things his own way, but most men did, didn't
they? She could live with that, as long as the other
stopped. And it would, now. She'd done the right
thing, leaving him for a while. He'd learned his lesson, and now everything would be perfect. They
would be married, and start a family right away.

"Oh, Joel, I love you. We're going to be so
happy!"

"I know, baby. It'll all be different this time,
won't it?"

She sighed happily, leaning back against the
lounge cushions. "I know it will. Just think, a new
life together, just the two of us." She blushed as she
added, "Well, until baby makes three, anyway."

"Baby?" He sat up abruptly, staring down at her.
She quickly realized he was thinking she was
telling him she was already pregnant. She sat up
quickly and turned to face him.

"Oh, no," she assured him. "I just meant when
the time comes."

"That time," Joel said, "will never come. You
think I want you fat and ugly, and then have you
spend all your time on a squalling brat? No,
thanks."

She stared at him, bewildered. "But when you
said we could add on to the cabin—"

"I meant for us, you idiot!"

"But the other bedroom—"

"Is still Pop's, of course. He says he's ready to move up there full-time."

She felt her dream begin to crumble around the edges. "You want us to live with your father?" she asked in a tiny voice.

"Sure. It's his place. We're lucky he's nice enough to let us live there with him."

"I . . ." She swallowed tightly. *Things are going to be different now, you're allowed to disagree,* she told herself. "I'm not sure I can do that."

He frowned, and the crumbling accelerated. "Of course you can. He's easy to get along with."

"He hates me."

"Don't be stupid. He just doesn't like it when you get out of line, that's all. But since you're not going to do that anymore, it's no problem."

The sound of her illusion shattering completely was almost audible in her ringing ears. She took in a deep breath, and gathered every bit of strength she'd gained since going to Rachel's House.

"Is that what you meant when you said it would all be different this time?"

"What?"

"Did you mean that I would change, not you?"

"There's nothing *wrong* with me, baby. You're the one who keeps screwing up."

It came back in a rush then, all the awful memories her hope had buried.

"Pop didn't want me to give you a second chance, but I told him I'd keep you straight this time," Joel said.

"You'll keep me straight," she repeated numbly.

And suddenly Regan Keller's voice was echoing in her head.

"Regan was right," she whispered. "You'll never change, will you?"

He leapt to his feet. And the old Joel, the one who had terrified her, was staring down at her.

"I don't need to change a damn thing. You're the one who needs to change. What kind of crap did they feed you in that damn place?"

"The truth," she whispered, unable to betray Regan and Rachel's House even now.

"Truth? You mean that all men are bastards or some other feminist bullshit?"

Slowly, she stood up and faced him. Reality was staring her in the face now, and it was uglier than she had ever remembered. And even knowing what it might cost her, she said with the certainty that safety and distance—thanks to Rachel's House—had given her.

"No. That kids who grow up in an abusive home are a thousand times more likely to become abusers themselves. You never had a chance, Joel."

From the corner of her eye she saw his arm move, and an instant later pain exploded in her head as he backhanded her.

"You little bitch!" He slapped her again. "Who the hell do you think you are?"

The proof Regan was right, she thought.

He grabbed her arm and threw her up against the screen door into the apartment. The metal mesh ripped, the frame bent, and she fell backward into the living room, crashing into an end table, sending a brass lamp careening to the floor. She felt something snap, and when she tried to move her left arm pain shot through it and up to her neck. She rolled over on her right shoulder, trying to get her back to the broken door. She hit the brass lamp with her head, but barely felt the pain.

Joel was striding through the ripped screen door like something out of a horror movie. And somehow, the woman she'd become at Rachel's House found the courage. She grasped the brass lamp in her right hand. And when Joel came at her she swung it at him with all her strength. The metal vibrated against her hand, just as Joel's roar of rage, words she'd heard so many times before, vibrated her eardrums.

"You fucking bitch, I'll kill you!"

The hail of blows that poured down on her went beyond pain, beyond enduring. It went on and on, until she could no longer even whimper through her battered mouth. Then she had a vague sense, through the agony, that she was flying, and realized he'd picked her up and thrown her once more. She slammed against something hard, her head snapped back.

Her last conscious thought was that he'd finally made good on his threat.

Alex settled back into his rhythm of hammering. He'd finish this section of roof today, which would leave only the back section and the porch roof. The gable there would slow him down a little, but he was still going too fast. But any slower and Regan was liable to notice he was dogging it. For the hours he was spending here, he should have been further along by now. And Regan didn't miss much. He had discussed the problem with his mother and she had promised to deal with it.

He barely missed his thumb and yanked the hammer back.

"Damn it," he muttered, knowing even as he said it that the curse had little to do with the near miss.

He'd spent every night this week telling himself why he couldn't do what he wanted to, which was ask her out again. He told himself he couldn't get involved with her, not when she had no idea who he really was.

"That's exactly why you should," he told himself. "It's Alex Edwards she likes, not Alexander Court of the Court family."

He'd never spent so much time with a woman without her knowing who he was. He'd kept his real identity hidden before, but it always came out sooner or later. And when it did, everything changed. Suddenly all the woman could see was the Court name, as if it hovered over him in gold lights. No matter what the woman's reaction, the relationship had never been the same.

He didn't know how Regan would react when she found out, as she inevitably would. When she found out not only who he was, but that he'd been lying to her from the beginning.

He was still thinking about it when his mother arrived. She'd forgone her limo, which she often used so she could work in transit. Instead, she was driving a bright blue, small SUV, a vehicle not exactly to her taste. But Alex could see the reason for it. Her connection to Rachel's House was well known, and someone who wanted to find the shelter might think to follow her.

The disguise went further. His elegant mother was dressed in blue jeans, tennis shoes, and a baggy T-shirt emblazoned with the logo of an alternative rock group he was certain she'd never heard of, let alone heard. But most incongruously of all, a San Diego Padres baseball cap sat on her silver hair. With her youthful carriage and energetic way of moving, it made her look like a soccer mom gone prematurely gray.

It was nearly an hour before she left again. This time she waved at him, no doubt because Regan had come out with her. The moment the car started to pull away he came down the ladder before Regan could get back inside.

"Was that a disguise?" he asked.

Regan laughed. "Effective, don't you think? You'd never guess she is who she is. Oh, she said she talked to you about doing some other work around here after you're done with the roof."

"Yes."

He said it with some relief, thinking he'd gotten past the danger point. He'd had dinner with his mother last night, and she'd caught him up on the results of her trip, and he'd updated her on the status of things at the shelter. He was glad she remembered his timing problem and came up with a solution.

"I'm clear at the moment, so now's a good time. She said you'd put together a list for me."

"I'll come up with one. Later," she said, sounding a bit harried.

"Was the royal visit that bad?"

Regan laughed. "No. It never is once it's happening, she's so nice, but the anticipation is nerve-wracking."

"So let's go un-wrack those nerves. With dinner tonight."

She stared at him, as if he were a puzzle she was trying to solve but wasn't sure she had all the pieces. He couldn't blame her. After he'd brought her back that night, he'd never said another word about it, even though he saw her every day.

"Thanks to Mrs. Court, I think I can even afford wine tonight," he said, meaning it as a joke, but cursing himself again when he saw the change in her expression, realized she thought she had that missing piece, that he hadn't asked her out again because he couldn't afford it.

"I'd like that," she said, and then proved his guess correct by adding, "but only if I get to buy the wine."

Great. He'd only managed to get himself deeper into the morass, and was utterly unable to pull himself out.

You don't want out, he told himself.

And later that evening, when Regan sat across from him, he knew it was true. She had on a deep green sweater, and he supposed that must be what made her eyes more green than hazel. She'd left her hair down, and its red fire far outshone the candle on the table.

He'd wanted to take her to the Shores Grill, his

favorite restaurant, but he was too well known there. The whole Court family was. So instead he'd chosen a new Mexican place that had just opened, only barely remembering to make sure he had the wallet with the credit card and ID in the Edwards name.

Conversation over dinner was tricky. Even the simplest question, the kind anyone would ask on a date, meant he had to tap-dance around, giving her the truth but not all of it, and he hated it.

"So you grew up here?" she asked.

He nodded. "I'm that rare beast, a native Californian."

"Is your family still here?"

"There's only my mother and I here. My dad was an orphan, and except for one brother and his girls, the rest of my mom's family is back east." He grinned. "They tell me there really is life east of the Rockies, but I'm not sure I believe them."

"Your father is . . . ?"

"He died. Years ago, when I was a kid."

"I'm sorry."

From most people, it was a platitude, but he knew Regan had been there. At nearly the same age.

"So was I. You know how tough it is. But we made it," he said, gesturing to include her in the statement.

She nodded. "Yes. I had my aunt Mary, thank God. She couldn't have kids of her own, so she spent her maternal energy on me."

This was the kind of chat, the tentative getting to know you kind of stuff that he'd wanted, yet knew was so dangerous. But he couldn't seem to stop himself.

"Do you still see her?"

"Yes, often. She's only down in San Diego. And makes the best home-baked cookies in the state, I might add."

He widened his eyes. "Do you think she might spare a couple for a poor, hungry roofer?"

"Just turn those baby blues on her, you'd get the whole plate. She's a sucker for a good-looking man."

Alex blinked. It wasn't that he wasn't used to compliments on his looks, he got them often enough, they just weren't usually so neatly delivered.

"Thank you," he said.

Regan shrugged as if she'd only been acknowledging a fact, which made it all the more effective.

Their meal arrived, smelling delicious, but she'd only had three bites of her enchilada when her phone rang. Her gaze shot to him as they both remembered what the last call like this had been. She dug her phone out and answered.

His heart sank when he saw her expression change. Another one? Then she spoke, and he was both relieved and concerned.

"Where is she? How bad is it?" She listened for another moment. "Did they catch him?"

Alex watched as anger joined the dismay on her face.

"Bastard," she said, startling him. "I'll be right there."

She slammed the flap of the cell phone shut, breaking the connection. She looked at him.

"I'm sorry, Alex, but—"

He shook his head, already waving down their waiter. "I'll have him box up your dinner. You may need it later."

She gave him a relieved look. "Thank you."

"Where are we going?" he asked when, food boxed and in a bag on the floor, they were back in his truck.

"You don't have to go. You can drop me off and I'll take my car."

"Where?"

"Western Medical Center."

"That would be backtracking, then," he said, and headed out without giving her any more chance to argue.

He could feel the anger radiating from her.

"Want to tell me, or is it none of my business?"

She clenched her hands into fists in her lap. "Mindy's boyfriend got to her."

He swore. There was no mistaking what that meant, not when they were heading to the main trauma center hospital for the county.

"How bad?"

"Bad," she said. "Last time he cost her half her hearing in one ear. This time . . ."

Her voice broke. He reached out and took her hand, wrapped his fingers around the tight knot of her fist.

"This time," she whispered, "he may have killed her."

CHAPTER 9

"She did it. I know she did it."

Lynne looked up as a clearly agitated Nick Kelso yanked off his jacket and tossed it over the back of his chair.

"Who?" she asked.

"Wheeler's wife."

"Did you get a match on the partial print CSI found on the watch?"

"Not in our files. I've sent it to IAFIS."

The Integrated Automated Fingerprint Identification System, Lynne knew, should have an answer in less than two hours. "Does she have an alibi?" she asked.

"She claims she was at a party."

"Should be easy to verify, then," Lynne said neutrally.

"I've already checked it. People say she was there, but nobody can swear she was there the whole time."

Lynne thought he was stretching a bit, but said only, "Must have been a big party."

"Yeah, some useless society woman thing."

Lynne winced inwardly. A memory stirred, that Nick's ex-fiancée had been from a socially prominent family. She hoped he wasn't letting that get in the way.

"What's she like, the wife?"

"Typical. Polished, refined. One of those fragile-looking ones, the kind that milk it."

"Not a big woman, then?"

"No."

"Odd. He was a big guy."

Nick yanked his chair out and dropped down into it. "Yeah, yeah, I know. Maybe she didn't do it herself, but she's in it up to her gold-draped neck, I'll swear to it."

"You think she hired somebody to do it?"

"Or seduced them into it."

"Wouldn't be the first time," Lynne said, although she wasn't liking his sour tone.

"Yeah."

Nick shoved his fingers through his hair. She thought again what a walking California poster boy he was, great bod, golden hair, the frequent killer grin. And then another image overrode the man before her, an image of a man with thick, dark hair, smoky gray eyes, and a grin that rarely appeared. Her mouth tightened. Why couldn't she fall for an open-book guy like Kelso? But no, she always went for the dark ones, in looks and nature. Quite a track record she'd compiled.

And now she was about to run head-on into the biggest speed bump on that track.

She stood up abruptly, needing to move, to get

out. She fastened the belt clip holster with her two-inch Smith & Wesson at the small of her back, then pulled on her lightweight linen blazer to conceal it.

"You're headed out?" Nick asked.

She nodded. "I'm going to stop by Rachel's House. They've probably heard about your case by now, so I want to let them know it isn't related."

"What difference does it make to them?"

She blinked. "They're pretty upset, Nick."

"Why? It's the guys who are getting offed."

If he didn't get it, she didn't have time to explain it to him now. So instead she changed the subject. "You still have those crime reports you pulled for our case?"

"The DVs? Yeah."

"Put them on my desk, will you?"

"I finished going through them already. No help there."

"Still, I'd like to have them handy. Wouldn't mind having your notes, too."

"I'll dig them out and get them to you first chance I get."

She wanted to demand them now, although she wasn't quite sure why. So instead she tried to be tactful. "Soon as you can. I'd like to get it in my head before the cavalry arrives."

"I said I'll get them to you."

He seemed tense about it, but he had just had a murder case dumped on him when he was supposed to be only on loan in the first place.

"Okay, thanks."

He unleashed that grin. "It's just that I like to finish a job, even when I didn't want it in the first place."

"Yeah, yeah," Lynne said to his mock whine as she left.

Reminded by their conversation, she stopped to thank records for pulling all those old domestic-violence files, something she'd been meaning to do, since Nick had a tendency not to bother to acknowledge anyone else's efforts. As she left there, she ran into Captain Greer coming from the direction of the chief's office.

"No task force yet," he told her. "But Investigator Garrison will be reporting here from the sheriff's office this afternoon."

"Yes, sir," she said levelly.

"You're sure there's no problem?"

"We're actually quite civilized," Lynne said.

"I'll leave it to you, then," Greer said. "It will make up for Kelso being pulled off your case."

"For which he'll be eternally grateful," Lynne said.

"I doubt that, as hard as he pushed to get assigned to it."

Lynne drew back slightly. "He what?"

"He must have been in my office three times a day, asking to be put on the case."

"Oh."

She didn't say any more, just thanked him and continued toward her car. It didn't make sense, she thought, remembering when Nick had first come to her.

I've been assigned to your case until it's cleared.

You have?

Told you my luck was rotten.

She would write it off as just typical cop griping if he hadn't kept at it so.

Since they stuck me on this thing, I'll pull my weight.
Damn, I didn't want this assignment anyway.

She shook her head. By the time she had arrived at Rachel's House, she had decided she was going to get a hold of Nick Kelso's files as soon as she got back to the station.

She parked down the street and waited for any sign that anyone was paying any attention to her. When she saw nothing, she got out of her car and began to walk door to door, holding her notebook as if she were some kind of survey taker. If anyone was watching, they would have no way of knowing what house she'd really intended to go to.

When she got to Rachel's House, she thought again how it looked like any other house in the quiet neighborhood. She wondered if the cul-de-sac location had been chosen purposely, then decided it probably had. If anything went wrong, there was only one exit to watch.

As she went up the walkway, she changed her mind; the front yard, at least, looked better than most on the street. She'd noticed when she'd come here for the interviews that flowers bloomed profusely, bright spots of cheerful color that seemed to almost glow in the sunlight. Somebody had a green thumb, she thought. Ben had talked to the gardener already about the case, but she was tempted to track him down and ask him for some gardening hints.

And somebody, she thought as she heard hammering from above and looked up, had great taste in roofers. That was one prime segment of the male population up there. She remembered the note Ben had left in the file, that he'd been vetted by Court Corporation, had been doing work for them for years.

The man glanced down at her, and smiled when she did. "Detective?"

The roofer came down the ladder with an easy grace that told her he'd done it often before.

"Yes, Mr. Edwards, isn't it?"

"Yes. I was just wondering . . . I know it's probably routine that you check everyone out, but . . ."

"Are you wondering if we checked you out?"

He blinked. "Actually, no. I assumed you had, since I'm working here."

Lynne smiled. "I wish more people would take that so casually."

He shrugged. "No, I was wondering about . . . the guy next door. Gene Pilson."

Lynne frowned. "I'm sure he was covered in a canvass of the neighborhood, but I don't recall anything specific, why?"

"I don't know. But he is over here a lot, and seems to have the run of the place. It's probably nothing, but I didn't know if you knew he had a lot of access."

"No. I didn't know that," Lynne said. "Thanks. I'll look into it."

The man nodded, went back up the ladder, and she heard the sound of hammering resume almost immediately.

Thoughtfully, she stepped up onto the porch.

When she knocked, Regan herself answered the door.

"What's wrong?" Lynne asked instantly. Regan's demeanor, along with her reddened eyes, fairly shouted that something was.

Regan opened her mouth, then shut it and waved a hand in a defeated gesture. Lynne hadn't known her very long, but she had a good idea what it would take to beat down this woman. She took her arm and led her back inside.

In the living room, four women were seated on the sofa. All of them wore expressions very like Regan's.

"What happened?" she asked.

"Mindy. One of our residents," Regan managed to say this time. "I just came from the hospital. She's in a coma."

Lynne went still. She knew better than to think the woman was simply ill. Not when she was living in a place like Rachel's House. The women on the couch were watching her, not knowing who she was but, she guessed, ready to judge her by whatever she said here.

"Who did it?" she asked softly.

It was the right question. The women's tension eased.

"Her boyfriend found her last night. We don't know how, but he did."

"Did you call it in?"

"Yes. I gave them everything I knew. They took a report, said they'd look for him."

"I'll rattle their cages," Lynne promised.

"You're a cop?" One of the women, dark-haired with rich brown eyes, had stood up.

"I'm sorry," Regan said quickly, ushering Lynne toward the group. "This is Detective Garrison. She's working on the murders. This is Marita, and that's Laura, Trish, and Belinda. The others will be here later."

They were all looking at her warily. And Lynne didn't miss the usage of first names only, although she knew what went with them from the files.

"I'm on your side," she tried to assure them.

"Oh?" The one who had stood up, the one Regan had said was Laura, spoke with a world of weary disbelief in her voice. "Is that why when I called the cops they said I should just not provoke my husband? Or told me I should just drop it because if it went to court no one would believe me?"

Lynne winced. "God, I hate hearing that crap."

Her honest reaction seemed to appease them, for the moment at least.

Regan gestured her to a chair. "Was there something you needed?"

Lynne took the offered seat. "Yes." She glanced at Regan. "You told them about our conversation last night?"

She nodded. "You didn't say not to, so I—"

"No, that's fine, I knew it was going to hit the papers anyway." She looked at the others. "I just wanted to confirm for you that on this one there doesn't appear to be any connection to any of you, or to Rachel's House."

"Thank goodness," Marita muttered.

"However," Lynne said reluctantly, "you may

not be out of the woods as far as the serial killer goes."

"Why?" Regan asked.

"This is what I couldn't tell you, but it's going to be released this afternoon. We're ninety-nine percent certain this wasn't the same killer."

After the buzz of reaction died down, Lynne explained that she couldn't tell them the details, and stressed that they should continue to be wary, and take the same precautions of accounting for their time and whereabouts that they had been.

"Thank you," Regan said when Lynne rose. "I know you must be terribly busy, and it was kind of you to come out here to let us know."

Lynne turned to face all of them. "When this is over, I'm looking forward to working closely with Rachel's House. My goal is to be so darn good at my job that it's the bad guys who have to hide, not you."

That got her a set of smiles from women she doubted had much reason to smile in their lives.

When Regan offered to show her out, Lynne shook her head. "You stay together. Oh, and let me know how Mindy is, will you?"

"I will."

"Is her family with her?"

"Her mother's bedridden, and can't travel. She lives with Mindy's brother. When I spoke to her, she said Marty was out on the road but she'd try to reach him. He's a trucker."

Lynne remembered that, from the first round of interviews with the Rachel's House family members. She also remembered Marty Baker from

Kelso's interview as a angry young man, at least on the subject of his sister's boyfriend.

"If she hasn't reached him by tomorrow, let me know. I'll put out an all-points for him."

"Thank you," Regan said. "I'll do that."

When she stepped outside, Lynne was startled to find the good-looking roofer sitting on the porch, close to the door. He was sipping a can of soda, so she gathered it was break time. When he saw her, he got to his feet.

"Sorry, didn't mean to be in your way. I'm Alex," he said, holding out his hand.

"Detective Garrison," she returned, not seeing any reason to go beyond that.

She half expected him to ask, as most anyone on the fringes of a murder investigation would, about the case. But he only nodded, said something about getting back to work, and retreated to the roof.

A small pickup truck pulled up directly in front just as she reached the sidewalk. It was full of gardening tools, and a man got out. Instinctively she noted his average height and build, deep tan, and the black baseball cap with the words "Howe Landscaping" embroidered across the front.

"The yard looks lovely."

"Thank you," he said. "I've got to catch up, though. I was sick for a few days. But I've worked on it for a long time."

"It shows."

He hesitated, then asked, "You're one of the detectives, aren't you?"

"Yes."

"I think it's rotten, that they're getting dragged

into this," he said with a glance toward the house. "Their lives have been bad enough."

He sounded protective, Lynne thought. That was kind of sweet. "We'll have it cleared up soon." *I hope.*

"If there's anything I can do to help," he offered.

"Just keep an eye out."

"I always do."

She walked back to her car thinking that for a battered women's shelter Rachel's House had a couple of decent men around.

At the rustle of sound at the door, Regan turned from the painful sight of Mindy's swollen, unrecognizable face to look at Pamela, the day-shift ICU nurse who had just come on duty.

"Someone left a huge bunch of flowers for her," Pamela said, her slight Southern drawl a welcome softness in this sterile place. "I'm sorry we can't bring them in. The man left them at the floor desk."

Mitch, Regan thought instantly. "Sandy hair, sort of cute, very tan?"

"Actually, dark hair, extremely cute, with a scar that tweaks one eyebrow."

Regan sucked in a breath. "Alex?"

Pamela nodded. "He said he brought them in from someone named Mitch, though."

"Ah. Mitch has been sick, he probably didn't want to risk coming himself."

"I wish everybody had such good sense."

Regan backed out of the way as Pamela checked the computer screen that hung over the bed, and the tubes that were connected to Mindy, helping connect her to life.

"She's holding steady," Pamela said encouragingly. Regan gave her the best smile she could manage. The woman was obviously dedicated, and never failed to save time to speak to worried family members, even at this early hour. She started toward the next alcove and her next patient, then stopped and looked back at Regan.

"He's still here, by the way. In the waiting room. He said if you had a chance to come out . . ."

Regan nodded, rather numbly. Alex had stuck with her that night, been an incredible support during those first few hours when they'd feared Mindy would die. He'd been a buffer as the police had pushed for details she didn't have, and a rock when she'd had to call Mindy's invalid mother in Arizona. But she was surprised he'd come back.

She whispered to Mindy that she would return, and walked out of the ICU. As she went into the waiting room, she caught a glimpse of riotous color at the end of the hall. Mitch had outdone himself this time.

Alex rose the moment he saw her. Without a word, he came to her and pulled her into his arms. He hugged her tightly, and as unexpected as it was, Regan allowed herself to let go, to let someone else hold up the world.

She buried her face in his shirt, listening to the strong, steady thud of his heart. His hand came up to cup the back of her head, then stroke her hair. She thought his heartbeat sped up a little, but then he was tilting her head back with both hands. He kissed her.

On the forehead.

"Everybody said to tell you they'll be fine, you just stay and take care of Mindy. Mr. Pilson was upset, too, and said he'd watch out for everyone."

Disgusted with herself for being let down by that brotherly kiss, especially here and now, Regan didn't trust herself to speak and nodded instead. She took a step back, and he let her go.

"How is she?" he asked.

"She's still alive. That's about all the good news at this point."

"Better than the alternative."

Regan didn't mention that it quite possibly might not be, that Mindy might not come out of that coma. Or that if there was permanent brain damage, she might be better off if she never did. Alex was a smart man, she was sure he'd thought of all that.

"I swear, if I saw that guy right now, I'd want to put him in the next ICU bed," Alex said, his voice grim.

"It wouldn't help. He'd just make it all her fault and take it out on her again."

Alex swore under his breath. "I never thought I'd say I understood a serial killer, but damn . . ." He shook his head. "How are you holding up?"

"I'm fine."

He grasped her shoulders and turned her to face him. "You're exhausted."

"I'm upright and walking around. Mindy's in there, full of tubes and needles."

"That doesn't make you any less tired. Give yourself a break, Regan."

"How can I—"

She broke off as someone stepped through the doorway.

She had never seen Mindy's brother before, but it didn't matter. He looked enough like Mindy to be her twin rather than three years older.

"Marty," she said.

His hollow-eyed gaze flicked from her to Alex, then back again. It seemed to take him a moment to process what he was seeing.

"You're Regan?" She nodded. After a second's delay, he nodded, too. "She said you were pretty." Marty shook hands with Alex as he asked, "How is she?"

"She's still with us." Regan wished she had better news.

Marty rubbed his bloodshot eyes. "I got here as fast as I could. My mother called me in Portland, and I dropped my load and headed straight back."

"You're here now, that's all that matters."

"Will they let me see her?"

"I'm sure they will," Regan said. She reached out and laid a gentle hand on his arm. "Be prepared. It's not very pretty."

"That stinking *bastard!*" Marty's jaw clenched. "Did they catch him yet?"

"No, not yet. They're looking for him. They'll find him."

"Son of a bitch should be dead. I shouldn't have let her stop me the last time he did this to her. But this time I'll finish the job. I swear, I'll kill him."

Regan sensed Alex tensing, and glanced at him before saying, "This might not be the best time to be making threats."

"You mean because of that killer? I say good for him, whoever he is!"

"Sometimes," Alex said, "so do I."

Marty gave Alex an assessing look, then a sharp nod. "Where is she?"

"It's around the corner and through the double doors. Pamela's her nurse today," Regan said. She pointed at the wall phone by the door. "Call from here and she'll let you know if you can come in now."

He did, and was cleared. Regan impulsively gave him a hug. "Talk to her," she said. "Let her hear your voice. The doctors may say she can't hear you, but Pamela says you never know, and on this at least, I trust the person on the front lines."

After he'd gone back into the ICU, Regan sank down into a seat. Alex knelt before her, putting his hands over hers on the arms of the chair.

"I can imagine how he feels," he said, "but I hope he's got the sense to keep his mouth shut."

Regan nodded wearily. "At least the medical costs won't be a problem for her family, thanks to Mrs. Court."

"She takes care of her own, and she includes Rachel's House in that contingent."

She looked up at that. "Yes, she does. Does she include you, too?"

"Sometimes," he said, sounding a bit odd. He glanced at his watch. "It's a little early, but let's go get some lunch while Marty is in there. You need to eat."

She wasn't sure she wanted to leave, but as if he'd read her mind he added, "We'll go someplace close. They have your cell number, right?"

She gave in. She wasn't at all hungry, but supposed he was right, she did need to eat, so she could keep going.

"All right."

It wasn't until they were seated in a little shop a block away, with a couple of healthy-sized sandwiches before them, that he said, "I was almost afraid to ask you to do this. You and I in a restaurant seem to attract bad news."

"We do, don't we?" She gave a halfhearted chuckle. "I think I forgot to thank you for all your help the other night."

"No thanks are necessary."

"Yes, they are. I don't know what I would have done without you."

"You would have done what had to be done."

Soon they were walking back to the hospital. As they approached the main entrance Marty was coming out, heading toward the parking lot. He was walking like a man with a mission, and even from here his expression was dreadful. Concern spiking through her, Regan called out to him. He kept going.

They took the stairs to the third-floor ICU, not wanting to wait for the annoyingly slow elevators. Pamela reassured them that there was no change in Mindy's condition.

"I was scared," Regan said. "We saw her brother leaving, and he looked so angry. . . ."

"He was," Pamela confirmed. "But there's been no change. It may have just been the sight of her, so beaten up."

Relieved, Regan went back in to sit for a while with Mindy. Alex even came in briefly, talking to the girl in the teasing tone he'd always used with her, as if he knew she had a bit of a crush on him but also knew it was all in fun. And he stayed, although Regan had told him he didn't have to.

At four, Regan decided she would go back to Rachel's House and give them the latest news. Alex followed her in his truck, saying he wanted to finish up more work before he wrapped for the day.

When they arrived, Mitch was out front, watching Ricky Grant playing with a toy truck in the yard.

"Hello, Ricky," Regan said.

"Hi." He glanced at Mitch, then back to Regan. "He said it was okay if I played outside, as long as he was here."

"It's fine," Regan assured the boy, flashing a smile of thanks to Mitch.

"How is she?" Mitch asked.

"Holding on," Regan said. "The flowers were beautiful, Mitch."

He shook his head as if the gorgeous bouquet was a negligible effort, but thanked Alex for playing delivery boy before saying, "She's always so nice to me. Did you know she sent my mother a birthday card? All I did was mention that I didn't dare forget it was coming up, and she remembered."

"No," Regan said, "I didn't know." But she wasn't surprised. For all her occasional youthful carelessness, Mindy had a kind heart.

Marita appeared in the doorway. "Spaghetti's on," she announced, and Ricky abandoned his truck and ran inside with all the eagerness of a growing boy. "Stay and eat, Alex," Marita said. "You, too, Mitch."

She was bending the rules, but in this case Regan thought it might do them all some good. Alex accepted with a grin.

"Mitch?" Marita asked.

"I can't, I have an appointment," he said, looking genuinely sorry. "But thanks. Thanks a lot."

"Next time," Regan said.

"Yes, next time." He looked toward the door where Ricky had run inside. "He told me about his father. How he wants to kill him and his mother, that he even tried twice. The last time just a couple of days ago."

Regan felt the old familiar churning in her gut, and quashed it with an effort. "An old, ugly story," she said.

"A man who could do that to his own son . . ." Mitch began, then trailed off. Regan had no answer for him, and after a moment he turned to packing up his gear and she went inside.

It was a pleasant evening after all. For the first time since they'd been there, Donna and her son joined them at the table, and Alex managed to keep the boy laughing through most of the meal. Donna herself seemed edgy, however, and although it wasn't unusual for a newcomer to be nervous, especially when this was her first time in a shelter situation, Regan made a mental note to take the woman aside and see if perhaps there wasn't something else bothering her.

For dessert they made hefty inroads into a gallon of ice cream, with Alex reducing them all to laughter with his efforts to get Ricky to come up with things that rhymed with spumoni.

Later, after Donna took the boy upstairs to tuck him in, the rest of them sat around the living room, listening to more of Alex's stories about his travels, and the various troubles he'd gotten into through lack of understanding of local customs. It did them all good, Regan thought, to sit around and laugh with a man. When the phone rang Regan, still chuckling, had to catch her breath before answering.

When she realized it was Detective Garrison, the last of her amusement faded. Her fingers tightened around the receiver.

"I'm sorry, Regan. But there's no doubt on this one."

She knew, instantly. "It's Joel, isn't it?"

"I can't state positively, but that's the preliminary ID."

"And it's like the others, not like the last one?"

"Yes."

The Rachel's House Avenger had struck again.

CHAPTER 10

"I'm glad he's dead. He was a stinking coward, and he deserved to die."

Lynne Garrison sat looking at the young man across the table from her. She took in the rebellious set of his jaw, the fierce anger in his eyes. But most of all she saw the resemblance to the young blond woman she'd interviewed at Rachel's House, the woman who now lay in the hospital in a coma.

"Personally," she said, keeping her voice even, "I think dying's too easy, because then it's over for them. I think they should be put in whatever situation it takes to terrorize them, for as long as they terrorized their victims."

Marty Baker went very still, studying her. A little of the anger receded, but the stubborn set of his jaw remained.

"Marty," she said, leaning forward slightly, "you know why you're here."

"I said I was glad he's dead. But I didn't kill him."

"You threatened to kill him last year."

"When he nearly killed my sister the last time? Yeah, I did. So?"

"I'm not saying you didn't have reason to feel the way you did."

"I didn't do it then, either. He was still alive, wasn't he?"

"But you were angry enough to kill him."

"Mindy begged me not to. So I took a long-distance haul, to cool down." He crossed his arms over his chest. "He got what was coming to him. And I'm sorry it wasn't me that did it," he ended with emphasis.

"Where'd you get that cut on your hand?"

"I told you, I slammed my fist against my truck door. There was something sharp sticking out."

Lynne wasn't sure she bought that story, if for no other reason than Marty's truck had been immaculate, polished to a high gleam, and spotless inside and out. He was obviously very particular, detail-oriented, and tidy. Which fit the profile of their killer.

"I'm already having your truck impounded for investigation."

"Hey! That truck's my living!"

"And this is about death, Marty. They'll go over every inch of your truck. Are they going to find your blood, or somebody else's?"

"You think I'm stupid enough to kill some guy and lug him around in my truck?"

Lynne sighed. She tried another tack. "Tell me something. Why do you think your sister stayed with Joel?"

She'd read the file on Mindy, she knew the answer, but she wanted to hear it from him.

"How should I know?"

"I think you do know. You grew up in the same house."

"You mean our old man? Yeah, sure, he slapped us around. And Mom." He frowned. "You mean that stuff about her thinking that's the way it's supposed to be, because of how he treated Mom?"

"I mean that children who grow up in abusive homes are more likely to accept violence as a means to resolve conflict. They may never learn self-restraint because they've never seen it practiced."

"You think I killed him because my father beat me up?"

"I think," Lynne said, "that there are a lot of things here that would look bad to a jury."

He went still. "Am I under arrest?"

"If you don't come up with a better story, that could happen. You saw your sister in the hospital, saw what Joel Koslow had done to her. You lost your cool, in front of witnesses. You disappeared for several hours, and when you came back, you told your comatose sister it was all going to be all right."

"I told her that because I'd calmed down, she didn't have to worry about me doing anything to him."

"But no one can verify your story of where you were during that time period. The time period in which Koslow was murdered."

"I told you, I was alone. I drove around."

"Looking for Koslow?"

"I just drove. Along the coast. And then I came back. That's when you guys grabbed me."

"You just drove for six hours?"

"That's what I do, I drive. You got a problem with that?"

At his belligerent tone Lynne decided it was time for some shock tactics. She stood, leaned, and slapped her hands down on the table in one swift motion. Marty jumped, startled.

"My problem," she snapped, "is that I've got four dead men, and so far you're my absolute best suspect!"

Marty paled. "Four? What the hell are you talking about?"

"Martin Baker, serial killer. Is that the title you're after? You want to go down in the history books along with Bundy and Ramirez and Dahmer?"

He shrank back in his seat. "You're crazy!"

"Or maybe you just like reading about your work in the papers, seeing it on the news. You like that name they hung on you, the Avenger?"

"*That's* what you're talking about? You're still trying to hang those murders on *me*?"

He looked astounded. Lynne noted it, but kept on. "Give me one good reason why I shouldn't."

"Because I didn't do it! You know that. I told you where I was when that first guy got offed."

He'd done more than told her. When they'd called him in after the connection to Rachel's House had been made, he'd shown her his logbook, that said he'd been on the road to San Francisco at the time of the murder. They'd confirmed the delivery had been made in San Francisco, and let him walk. Since last night she'd been wondering if perhaps they'd been a little premature.

Lynne sat back down. "Then talk to me. Make me believe you."

He took a couple of deep, audible breaths. She gave him that much time.

"I've got a captain and a police chief who are on my case bad," she said. "Tell me why I shouldn't just wrap you up and hand you to them."

"Why would I kill three other guys? It was Joel who hurt my sister. I don't give a shit about anybody else!"

"Maybe you're as smart as you think you are," Lynne said. "Maybe you planned to kill him all along, but killed the others to make it look like we had a crazy on the loose."

"But *that* would be crazy," Marty said, sounding desperate. "I'm not crazy. I can't say I wouldn't have killed him if I had the chance, but three other guys I don't even know?"

The buzzer on the intercom on the wall of the interview room sounded. Durwin's voice came through.

"You need to hear this."

The subtext, since he wanted into the room with their suspect, was that Marty also needed to hear whatever Durwin had turned up. She opened the door.

Durwin strode in, a piece of paper in his hand. He glanced at Marty with an expression she could only call a smirk. But she was fairly sure the attitude was for Marty's benefit. When he looked at her, glanced at the paper he held, then back at her as if signaling something, she was sure of it.

"We've got him."

"Oh?"

"I got to thinking we should have checked a little closer the first time. So I called that company he made the delivery to, up in San Francisco, asked them to dig a little deeper."

Marty shifted in his seat, as if he'd suddenly realized they were talking about him.

"And?" Lynne asked, playing along.

"When we called before, they just confirmed the delivery by asking the guy who'd been working that day. But now they checked their written records. Turns out, our boy made that delivery all right. About ninety minutes late."

"So?" Marty said. Following Durwin's lead, Lynne didn't look at him.

"Here's the original supplemental report on his interview after the second murder." Durwin handed her the paper. "Look at the timing."

She did. And then, finally, she looked at Marty.

"What?" he asked, brows furrowed. "So I was late. Happens all the time."

"Ninety minutes late," Lynne said. "And leaving an hour and a half after you said you did puts you right here in town at the time Cal Norman was murdered."

"That sound you hear is your alibi flying away," Durwin said.

"I didn't leave late," Marty protested. "I had a problem on the way, with an airbrake line."

"Nice try," Durwin said. "But I checked with the company you were driving for. There's no record of a callout for a repair."

"I fixed it myself."

"Convenient."

"It would have been stupid to call someone. It was only a gladhand rubber, but by the time I figured out what was wrong, found the spare, replaced it, and got rolling again, I was down an hour. Then I hit traffic coming into Frisco."

"You have any proof of that? Like the old part?"

He gave her a dubious look. "Of course not. I threw it away. It was useless, and I don't like things cluttering up my truck."

She leaned back over the table. "It's not looking good, Marty. You've got motive. You've got no alibi for the Koslow murder, never had one for the two before that. And we just blew your alibi for the first murder out of the water."

"I had a breakdown, damn it!"

"And no proof of that."

"I didn't do it," he said. "Any of it."

Lynne glanced at Durwin. His eyes flicked toward the door. She gave him a barely perceptible nod and said nothing as he opened the door and walked out. She began to follow, then looked back at Marty.

"I feel really sorry for your sister, Marty. If she does come out of that coma, she's going to be all alone."

"You can't be serious!"

Alex heard Regan's exclamation as he walked past the front porch. He stopped, glanced over to where Mitch was busily trimming the hedge along the front sidewalk, then put down the ladder he'd been carrying and went quietly up the steps.

"He's going to anger-management classes,

Regan. He really means it this time." It was Trish, he thought.

"Fine. After he's finished the classes, start with supervised visits."

"But he wants to see me now."

Regan's voice went chilly. "You've talked to him?"

"No, no, I wouldn't break the rules, you know that. But he gave my sister a note to give to me."

"I thought your sister hated him."

"That's what I mean. She says he's different now. Besides, he wouldn't dare hurt me now."

"Why?"

"Because of the Avenger."

There was a pause before he heard Regan say, in an incredulous voice, "You're trusting the man who beat you for three years because you think he's afraid of a serial killer?"

Whatever Trish said was too quiet for Alex to hear.

"And when they catch him? Maybe it is Mindy's brother, and they already have. What keeps him in line then?"

"You don't have to yell at me," Trish said, sounding thoroughly chastened.

There was a moment of silence, then Regan's voice again. Quieter, but Alex could still hear the tension in it. "I'm sorry for that, Trish. It's just hard for me to believe you'd want to risk yourself again. Think about it, will you?"

He heard footsteps headed his way, and backed up. Not quickly enough, as Regan barreled out the door and almost ran him down.

"Whoa!" he said, grabbing her arms to steady her.

"Sorry," she muttered.

"You," he said, "look like a woman who needs a break."

"That's an understatement. I'm going to see Mindy, then stop by the office."

"I'll drive you."

She looked at him. "Why?"

"Because you're upset. Because I'd like to check on Mindy, too. Because I'm feeling lazy and want a break myself."

"Oh."

"Right answers?"

A smile tugged at one corner of her mouth. "Acceptable answers."

She even let him drive.

"I don't know what Mindy will do if it turns out to be Marty."

"It won't be easy," he agreed.

She sighed. "I was just glad we didn't have to turn him in."

It would have been awkward for her, Alex knew. But the hospital staff had remembered his outburst, and when the news came that Joel Koslow was dead, they'd called it in themselves.

Mindy's condition hadn't changed, although the staff said they were being careful not to mention anything about Marty around her, just in case. Alex said a few words to her, all the while wondering what kind of man could do this to a woman who was all of five feet two and weighed maybe a hundred pounds.

He left Regan to sit with her for a while, and when she came out, he started to walk down the hall with her.

"You don't have to go to the office. I can actually walk from here."

"And get home how? Come on, if it's that close, it's no trouble."

She gave in, and within a couple of minutes she was directing him to pull into a small business building—a CourtCorp-owned building, he realized—and up to the glass storefront at one end. It was inobtrusively labeled "Rachel's House Information and Donation Center," and in the windows were taped lists of emergency and hot line phone numbers.

He followed her inside, past a large, spinning rack of brochures and flyers. It looked like any other office, except for the high front counter, and the fact that the only way to get behind it was through a locked doorway on one side. She greeted a young woman on the way in, then unlocked the door and led the way into the office area behind the high counter.

There were two desks, one with two multibutton phones, one with three. On the opposite wall he saw a large bookcase that held, from a quick glance, everything from road map books to what looked like a copy of the California Penal Code. On the nearest wall next to the door was a wall rack full of the same brochures and fliers. Yet what caught his eye was a large, framed photograph.

He stopped in front of it, staring at the image of a lovely young woman with a smile on her lips that spoke of bright summer days and an endless, exciting world ahead. Underneath was a small brass plaque. *Rachel Carreras, murdered at twenty-one by the man who swore he would never hurt her again.*

"So that's why it's named Rachel's House?" he asked Regan.

She nodded, and he saw both wistfulness and pain in her eyes as she looked at the picture. "She was my best friend since we were seven. I put it here because for so long after she died, I couldn't remember how she really looked. All I could think of was what was left of her face when I found her."

Alex's gut knotted. "You found her?" That hadn't been in the file, or he'd somehow missed it. Of course, Regan hadn't meant anything to him then.

"Oh, yes," she said, for the first time since he'd known her a touch of bitterness coming into her voice. "Her boyfriend made sure of that. He knew I didn't like him, didn't trust him, that I tried to get Rach away from him. So he took her body and posed it so it was the first thing I saw when I walked in the door."

Alex swore fervently under his breath.

"I only knew for sure it was her because of the necklace she had on. He'd raped her, beaten her, slashed her throat and then her face, until you couldn't even tell it was a face."

"My God."

He wanted to fix this for her, more than he could remember wanting anything. And it made him crazy to know he couldn't. There wasn't a damned thing he could do. Something a female cousin had once said to him echoed in his mind. She'd told him when they were teenagers, after he'd waded in and straightened out a boyfriend who'd treated her badly and she'd nearly slaughtered him for it, that sometimes a woman doesn't want you to fix it, but just to listen.

So he listened.

"I couldn't understand what she saw in him. She hadn't grown up with that kind of treatment, knew it was wrong. But he . . . fascinated her somehow. She'd break away, but then she'd go back."

He saw the pain in her eyes. It wrenched at him, and he felt that off-balance sensation she seemed to bring on.

"I even wondered if he'd drugged her or something, gotten her addicted and kept her supplied. But after . . . we found out she was clean. It was him she was addicted to."

He opened his mouth, then shut it again. *Just listen*, he told himself.

"I kept thinking if only I'd done more, if I'd just figured out the right way to get her away from him, she might—"

"Stop." He pulled her into his arms, not caring that there was another person there. "You did everything you could. You couldn't do it for her, Regan. No matter how much you wanted to."

"I still can't," Regan said into his shirt, her voice shaky. "I can't do it for any of them."

"But you're doing everything else that can be done." He hugged her tighter. "Give yourself a break, Regan."

He turned her to face the photograph. With a gentle finger he tilted her head back, making her look at it.

"That doesn't look like the kind of friend who

would want you to live in guilt the rest of your life over her."

There was a long, silent moment before he heard, softly, "She wasn't. Until she met him, she was the most alive person I knew."

He didn't know what to say, decided saying nothing was better than saying the wrong thing just now. So he just held her.

At last she pulled away. Alex noticed then that the young girl named Danielle had discreetly retreated to one of the two offices in the back corner of the big room.

He could almost feel her putting her mental armor back on as she drew herself up, not looking at him.

"Let me do what I came for," she said almost to herself. Then she did look at him. "Thank you," she said quietly.

"You're welcome." He smiled at her because he couldn't think of a thing to say beyond that.

She walked into the other office at the back of the room, talking as she went.

"I want to see if the police reports on Donna and her son have finally arrived. There's something about that whole situation that just doesn't feel right."

He'd seen little of either the woman or her son, so he had no idea what Regan meant. "Like what?"

"I'm not sure. She just doesn't seem . . . I don't know. As scared as most of the women with a child to protect who have come through."

"Maybe she just feels safe now."

"Maybe. We're still waiting to find out the official version of what happened to send her running."

"You mean you don't know?"

"No. Those are the reports I'm waiting for. She just came in with the boy, said her husband abused them, and had tried to kill her. In a case like that, we help first, ask questions later."

She turned and called out to the girl up front. "Danielle? Did that stuff regarding Donna Grant ever come in?"

"No, not yet. Mrs. Tanaka called them today, and they told her they were still having trouble finding it. She left you a message about it."

"Great," Regan muttered.

He watched with interest as she read the note she found on the desk, frowned a couple of times, then set it aside and went through a stack of paperwork with quick efficiency.

"Is it always this much work?"

"It would be worse if we weren't private. You can't imagine the paperwork involved with state or federal funding."

"Don't give me that bullshit! Where is she?"

The booming male voice from the front office made Regan go still. Her hand was on the phone, to call the police Alex guessed, when a loud thud and a scream whipped her head around.

"Danielle!" Regan leapt to her feet and started for the door of the back office, heedless of the possible danger. Alex barely managed to hold her back.

"Don't make it worse. Call the cops, let me go out. Maybe a man will calm him down."

He moved before she could protest, and as he stepped out the office door he heard her dialing the phone.

"I said I want that address, and I want it now!"

Calm him down? Alex thought as he stopped dead at his first sight of the outer office.

On the other side of the counter was a man who looked to be in his fifties, with salt and pepper hair receding from his forehead and a bushy mustache. He was small, wiry, but his size didn't matter.

He was holding a knife to Danielle's throat.

CHAPTER 11

Lynne dropped the stack of domestic-violence reports on her desk. Nick had finally given her his own notes, but she'd told him again she needed to go through the actual reports herself to get it all straight in her head; you never knew what tiny detail might be significant later. She'd asked him for the reports a couple of times more, but he kept forgetting to give them to her so she'd finally dug through his desk and retrieved them herself.

They had a good, solid suspect in Marty, but she knew that didn't mean she could quit looking. Following the roofer's suggestion, she'd examined Pilson's local history and found the thirty-eight-year-old—which had surprised her, she'd thought he looked over forty—solitary man fit the profile a little too well to ignore: few friends, a boring dead-end job as a night-shift supervisor at a local toy manufacturer. She planned to ask Regan about him soon.

She was going to make darn sure nothing could be second-guessed in this investigation. They were a small department unused to dealing with murder at all, let alone a string of them, but they weren't going to embarrass themselves if she could help it.

She settled in, thinking wryly that all those people whose images of cops came from movies and television would be bored out of their minds by the plodding, paperwork-laden reality. Those moments of pulse-pounding excitement came, of course, but you paid for them with hours of desk-bound routine.

Nearly halfway through the pile, she came across a report with a familiar name. Laura, the woman from Rachel's House who had been rather vocal when Lynne had first gone there, saying the police "told me I should just drop it because if it went to court no one would believe me."

Curious, she thumbed through the pages to the supplemental, written by the officer who had followed up the primary. She frowned as she read that Laura Dennis had supposedly refused to press charges, saying it was all a mistake. That didn't sound at all like what she'd heard from Laura herself.

More out of curiosity than anything else, she went back to the first report in the pile and started again, this time starting a fresh page of notes. Slowly a pattern emerged amid the pages of names, dates, locations, and details she compiled.

She finished with the last report, sat back in her chair, and let out a pained sigh. Report after report of domestic violence, of assaults and occasionally even batteries on women by men. And all tied together with an ugly thread they all had in common. Every woman had been talked out of pressing charges, or into denying it had ever happened.

And in all but two of the kissed-off cases, the officer doing the persuading had been Nick Kelso.

This was the absolute last thing she needed. In more ways than one. It would have been a difficult burden at any time, and now, in the middle of this investigation, it was horrible.

No wonder Nick had wanted to go through these reports himself. And, she thought, realizing it only now, no wonder he'd been so reluctant to give them to her. He'd known there was a chance she'd see the pattern.

If he'd done it only once or twice, she could have chalked it up to laziness, not wanting the hassle of taking the report, the statements, documenting injuries, and letting yourself in for what would be an ugly court case. Or even something as simple as catching the call near the end of your shift when you had important plans after work. It happened, she knew, even though it shouldn't.

But not this. Not on nearly every call.

He must have been in my office three times a day, asking to be put on the case.

The captain's words came back to her, and the sick feeling in her stomach grew. Had Nick truly pushed so hard to get on the case just to try to keep anyone from discovering that he'd been sabotaging abused women the entire time he'd been in patrol? And why? Why would he have done it in the first place?

She rubbed wearily at the back of her neck with one hand. She was glad Durwin was downstairs hammering away some more at Marty, and that she had the office almost to herself. It was going to take her a minute to gather this up and shove it out of her mind. No murder investigation was easy, a serial murderer was obviously worse than most, and now this.

If life could get any worse, she didn't want to know how, she thought, lifting her left hand to add to the massage that wasn't helping to loosen the knots of tension in her neck and shoulders.

"You're still wearing your wedding ring."

She froze. For an instant she cursed herself for tempting fate, even though she'd known this was coming.

Slowly, she lowered her hands and turned to face the ex-husband she had once hated.

"Take it easy, there," Alex said to the knife-wielding man. Regan watched from the office, her attention split between the awful scene before her and the voice of the police dispatcher in her ear. Alex was walking toward the man, holding his hands up to show he meant no harm.

The furious man's arms tightened around Danielle, and the girl whimpered as the knife nicked her and drew blood. He must have pulled her right up and over the counter. That had to be the noise they'd heard, Regan thought.

"I'll kill her. Right here, unless you tell me where she is."

Regan's grip on the phone tightened. "He hasn't seen me yet. I don't think he knows I'm here or calling you," she told the dispatcher, who reassured her help was already on the way.

"I don't work here, so you'll have to tell me who you mean," Alex said calmly.

"Don't try to fool me. You're one of those wimps who believes all this crap about women being victims when all they need to do is keep their damn mouths shut."

"Hey, look, man, I was just walking by." She heard a joking note come into Alex's voice as he added, "Saw the cute girl, figured I'd check her out. You know how it is."

The man-to-man, macho approach, Regan thought. "No, I don't know who he is," she whispered into the phone. "I've never seen him before." She answered the questions as best she could as the dispatcher compiled information on the dangerous situation.

"So, who is it you want? Maybe I can help," Alex said casually.

"Are you kidding? They guard those bitches like they were the queen of England. But I'll find her, so help me."

"This your wife you're looking for? She sneak out on you?"

Alex's voice was commiserating now, inviting the man to see him as a partner, not an enemy. Even from here Regan could see it was working. The man wasn't quite as frantic as he'd been seconds ago. Danielle was still terrified, but she'd ceased struggling, as if she sensed she was better off if the man was focused on Alex.

"Like I'd marry a cunt like that. I tried to tell Joey she was nothing but trouble, but she had him thinking below the belt."

Joey. Joel? Regan guessed. "We have two units arriving now," the dispatcher said.

"It happens," Alex said easily. "You can't blame the guy."

"But she *killed* him," the man burst out. "She killed my boy."

Oh, God, Regan thought. "He's still talking," she whispered into the phone, "but he's got the knife at her throat. From what he just said, he may be related to the last serial killer victim." She listened in an agony of tension as she heard the woman swiftly relay that information.

"This woman killed your son?" Alex was saying. God, how could he stay so calm?

Regan's breath caught as she saw a police car edging into the parking lot.

"Doesn't matter if she did it herself. Maybe it was that killer. But it wouldn't have happened if she hadn't made those reports for nothing. All he did was slap her a little when she got out of line."

The police car crept closer.

"It isn't fair, is it?" Alex said understandingly.

"No, damn it! She made him lose his temper, the way she flirted all the time. She was a slut, and—"

His head snapped to the right. He'd seen the police unit. As he moved, the knife lowered slightly, away from Danielle's throat.

In the same instant Alex hurdled the high counter, kicking out as he went. His foot caught the spinner rack, sent it crashing to the floor. The man jerked around toward the clatter. Then Alex was on him, wrenching his arm, pulling Danielle free. The moment the girl was clear, Alex took the man down to the floor, pinning him with a knee as he tightened his grip on the hand that held the knife. After barely a second, the knife dropped, hitting the floor with a resonant clang.

It happened so fast Regan forgot to breathe, let alone speak. "He's disarmed," she said belatedly into the phone. Then she dropped the receiver and ran to Danielle, to make sure she was all right.

There was too much to do for Regan to dwell on the amazing scene she'd witnessed just yet. The police quickly came inside and handcuffed the man.

"Nice work," the first officer on the scene said to Alex. "Stupid, but nice work."

Alex gave him a lopsided smile.

"Hey, I know you," the officer said. "Aren't you—"

"Alex Edwards, yes. I think we met last year. At that place that got broken into up on Pacific Boulevard."

"Yeah, that's it. But—"

"Thanks for the quick response. He had me scared."

"What's this about his son?" the backup officer asked.

"She killed him, damn you," the man said, but the ferocity was waning.

"I think his son was the man they found last night," Regan told them.

"Killed by the Avenger?"

She nodded.

"That little bitch set him up for it!"

Regan lost her temper, turning on the handcuffed man. "That 'little bitch' is in the hospital in a coma and may die, thanks to your precious son! He brought this on himself, and if there's any other fault in this, it's yours, since you're obviously where he learned to use violence!"

He spat at her. She was far enough away so that the spittle didn't reach her, but that didn't stop Alex from taking a step toward him.

"Easy," the backup officer said. "I'll get him out of here. And we'd better call Detective Garrison, if there's a connection to the Avenger."

The first cop nodded. "Hey, let's let her book him. I heard she's feeling pretty edgy right now, with her ex being on loan to work the Avenger case. Nothing she'd like better than to get her hands on a prize scumbag like this one."

The second officer laughed as he dragged his prisoner out of the office. *Ex?* Regan wondered, recalling the wedding band she'd seen on the detective's hand.

"Let me go get some report forms, and we'll get through your statements as fast as we can," the first officer said, and left to go back to his police unit.

"Start with Danielle so she can go home," Regan suggested. With a nod, the officer led the still shaken girl into Regan's back office. Regan used one of the desk phones to call her parents to come pick her up.

When she hung up, Regan turned back to Alex.

"Now," she said, "do you want to tell me where the heck you learned to fight like that?"

He shrugged. "I took some classes when I was a kid."

"That looked pretty darn freshly practiced."

"I try to keep my hand in. It's a scary world."

"Isn't it just," she muttered. She studied him for

a moment. "That really was incredibly brave. Stupid"—she grinned as she repeated the officer's assessment—"but brave."

"Hey, it worked. Besides, I didn't want it to get any worse, drag on for hours with all of us hostages in here and the cops out there. He was distracted when he saw the police car, so I took advantage."

"I've never seen anything like that outside a movie."

"I saw it in an old *Miami Vice* once. Cable TV is a great thing. I wanna be Sonny Crockett when I grow up."

"I loved Sonny when I was an impressionable young girl. But now I think that was his problem. He never did grow up."

"Well, I want the alligator, then. Great pet."

She laughed, and then wondered that she was able to, considering.

"That's better," Alex said, and she realized that had been his intention all along.

He put his hands on her shoulders and squeezed gently. She wanted nothing more than to cross that distance between them, to have the feel of his arms around her again. But instead she just smiled and stayed where she was. After a moment, he let go.

"Even though you still talk to the male of the species, you don't trust us, do you?"

The truth hit her with blinding clarity. Living with horror stories about brutal men every day had affected her. It had colored her reactions to any man. It had colored her reaction to Alex. She'd been fighting her response to this man from the moment she'd realized his interest went beyond just his work at Rachel's House.

"I think," she said shakily, "I need to go home."

"I'll take you as soon as we're done here. But I don't think you should tell them what happened here."

"I agree," she said, "but that's not what I meant. I want to go *home*. I need to talk to Aunt Mary."

He looked at her for a long moment. "Then I'll take you there," he said.

"Don't be silly. She's in San Diego."

"Don't be silly. You shouldn't be driving."

Regan fought the instinct to say no, to keep distance between them. Finally she said, "Thank you."

Drew Garrison was still the sexiest man she'd ever seen. The lean, rangy body was still the prototype of any man who made Lynne look twice. The bit of gray that flecked his dark hair at the temples did nothing to change that, nor did the crow's-feet at the corners of his eyes. They only made him look like what he was, a man, not a boy.

Lynne got to her feet, not liking the advantage his height gave him when she was sitting. She was a tall woman, so it didn't usually affect her, but with him it did. He was one of the few men who'd ever been able to make her feel as if five feet nine wasn't so very tall after all, even though he was only four inches taller.

But whatever she gained by standing she lost when he stepped forward and took her left hand. The hand that still wore his ring.

"I would have thought you would have melted it down and turned it into a toothpick by now."

"It helps keep the wolves away," she said, giving him part of the truth. A small part.

"Is that the only reason?"

"It also reminds me how big a fool I can be." His expression went blank. She shrugged. "You asked."

"Yes, I did, didn't I?" He changed the subject so obviously that it was clear he didn't care if she knew it. "Ironic, isn't it? I've been a homicide investigator for nearly ten years, but you're the one who gets the serial killer case."

"Think I can't handle it?"

His eyebrows rose at that, and Lynne knew she'd given herself away. For all his sins, Drew had never belittled her ability to do the job. In fact, he'd been her biggest supporter, as angry as she had been at the constant battles of a woman in this still mostly male world.

"Look," she said, "there's some other stuff going on, so I'm a little edgy."

"I'd be surprised if you weren't," he said. "But don't doubt you can handle it. You can."

Now there was the true irony, Lynne thought. She felt as if she were about to buckle under the added weight of the discovery about Nick, and here was Drew propping her up.

"Yes, I can," she said, determined not to let it show.

"Is it going to be a problem, me being assigned to help on your case?"

"It's Ben Durwin's case. I just got sucked in a side door." She saw by the flicker in his eyes that he knew she was dodging the question, so she added firmly, "No, it's not a problem. Unless you make it one."

"Me? I try never to make problems where there aren't any."

She nearly gaped at him. He couldn't mean that the way it sounded. If anybody had made problems between them, it had been him.

"Are you Garrison?"

The voice came from behind them, and at the sound of the name they shared, they both turned. A young man in uniform stood there, looking hesitant. Drew tactfully took a step back, since it was clear she was the Garrison he was looking for.

She'd seen the young patrol officer around. She glanced at his name tag. McDonald. She'd heard about him, that he'd only been on about two years, but was a go-getter. "You have something for me, or need something, McDonald?"

"I figured you'd want to know we just brought in the father of the last Avenger victim."

Great, Lynne thought sourly. "Joel Koslow's father?"

He nodded. "Jack Koslow. He went ballistic in the office for that shelter, Rachel's House. He was all crazy, blaming them for his son's death, them and the son's girlfriend."

"The one in the hospital, nearly dead herself?"

"Yeah. Crazy, like I said. He took a volunteer worker hostage."

"Anybody hurt?"

"No, thanks to some guy that was in there. He took Koslow down like a pro, real smooth. That's the other thing I wanted to talk to you about."

"That guy?"

He nodded. "I'm not sure whether this is important."

"Right now everything's important," she said
with an encouraging smile.

"Well, that guy . . . he lied about who he is."

"Oh?"

"He said his name was Alex Edwards, and that
he was a roofer working at that shelter."

Lynne flushed, remembering the good-looking
man she'd seen and admired. She became very conscious of her ex-husband just a few feet away, and
kept her eyes on the young patrolman. "They are
having some work done," she confirmed. "I've
seen him."

"But last year I got a big commercial burglary. I
remember it because it was my first big call on my
own. Anyway, this guy was there."

"Roofing?"

Bob shook his head, rather vehemently. "No. He
owned the place."

Lynne frowned. "You're sure of that?"

He nodded just as vehemently. "I went back and
pulled the original report. The name he gave then
was Alexander Court."

"Court? As in Court Corporation?"

"Yeah, that was the name of the business. It was
one of their property management offices."

Alexander Court. Of Court Corporation. The
main support of Rachel's House.

Well, well, well, Lynne thought.

CHAPTER 12

"Oh, honey, if I were you I'd grab that Alex and hang on!"

Regan took the tall, frosty glass her aunt handed her and shook her head. She'd felt the stress of what had happened begin to fade the moment she'd seen her aunt's face.

"It's not like that," she explained, wondering if she was trying to convince her aunt or herself. "With all this ugly stuff going on, he's just been really nice about helping."

"Nice? You call leaping over counters to save people from knife-wielding madmen nice?"

Regan gave Mary Day a sheepish grin. "Well, that was rather spectacular, I'll admit."

She took a long sip of the root beer float, a childhood favorite she now indulged in only when she was here. Alex had dropped her off with a promise to come back and pick her up after a few errands. He'd stayed long enough to be introduced to the woman who was more mother to her than aunt, and had clearly charmed her in the process.

"And I may be old, but I'm no fool," Aunt Mary said.

"Nor will you ever be," Regan said. She meant it; the curly hair might be gray, but the hazel eyes, mirror images of her own, were as sharp and quick as the mind behind them.

"Then listen to me when I tell you that boy's got more than being nice on his mind when he looks at you."

"I don't know . . ."

"You don't have to, I just told you." At times her father's older sister could be as commanding as he had been. "Now, what are you going to do about it?"

"Do?"

"Lord, I know I didn't raise you to be so oblivious, so it must be that place. You're not letting it convince you all men are like those few, are you?"

She was startled at her aunt's perceptiveness, then realized she shouldn't have been surprised. This wasn't the first time she'd cut through the vines to the root of the situation, as Mary so quaintly put it.

"I think maybe I was," she admitted. "But I'm trying to get over it."

"He'd be reason enough," Mary said with a grin that belied her years, and reminded Regan of her father. "Take my advice, honey, and open the door for that one."

Regan sighed inwardly. Easier said than done, she thought. And was grateful when her cell phone rang. She took it out of the side pocket on her purse.

"Regan? Lynne Garrison." Regan's stomach clenched. "It's all right, no news."

"Thank you," Regan said.

"I just needed to ask you about someone. Gene Pilson."

"Mr. Pilson?" Regan asked. "What about him?"

"Any problems with him?"

"Heavens, no. The opposite, he's been wonderful, ever since we moved in."

"So wonderful he has the run of the place?"

"The residents voted him access, yes."

"Would he have access to the files?"

Regan realized suddenly where this was heading. "I know you have to check on everyone, but Mr. Pilson? He wouldn't hurt a soul."

"Isn't that what outsiders say about most batterers?"

Regan flushed; the woman was right, and she couldn't believe she'd fallen victim to that fallacy that people who seem nice can't be hiding darker sides. She tried to remember the original question and finally said, reluctantly, "He did help me move the file cabinet once. I suppose he could have seen where I put the key."

"And does he generally know what happens with the residents? Like going to court, or run-ins with their abusers?"

Regan felt an odd tightness in her stomach. "Yes. Yes, he does. They talk pretty freely in front of him. And he's always popping in."

"In the interview with Detective Durwin, he said he worked a split shift."

"Yes, sometimes he goes to work at midnight, sometimes earlier or later. He works at some manufacturing plant, I think. I always have wondered when he sleeps, since he seems to be up all day, too."

"Has he ever said or done anything that seemed odd or unusual?"

"No, he's just a nice man," Regan said. *He has to be just a nice man.*

"Ever give you any indication of what he thought of abusers?"

Regan's breath caught. And just like that she was back to that sunny morning, picking up the paper on the sidewalk in front of Rachel's House.

Another piece of slime cleaned off our streets. . . .

My God, she thought.

Quickly she told Detective Garrison about that morning. And thinking some more, she reluctantly added something else.

"He always asks if there's anything he should be on the lookout for, or anyone who's had a recent problem with their abuser."

"And they tell him?"

"Yes," Regan said, feeling sick. "They never had any reason not to. He seemed so protective."

"Maybe he is," Lynne said, grimly.

"Something wrong?" Aunt Mary asked when Regan hung up.

"Just the same ugly thing going on," Regan said. "It's awful, trying to think who you know who could be a serial killer."

After a soothing amount of commiseration, Regan changed the subject to something more pleasant. It wasn't hard. Just being here, in the house she'd grown up in, with the woman who had moved in and taken her widowed brother's ten-year-old child and raised her as her own, and who despite her own racking grief had been the rock that had gotten her through first her father's death, and then her best friend's, restored Regan as nothing else could. As it always did. By the time Alex returned, she had her equilibrium back, and her certainty that Mr. Pilson could no more be the Avenger than she could. Plus a container of cookies that Alex eyed expectantly.

She also had Aunt Mary's advice ringing in her ears as they drove back to Rachel's House. Hearing "grab that Alex and hang on" was all well and good when he was nowhere around, but when he was barely two feet away in the suddenly cramped cab of his pickup, it took on an entirely new slant.

"You sure you're ready to go back?"

"I'm fine. One of Aunt Mary's root beer floats'll do it every time."

He gave her a sideways look and a grin that had her thinking about her aunt's advice yet again. "I should've taken her up on the offer."

. . . *open the door for that one.* "I go see her at least a couple of times a month. Come with me, and she'll make you as many as you could hold."

She couldn't believe she'd said that.

"I'd like to. Tell me when."

She couldn't believe he'd said *that*.

"All right," she said, barely able to get it out. "In the meantime, she sent home cookies."

"At least I can find out how good they are."

When they arrived at Rachel's House, he walked with her up to the door. Mitch was busily at work on the bird-of-paradise plant in front of the porch.

"Trimming again?" she asked.

Mitch smiled at her. "These things will go crazy if you let them. Did you know there's one farther inland that's twenty feet high and fifteen feet across?"

"I had no idea," Regan said, eyeing the plant cautiously. "It's worth it for the flowers, though," she added, gesturing at the unique orange and blue blooms shaped like a bird's head, giving the plant its name.

"I put some in your office. I know you like them," Mitch told her. "My mother doesn't. She's more of a traditionalist, roses, carnations, that kind of thing."

"Good thing she's got you to keep her supplied," Regan said with a smile, leaning over to look at one of the exotic blooms. Then she went on up the steps, Alex on her heels.

"Since I missed the root beer float this time," he said, "mind if I get some water? I'm out of soda, and I need something after devouring half your cookies."

"Of course not."

Then she nearly jumped as the door she was reaching for opened in front of her. Mr. Pilson was on the other side, and nearly jumped himself.

"Oh! My, I'm sorry, I didn't see you," he said, sounding flustered.

"That's all right," she assured him. "Did you need something?"

"No, no, I was just checking to see if anyone here needed anything. I'm about to run to the store."

"I don't think so, but thanks for thinking of us."

"I never forget you," he said.

Regan started to go in, but stopped when Alex didn't move, and instead stood there watching Mr.

Pilson go down the steps and hurry through the hedge toward his house, being careful not to step on Mitch's handiwork.

"Does he come and go like that all the time?"

Regan looked at him sharply. "You and Detective Garrison. She called me today, and had me half convinced he's the Avenger."

"Did she?" Alex asked, and he looked oddly satisfied.

"Of course it's silly," Regan said as she pulled open the door, "but I know she has to check out everyone."

Regan stepped inside, spotted Donna on the telephone, and gestured to Alex to go ahead.

"I need to talk to her," she told him.

"About what you were talking about in the office?"

She nodded. Alex glanced at the woman, then headed for the kitchen and the icemaker.

Donna hung up the phone and turned to Regan, a look of glittering excitement on her face.

"That was my attorney. He's pretty sure I'm going to win!"

"You're going to court?"

"Tomorrow. I don't want Richard near Ricky."

"If you go to court, he could end up with visitation rights. Is that what you want right now? To have to face him on a regular basis?"

"He won't get visitation."

"You can't be sure of that. I've seen abusers get visitation before."

Donna's happy expression vanished. "God, do

you always have to be so negative about everything?"

"Realistic," Regan stated, irritated by the woman's attitude.

"Yeah, yeah."

"Fine. We'll talk about it later. Right now I wanted to ask you if you ever remembered what officer took your report."

"I told you before, I can't remember his name." She grimaced dramatically. "I was upset, all right?"

"They can't find any paperwork."

"I can't help that."

"Do you have any idea why they can't even find a record of the phone call?"

"How should I know?" She waved off the query as if it were negligible. "Maybe I was wrong about the date. I was pretty shaken up, after all." She glared at Regan. "What's up with the third degree? This is supposed to be a shelter, right?" Her voice was rising.

"Rachel's House is a shelter," Regan agreed. "But it's not a free ride."

"Look, I'll tell you again, just like I told Mr. Pilson. He beat me up." Donna's volume went up again. "And he hit Ricky, too! Hit him all the time. He doesn't deserve to be his father!"

The shouted words seemed to echo in the room. Only then did Regan realize Alex was standing in the doorway of the kitchen, watching warily, standing by in case she needed help.

As if realizing she'd gone too far, Donna whirled and ran upstairs. Alex waited until she was out of sight, then headed toward Regan as she walked toward her office.

"Something wrong?"

"I don't know," Regan said.

She turned to look at the eternal bouquet. The bird-of-paradise flowers were there, just as Mitch had promised, looking striking amid the more common flowers and greenery. But all she could think about was Donna and her story.

"Something," she muttered. "Something."

Lynne leaned wearily against the desk behind her as she watched the interview through the two-way mirror. She had the sound on the intercom turned off. She wasn't here officially and didn't want to end up a witness. She wasn't sure why she was here at all when it wasn't her case, it was Nick's. Especially after the sleepless night she'd had; it wasn't even noon and she was exhausted.

Maybe it was disbelief, she thought. Disbelief that Nick could have done what those reports showed he had done, condemn woman after woman to continuing her life of despair and brutality, talking her out of any attempt at escape by using the age-old arguments of the batterers themselves: no one will believe you, you can't make it on your own, you'll be humiliated when your friends find out, you'll lose your children . . .

Why? It made no sense. Nick Kelso, division Romeo and department flirt, always so charming to every woman around. If it was all a front, then what was behind that charming facade? What was he thinking—

"You spent some time on Koslow."

Lynne hadn't even heard Drew come into the observation room. She thought he was still down in the jail, where she'd spent an hour hammering at the man who'd taken the Rachel's House worker hostage at knife point.

"I had to eliminate him as a suspect," she said, staring through the mirror as if she'd been paying attention all along instead of dwelling on Nick Kelso's perfidy.

"Sounds like he wants to kill the women, not the batterers."

"I'm dealing with a serial killer. They don't think like the rest of us. Who knows what kind of glitch might have shifted his focus."

"I know."

Lynne flushed slightly. Most of what she knew about murderers in general, and serial killers in particular, had been taught to her by this man. She'd lived with him for nearly three years, after all.

"I've got another possible working, though," she said. "A neighbor of Rachel's House, who's worked his way into their confidence there. Apparently he's got the run of the place."

"A man? Unusual."

"Yes. And he fits the profile, right down the line. Regan Keller admits he comes and goes a lot at Rachel's House, and might have been able to get access to the files. I'm going to dig deeper on him. He works varied hours, so I'm having them pull his time cards to match them up to the times on the cases."

Drew nodded, then looked back at the interview in progress. "He's working her pretty hard," he said, and she sensed rather than saw his gesture toward the two-way mirror.

"Yes," she said, glad of the change of subject. He was right, Nick was going at the wife of the non-Avenger victim pretty hard. "He's convinced she either did it or had it done."

"You're not?"

She didn't want to get into explaining that it was Nick's early settling on the woman as the only suspect that had her withholding agreement. Her gut had her thinking the woman wasn't the cool, calculated society ice princess Nick was painting. There was something about her, something in the way she held herself, in the way she watched Nick's every move . . .

"It's Kelso's case, not mine," she said.

She could feel Drew looking at her. "What's up, Lynne? If it's not your case, why are you here, and giving Kelso that look?"

"What look?" She still refused to meet his gaze.

"The one that says 'If I was less civilized, I'd rip your tongue out.'"

Her head snapped around. "What?"

He nodded toward Kelso. "You were looking at him like this glass was the only thing between you and a particularly despised species of snake. He giving you trouble?"

Frustration swamped her. Here she was, face-to-face with one man she knew for certain would understand, and she couldn't tell him. Once, she would have spilled it all, and he would have helped her work through it, decide what to do. But he wasn't that man anymore. And she didn't dare spill to him anyway. She could never be that vulnerable to him again.

"If he was, I'd handle it." Her tone was a little sharp, but Drew's expression never changed.

"You always did," he said.

"I was thinking about something else," she said, and turned back to the interview scene.

"You've got enough to think about," he agreed mildly. "I've been through all the files again, gone through the data added since I did the profile."

She watched as Nick leaned forward, using his considerable bulk to force the woman back in her seat without touching her. Lynne frowned, but only said to Drew, without looking at him, "And?"

"For what it's worth, I agree with you and Ben on this one." He jerked a thumb toward the interview room. "It's not the same killer."

Lynne finally looked at him, knowing this was his due. No matter how she felt about the man, she still respected him as a cop. "It's worth a lot, coming from the premier homicide investigator in the county."

He'd never been a man to give away much, but she thought she saw a flicker of emotion in his eyes. She knew she'd been right when he looked down at her left hand.

"And coming from the man who put that ring on your finger?"

A chill came over her. "It's worth," she said, "just what the vow that went with it was worth to you."

She turned away again before she added the final word.

"Nothing."

CHAPTER 13

"So there it is, out in the open. You still hate me."

Lynne glanced at her ex-husband. "No. Hate is an active emotion that requires stoking."

"And I'm not worth it?"

"You said it, not me."

He looked at her, his mouth quirking at one corner. "I always said I didn't ever want to get on your bad side."

"Too bad you didn't follow your own advice."

This time the look was long and considering. "I'm never going to be able to convince you, am I?"

She turned to face him then. "Convince me of what? That you never slept with her?"

He shoved a hand through his hair. "I didn't. Not . . . technically."

"Keep that line handy in case you get elected to office someday."

"I was undercover, I had to keep up the front. It was my job, Lynnie—"

"God, you just don't get it, do you?" she burst out, prodded by the nickname only he had ever used. "Whether you slept with her or not barely matters at all! What matters is that she became more important to you than your marriage, your wife, and that honor you were always so proud of."

"She was in trouble. Scared. She had no one else."

"And as it turned out, so was I."

He winced visibly. "If I'd known—"

"But you weren't around to know, were you? Do you have any idea what it felt like, to lose that baby alone, knowing my husband couldn't be bothered to even call?"

"I would have been there if—"

"If you could have torn yourself away from your drug-addicted hooker?"

"She paid the price, Lynne. She died."

"So did your son. Win one, lose one."

"Win one?" he asked, sounding bewildered. "What did I win?"

"What you wanted. You never wanted our baby, so presto, you got your wish."

He gaped at her. "Never wanted— Where the hell did you get that idea?"

"Where?" she asked sweetly. "Perhaps when you told your captain my timing sucked, and what a nuisance it was? As if I'd managed to get pregnant all by myself?"

He paled. "You . . . heard that?"

"Amazing what you hear when you live in the same house."

"I was just . . . God, Lynne, he was pissed because we were so close to breaking that case. We'd put so much time in on that operation, I was just trying to placate him, go along with his griping."

"Forget it," she said, suddenly weary. "This is old, tired ground, and I don't want to walk every inch of it again."

She turned and headed for the door.

"Lynne," he said.

She paused without looking back. When he didn't say anything more, she kept going. She went to the lunchroom. Ate a vending machine sandwich she could barely taste, which was probably for the better.

Her phone was ringing when she got back to her desk, but it had been nearly nonstop since the press release asking for help from the public had gone out, with her phone number on it. The detective secretary was tearing her hair out, so Lynne tried to catch as many as she could when she was in the office.

That there was a connection to a specific women's shelter had been part of the release, although they'd still kept the name of Rachel's House out of it. Lynne had had to fight for that one. Finally her argument that they had no guarantee the killer would continue to limit himself to only Rachel's House abusers won out.

She picked up the receiver. A timid voice, a child of indeterminate age or gender, asked if this was the detective in the newspaper.

And me without my Officer Friendly hat, she sighed inwardly. But she believed in the "be nice to kids, you may be forming their attitude toward police forever" adage, so she gathered up what little patience she had left and answered pleasantly.

"I'm Detective Garrison, is that who you want?"

"I think so. Was your number in the newspaper?"

"Yes, it was. And my name. What's your name?"

A pause. "Do I have to tell you?"

Uh-oh. This one was already wary. "How about just your first name? That can't hurt."

Another pause. "I guess. It's Tyler."

"Okay, Tyler. How old are you?"

"Seven. Today's my birthday."

"Well, happy birthday," Lynne said, wondering what had the boy calling the police on his birthday. "What can I do for you?"

"Is it true that 'venger guy is killing dads who hit?"

Lynne got a sinking feeling in her stomach. "Where did you hear that, Tyler?"

"I heard my friend's mom talking about it. Is it true?"

Truth or lie? Lynne asked herself. Did you tell a child so young the truth, or try to protect them with a lie? A lie they might find out, and blame you—or the police in general—for?

"Why do you need to know?"

"I just do."

She took in a breath. Truth, she decided. Even kids should have someplace to go where they knew they'd get the truth. "Some people have been killed, yes. And they were people who hit their wives or their children."

"Oh."

He sounded very much like a child who had hoped it was all a mistake. "Is there something you'd like to tell me, Tyler? Maybe I can help."

"I don't know. . . ."

"That's what I'm here for, you know, to help."

"Can you help my dad?"

"Help him?"

There was a sound that was suspiciously like a sniff. Then, abruptly, the dam broke. "I don't want him to die! He's mean sometimes, and he hits us, but I don't want him to die!"

Oh, God. "I'm sure you don't, Tyler. Why don't you tell me where you are, and maybe I can help."

"But he told my mom if she ever told and he got in trouble that he'd come back and make her sorry. That he'd take me away. I don't want to leave my mom. But I don't want him to die! I don't know what to do."

The voice was so young to be dealing with such ugliness. Every once in a while, Lynne thought, you got one that broke through the armor you had to put on to survive.

"Let me help," she urged. "I'll come get you, and your mom, so nobody can hurt you."

"But what about my dad?"

The fear in the child's voice tightened that vise around her heart. *Let him hang,* she thought. "We'll protect him," she said instead.

There was a long silence before the dreaded question came. "Can't you just make him not be mean anymore?"

"If only I could," she said. Then she heard a noise in the background, another voice. "Are you at home, Tyler?" she asked quickly, afraid he'd hang up before she had enough information to track him down.

"No, I'm at my friend's house," he said, and the voice in the background grew louder. "I gotta go."

"Give me your phone number at least, so I can call and make sure you're all right?"

"Can't. Bye."

He hung up.

She sat listening to the dial tone for a long time. There were ways, she knew they could eventually trace the call, but right now she couldn't bestir herself to take the first necessary action. Finally, slowly, feeling as battered as the women of Rachel's House, she replaced the receiver.

"My God, Lynne. What happened?" Again she hadn't heard Drew approach.

"Nothing much," she said bitterly. "Just a scared little boy wanting to turn his dad in before the Avenger gets him. The dad who hits him and his mom and threatens to take him away if he gets caught, but he doesn't want him to die."

"Jesus," Drew muttered.

"'Can't you just make him not be mean anymore?' That's what he wanted."

Drew crouched down before her, put his hands on her knees. She pulled away. *No more. I just can't take it right now.*

She didn't say the words, but he seemed to have heard them anyway. He'd always been good at that. And reading her face. When he'd been around.

She stood up abruptly. Called out to the secretary. "I'm going to Rachel's House. I'll be on pager or cell."

A harried wave indicated the efficient but at the moment beleaguered woman had gotten the message.

"Lynne."

"Not now, Drew. Not now."

He let her go. A small, frightened voice echoed in

her mind. And for the first time in a very long time, she wished she'd gone into another line of work.

"I see your roofer's found something else to do," Lynne said to Regan. *Ah-hah*, she said to herself when she caught the faint rise of color in the red-head's cheeks. *I thought so.*

Now all she had to do was probe, tactfully. Which seemed downright simple next to everything else on her plate just now.

"Yes," Regan said, "he's nearly done with the roof, so he's doing a lot of fix-up things around the place."

"Nice." She winked. "In more ways than one."

Regan colored again, but she didn't dodge. "He does improve the aesthetic appeal of the place, doesn't he?"

Lynne laughed. "The flowers are beautiful, but so is he, in a very male way."

"Yes," Regan said simply.

"Where on earth did you find him?"

"Mrs. Court did. She's paying for all of it, even though it's not in this year's budget."

"Bless her," Lynne said, meaning it. "What's his name? Alex something?"

"Alex Edwards. He's done a lot of work for Mrs. Court, so she trusts him."

I'll just bet she does, Lynne thought, feeling more than a little irked that both Mrs. Court and her son were lying to this woman. She liked Regan, and the idea of her being deceived by people didn't sit well. Especially when it seemed she was interested in that piece of aesthetic value in a very personal way.

She was tempted to blow him out of the water

right now. But she also knew the kind of weight the Court name carried in this town. Maybe there was a reason for what he was doing.

"Mind if I talk to him?"

Regan gave her a startled look. "That's up to him, of course, but why?"

"Just routine," she assured her. If Regan's worried expression was anything to go by, the woman had in fact passed merely interested a ways back, Lynne thought. Which only made her less kindly inclined toward him.

Regan walked her out to the porch and turned to go, but Lynne touched her arm to stop her. Then she called up to Alex. He tossed down a hammer and headed for the ladder.

"I wanted to tell you both," Lynne said when he was with them, "it doesn't appear the guy that went crazy at the office has any connection to the killings, in case you were wondering."

"I did wonder, with the knife and all," Regan said. "It didn't make sense, but then, none of it does."

"I know. But that was an entirely different weapon. The killer uses something much bigger, probably with a curved blade."

Regan grimaced, no doubt at the thought of something bigger than the six-inch blade Jack Koslow had brandished. "Thanks for letting us know."

Lynne nodded, flicked a glance at Alex and back to Regan. She took the hint and stepped back inside.

Judging by the look on Alex's face when Regan left them, some of her feelings were showing. Perhaps this wasn't the best time for this, when she was just about running on empty, but she wasn't happy with the idea of just letting this go on, either.

"Problem, Detective?"

She decided to take the shortest possible route. "That depends, Mr. Court."

He went very still. To his credit, he didn't deny it, or even ask how she'd found out. Perhaps he'd put it together himself after the encounter with the officer at the Rachel's House office.

"There's a reason," he said.

"Which is?"

He glanced around as if to be certain they wouldn't be overheard. "You know the Court Corporation's connection to Rachel's House? In particular my mother?" She nodded. "She sent me here."

"Why?"

"Because of your case, the Avenger."

Lynne frowned. "Does she have reason to think anyone here is in danger from him?"

He met her gaze levelly; he was a cool one, she thought. "No. She wanted to be sure they weren't in any danger from you."

Lynne drew back, startled. "Me?"

"Not you specifically, just any overzealous investigator who might put more pressure on them than necessary."

Nick, Lynne thought suddenly. *He'd be the type.*

She pushed that aside. "And the 'Alex Edwards' ruse?"

"It's a name I've used before, during in-house investigations for CourtCorp. She asked me to come here anonymously, so that neither Regan nor the residents felt any added pressure, didn't feel as if

they had to put up a good front all the time because
of the financial support connection."

"I see."

Annoyingly, she did see. It made sense. And in
fact, was a thoughtful gesture on Mrs. Court's part.
She studied him for a long silent moment.

"Do you do this often?"

"I'm sort of the troubleshooter for the family
business, so yeah, every now and then."

"Do you always get personally involved with the
people you're lying to?" she asked bluntly.

Bull's-eye, she thought as her shot rattled his cool
demeanor. She'd been guessing pretty well today
so she'd risked it, and obviously her thought that
he wasn't real happy with the situation just now
had been right.

"Did she say something to you?"

Lynne noticed he didn't specify who he meant,
which she found nearly as telling as his reaction.

"Shouldn't you be worried whether I said something to her?"

He paled. *Good*, she thought, glad to see this sign
that Regan's interest wasn't one-way.

"Did you?" he asked, tension fairly humming
from him.

"Not yet," she said. "But if you plan on taking
whatever's going on between you any further, I
suggest you tell her yourself. She's good people,
and I'd hate to see her hurt."

"So would I," he said, and Lynne knew she hadn't
imagined the harshness in his tone.

He wasn't stupid; he'd gotten her message. Deciding she'd meddled enough in the personal af-

fairs of near-strangers, she headed for her car. But she didn't miss the way Alex Edwards aka Alexander Court turned to stare at the house.

This visit to Rachel's House had settled her, and as soon as she was in the driver's seat she got out her phone. She called the detective secretary, and asked her to start a trace on the nine minutes after noon call she'd received on the line that had been published in the paper.

"But . . . that trace has already been done."

Lynne blinked. "It has?"

"Yes. Your . . . Investigator Garrison already ordered it. In fact, I believe he's already out at the address it came from."

"Thank you," she said, feeling a bit numb as she hung up.

Damn you, Drew.

Just when she thought she'd dealt with the debris of her fractured marriage, thought she was finally free and clear of the tangled emotions, he went and did something like this.

She sat there, trying to wrestle with her feelings. It wasn't working. Distraction, she thought. She got back out of her car and walked up to the house next door. She knew Pilson was at work, and she planned to come back tomorrow to talk to him, but she figured it couldn't hurt to take a look around now.

She went to the front door just in case. He supposedly lived alone, but you never knew. She knocked, and rang the bell. After waiting several minutes, she started to walk around the house. She found a kitchen window and peered in. Nothing odd there, other than it was extremely tidy. She

went through a side gate that went across the driveway, but the next two windows had curtains that
were closed. She walked around the back. There
were shutters on two back windows, but they were
slanted so that she could peek in. It appeared to be a
den, with a big screen television and a computer in
one corner. Here again it was very neat, not even a
magazine on any of the black gloss finish, Japanese-
style tables. Unusual for a man living alone, but not
necessarily the sign of a sick mind, she supposed.

The last window was blocked by a standing
screen of some kind with an oriental design, so she
gave up for now. She'd have to see what she could
see when she came back to talk to the man. She
turned to go, then realized the detached garage behind the house had what appeared to be a storage
room behind it. She walked over there, to the window beside the door, and looked in.

She drew back sharply, her breath stuck in her
throat. She blinked, then leaned forward again to
look into what looked more like a shrine than a
storage room.

And hanging on one wall was a pair of crossed,
curved swords.

"Do you always do this, go to court with them?"

Regan leaned out from under the porch roof to
look upward. She was dressed up in a neat gray suit
that matched the slightly foggy sky this morning.

"Not if they have someone else to go with them.
But Donna doesn't, so I'm going."

Alex frowned. "I thought you weren't very
happy with her."

"That has nothing to do with this."

That was like her, he thought, to put her own feelings on hold to help someone. "What about the boy?"

"He's over at the transitional housing child-care center for the day."

Donna came out the front door of the house. She wore a bright red dress that made him suddenly aware of the more quiet, subtle colors Regan wore. He supposed when you had hair the color of fire it didn't do to compete with it. But all the women of Rachel's House wore quiet colors, he realized now. Maybe because they didn't want to be noticed, at least not in the way Donna's rather slinky dress hollered for attention.

"I'm ready," she said, sounding breathless.

Alex wondered what for, considering she looked made-up for a night on the town.

He noticed Regan looking her up and down as well, and wondered what she was thinking. But as he would have expected, she said nothing, just picked up the satchel she'd put down when she'd come outside.

Alex walked with them down to the sidewalk. Regan was driving them and her car was, as usual, a few doors down. But just as they reached the end of the Rachel's House walkway, a vehicle pulled up in front.

Regan froze, and Alex sensed her tension as a man got out. Alex guessed he was in his early fifties, although just now he looked older, thanks to the dark circles under his eyes.

"Detective Durwin," Regan whispered to him.

That explained the eyes, Alex thought. Working a serial killer case probably didn't allow for much sleep.

"Miss Keller," the man said. "Sorry to bother
you, but I need to speak with a Mrs. Grant. I understand she's here?"

"Why, that's me," Donna said with an artful smile.

"Donna, this is Detective Durwin, from Vista
Shores PD," Regan introduced them noncommittally.

"Is there someplace we can speak in private, Mrs.
Grant?"

"Oh, no, you see I'm on my way to court this
morning, and we're already late."

Durwin flicked a glance at Alex, a longer one at
Regan, before he said, "You won't be needing to go
to court, Mrs. Grant."

Donna looked at him blankly. But Alex heard
Regan's breath catch in the same instant his own
stomach knotted.

"What do you mean?"

Could she be that stupid? Alex wondered. Or
was she just too new to Rachel's House to have
picked up on the constant aura of tension?

"I think you'd better go back inside," Regan suggested.

"No," Donna said, setting her jaw stubbornly. "I
want to get this over with today. This whole thing
is just too boring."

Again Durwin looked at Regan, who tossed it
right back to him with a gesture of one hand. Durwin
nodded and turned back to the puzzled woman.

"It is over, Mrs. Grant. I'm sorry to be the one to
tell you your husband is dead."

Donna stared at him. "What?"

"Number five," Durwin said bluntly.

"I don't understand."

"The Avenger," Regan said quietly.

Donna's eyes widened. "The Avenger? You mean that killer?"

"We found him in the parking lot of his office early this morning," Durwin said.

Donna's jaw gaped inelegantly. "No, that can't be."

"I'm afraid it is, Mrs. Grant. One of his business partners made the identification."

"But . . . why would that Avenger kill Richard?"

She looked bewildered, so Regan explained gently, "I know you've probably been too distracted to follow the story, Donna, but he's been killing abusers."

She wasn't devastated. She wasn't heartbroken or gleeful. She was quite simply dumbfounded. And misgiving suddenly sparked to life in Alex's belly.

"I know that, but why—" Donna broke off then, a look of horror spreading across her face. "No! No, it's not possible. It can't be!"

She backed up a step, shaking her head. For the first time since he'd known her, Alex heard Regan swear.

"Damn," she said, advancing on the woman. Alex took a step toward them, but Durwin reached out and held him back, shaking his head as he watched the two women intently.

"It can't be," Donna said again, her voice wavering.

"Why, Donna? Why can't it be that the Avenger, who only kills abusers, murdered your husband?"

Alex had never seen a more distraught woman

than Donna Grant in that moment. But he'd also never seen a more furious one than Regan Keller.

"I didn't— I never meant—" Donna waved her hands helplessly.

"I knew there was something wrong about your story, I just knew it! How dare you? How dare you come into this house under false pretenses, among these women? You used us, you used me. You even used your own son!"

The tears started then. Regan ignored them.

"There never was any police report, because there never was any abuse, was there?"

Soundlessly, the broken woman shook her head.

"Why? Why, damn you?"

"I . . . he was going to divorce me. After I had his precious Ricky for him, all that pain and looking so ugly for months! He humiliated me. I wanted to take Ricky away from him, that's all."

"And instead you've killed Ricky's father as surely as if you'd held the knife yourself."

The reality of what had just happened sank to the pit of Alex's stomach. Thanks to this vindictive, petty woman, the Avenger had just executed an innocent man.

CHAPTER 14

Lynne hurried in, shut the door of her apartment, and sagged against it. It was nearly two a.m., and she'd had maybe five hours of sleep in the last forty-eight. She felt more wasted than she ever had in her life, except once.

She doubted anything would ever surpass the night she'd lost her only child before he'd even had a chance to live. The night she'd been in pain alone, in fear alone, and finally had mourned alone. She managed to put it out of her mind for weeks, even months at a time. She put Drew and his betrayal out of her mind for even longer stretches than that.

But that was all blown to bits now; he was not only back in her mind but back in her life, until this was over. And with him came the memory of that tiny spark of life they'd created, gone before it had really begun, leaving her with a hollow ache inside. It had lessened, over the years, but she didn't think it would ever go away completely.

She was exhausted, but at the same time she knew the adrenaline was still too high to let her sleep. The discovery of the Avenger's fifth victim had been bad enough. The revelation that he'd been innocent of anything except poor taste in wives had been a body blow. Especially after she'd gone straight to the manufacturing plant and had found out while Pilson had indeed been working, he had also taken an hour lunch break. She didn't think so, but she was going to have to drive it, see if there had been time. If she could have stopped this, if one of those swords was indeed the murder weapon . . .

They'd spent hours going over the crime scene. Again it was a commercial location, probably because it made the likelihood of witnesses much lower, not to mention that the pavement kept things cleaner. And since they were dealing with outdoor areas that were unsecured for an unknown amount of time after the murder, they didn't know how many people might have contaminated the scene, leaving unrelated fingerprints, dropping cigarette butts or beer bottles.

Evidence? Lynne had thought as she watched the CSI tech examine a crumpled Twinkies wrapper. Or just trash?

In the end, the area sweep results were as skimpy as usual: no fingerprints or footprints, and minimal trace evidence. One oddly shaped smear of blood on the pavement a few inches from the body. A few tiny fibers, a couple of hairs, which did no one any good without a suspect to compare them to. The consensus on all the cases so far was that the killer wore gloves, judging by the few marks they'd found. That the victims were killed at the scene, and only the victim's blood was found at the scene. That the killer continued to pose the bodies after death. And that was darn near all they had.

Lynne rubbed her eyes, almost hoping for the crash. She headed for the kitchen, thinking something warm to drink might do it. She should eat, she supposed, but she didn't have the energy to fix anything. Managing some hot chocolate or even warm milk was going to be about all she could handle.

The knock on the door made her groan. Whatever it was, she could not deal with it until she had some sleep. She headed for the door, only finding when she looked through the peephole just how right she was.

Drew. Here. On her doorstep. In the middle of the night.

Of course, he'd cleared the crime scene not all that long ago, too. It had been Drew who had suggested, after examining that odd bloody smear at the scene, that the suspect might be wearing some kind of cloth over his shoes, to avoid leaving any kind of recognizable tread print if he accidentally stepped in blood. Which meant he was as thorough and careful as they'd feared.

He knocked again. With the light on behind her, she guessed he'd probably noticed the darkening of the peephole and knew she was here and still awake. She pondered the feasibility of simply not opening the door. But there was a slim chance he might be here for official reasons. With a sigh, she opened the door.

Two things happened simultaneously. Drew gave her that crooked grin that had always made her heart flip-flop, and her stomach gurgled when the aroma of hot food hit her nose.

"I was starved," he said, lifting up a bag that was clearly full of some evil and luscious fast food. Another bag, she'd guess holding drinks, was in his other hand. "And I figured you hadn't eaten either."

"I'm too tired to eat," she said.

"Uh-huh," he said as her stomach loudly called her a liar. "It's all right, Lynne. I won't overstay my limited welcome."

She was too tired to be gracious, too tired even to be rude. So she ended up saying nothing and simply stepped aside to let him in.

Without a word he walked to the coffee table in front of the big, overstuffed sofa. If he realized that under the bright yellow slipcover it was the same one they'd had in their house, he didn't react. He efficiently emptied the first bag of hamburgers, fries, and napkins. He spread out a napkin like a place mat, arranged the food, then reached for the second bag.

"I skipped the caffeine," he said as he pulled out tall, covered plastic cups. "I hope you still like lemonade."

"That's fine."

She dropped down onto the couch, leaning forward toward the food on the table. Somehow it wearied her even more that he remembered she liked lemonade. He'd always been good at that, remembering her little likes and dislikes. He proved it in the next instant by pulling the pickles out of her cheeseburger before handing it over.

She decided to eat and when the first mouthful hit her empty stomach she was glad of it. She took another quick bite, then a couple of fries, before the growling ebbed.

She was afraid Drew was going to start a personal conversation, so she spoke first.

"Thank you again for checking on that little boy."

The moment she said it, she realized she had in a way done just what she'd tried to avoid, brought up a topic that could easily become personal. But when he finally answered, after some quick consumption of his own, it was purely business. "It didn't take long."

"What was the situation?" All he'd had time to tell her before, at the crime scene, was that he'd found Tyler and that he was all right.

"Typical. So far the abuse has been limited to his mother. Alcohol-induced, from what I could tell. I talked to his mom, gave her the hot line number, but I doubt she'll call. She's still in the 'I know he'll change' stage."

Lynne sighed.

"I did have a little man-to-man chat with ol' dad, though."

He hadn't told her that. "You did? You didn't tell him Tyler had called, did you?"

"No, I didn't want the boy in his sights." He grinned. "I sort of hinted that our serial killer had a list, and he was on it."

Lynne's eyes widened, and a smile curved her mouth. "Oh, really?"

"I told him not only was he a coward and pond scum, he was in the worst possible place to be. He had a serial killer hunting him on one side, and me on his ass on the other. One step out of line and his wife and child wouldn't have a thing to worry about anymore. The only question would be who got to him first. And he'd better hope it was me."

"Thank you," she said.

He didn't try to milk it, for which she was grateful. "Like I said, it didn't take long. And I don't know how much good it will do."

"Probably a lot. At least as long as our killer is active."

"Which may be a while. This one doesn't want to get caught," he said.

She felt relieved at the turn in conversation, then vaguely amused about thinking a serial killer as dinner conversation was a relief.

"At least, not yet," Drew added.

"You think it's more than him just being an organized killer?" she asked, referring to the general division profilers had come up with between organized and disorganized criminals. "He fits all the criteria, he's careful, leaves no evidence, and it's obviously premeditated."

"I think so. He's not just careful because that's his nature, although it probably is. He's on a mission."

She'd already determined that. This was no hedonistic killer, nor one after power or control. This was the other kind of serial killer, the man following his own twisted vision. She munched on another fry, thinking they'd never tasted so good.

"What do you think about Pilson?"

"He's a likely," Drew said. "Fits the profile on all but a few minor points. And from what you say, he had access to the information he'd need to find out about the victims."

"When I pushed Regan, she remembered that he was around on several occasions when the victims' latest attacks on the Rachel's House women were being discussed. She couldn't be sure he knew about them all, though."

"What about alibis? I recall something about him working nights?"

"Only sometimes. He works a split shift, some nights, some graveyard shifts." She grabbed another fry, ate it, then told him, "I checked the distance from his work to where the last body was found, and then back. Assuming he doesn't drive like a maniac—"

"Which he wouldn't, because he doesn't want to attract attention."

"That's what I figured. Driving the speed limit, it leaves only fifteen minutes for picking up his victim, the actual murder, and arranging the body."

"Tight. But I can't say impossible."

"My background check does show he's had an interest in Asian culture, and those swords looked Japanese. It may be innocent, but I still want to ask for a search warrant to pick them up."

"Good idea."

"Would our killer be the sword collector type?"

"Maybe. They can pick anything as a symbol, or part of the ritual. I can easier tell you what he's not.

He's not the 'What's one less person on the face of the earth anyway?' kind of killer."

"What?"

"That was Ted Bundy's rationalization." He shrugged. "This guy's more specific."

"To rid the world of abusers?" she asked. "Sounds almost sane."

"If that's what, in his mind, he's really doing."

She took what normally would have been her last two bites as one, then wiped her fingers. "What else?"

"I don't know." He chewed a bite of his own burger and took a sip of the lemonade before continuing. "He's obviously getting some psychological gain out of it. Maybe he was abused, and is killing his own abuser over and over."

"Seems a little too simple for this guy."

Drew smiled. "Good for you. Somebody taught you well."

For a moment the conversation threatened to turn in the direction she didn't want it to go. Quickly she tried to divert it.

"I've been refreshing my memory," she said. "So I know it's likely it started in childhood. Isolation, no bond with parents, all that. Never learning to relate to other people, so that other people never seem quite real to them."

He nodded. "And the triad."

"I know, fire-setting, bed-wetting, and torturing animals, the red-flag triad of serial killers in the making. Add the brutal dad, controlling mom." The last three fries vanished, as did the empty feeling in her middle. "Pilson's parents died several years ago, back in Cincinnati. I put a call in to the local cops there, to see if there's any record of family abuse or domestic violence, or if there's a juvie record on him."

"Good. I'd rather not wait until he makes a mistake. And as a rule, serial killers get better with practice."

"He just made a big mistake," Lynne pointed out, although she knew the Avenger's mistaken choice of victim wasn't what he had meant.

Drew nodded. "It's going to be interesting to see how he reacts. Will he count it as just a detour, or will it disrupt his careful pattern so much that it rattles him into screwing up?"

Deciding she'd finish the lemonade in a minute, she leaned back on the sofa, pulling her feet up beneath her. "Enough to make the kind of mistake we need?"

"We can but hope," he said.

He leaned back as well, putting his feet up on the coffee table as he'd always done, although he nudged a magazine over to protect the wood; that was new, she thought.

And then all thought fled as she stared at the set of keys next to his foot. He'd dropped them there when he set down the bag of food, but she hadn't noticed them until his movement had drawn her gaze. And she especially hadn't noticed the one item on the key ring that wasn't a key.

His wedding ring.

There was no mistaking it. It matched hers, a simple diamond cut gold band with grooves near the edges that were black. The sight of it took her breath away, and her mind raced, trying out meaning after meaning, unable to settle on one.

He saw her looking at it, and sat up. He picked up the keys by the wedding band. And abruptly he swung open the door she tried so hard to keep shut.

"Did you ever wonder why I didn't contest the divorce? Why I didn't fight you over anything?"

"Back then I wasn't wondering about anything except how I was going to get through the next hour."

"I didn't fight because I felt so damn guilty. I felt like you had every right to hate me. Our baby died before he had a chance to take his first breath, you nearly died with him, and I wasn't even there. For three days, I wasn't even there."

She bit down hard on the inside of her lip, using the pain to fight down emotions she had to beat before she could trust herself to speak. "Believe me, I remember," she said finally.

"I knew the only thing I could do for you was to make leaving me as easy as possible. Even though it was tearing me up inside."

And he was tearing her up inside now.

"Stop it, Drew. Just stop."

He dropped the keys back on the table. His feet went back up. And for a long, strained few minutes, neither of them spoke. At last Drew broke the silence.

"I forgot to tell you. Kelso broke his case."

She forcibly yanked her attention away from the telling sight of the ring, still wishing she knew exactly what it was telling her.

"He was right? About the wife?" She hadn't followed the case after that day of observing Nick's technique, hadn't wanted to be anywhere near him while she had all this other stuff on her plate. She figured she'd hear when something broke, and beyond that she was better off not being involved.

Drew nodded at her question. "Apparently the husband had been beating her for years, and she finally saw a way out. So she hired a guy."

"That was it," Lynne whispered, almost to herself.

"What was it?"

"I kept thinking there was something familiar about her, but I couldn't put my finger on it. Not like I knew her, but that she reminded me of someone. And I just realized what it was. She held herself like the women at Rachel's House. Carefully, as if she thought she might have to dodge a blow at any moment."

"Sometimes your gut knows before your head," Drew said.

"So she figured as long as abusers were being killed, she could kill hers and pass it off as one of the Avenger killings?"

Drew nodded. "She didn't want to just leave, she'd signed a pre-nup and wouldn't get anything in a divorce. Lot of money there, I guess."

Lynne nodded. "She looked it."

"Kelso said she'd never worked a day in her life."

"So she thought she couldn't survive on her own. That's one of the intimidation tools they use."

"I just hope Kelso played by the rules. He was

riding her pretty hard, and talked her out of a lawyer more than once. If she'd had counsel, she might never have given it up."

Lynne frowned. It would be like Nick to use the woman's already battered psyche against her, to break her. "She gave up the actual killer?"

"Yeah, and the guy rolled right over on her when Kelso finally tracked him down today. Cleared the case in two weeks."

"Good for Nick," she said. And meant it, although the spectre of what she'd learned about him still hung over her.

"Yes," he said, his tone neutral. "Not for the guy, though. She gave him some jewelry, because she was never allowed to have much cash. That's how Kelso found him, when he tried to fence the jewelry. Diamonds, emeralds, platinum, high-class stuff, and he takes it to some two-bit fence who about has a heart attack."

"The rich," she said tiredly, leaning her head back on the soft sofa cushion, "live lives I can't even begin to comprehend."

"It'd be nice to try, though, wouldn't it?"

She smiled, her eyes drifting closed. "Give me the chance to prove money won't change me?"

She fell asleep. Just like that. She must have, because she dreamed she heard Drew say softly, "Or harder still, give me the chance to prove . . ."

She woke up hours later, wrapped carefully in a blanket that had been in the trunk at the foot of her bed, and wondering what she'd dreamed Drew wanted a chance to prove.

* * *

"It's got to be somebody connected to somebody at Rachel's House somehow."

Alex leaned against the porch railing. Regan had come outside to sit on the bench, looking very much as if she'd hit the wall. She had on worn jeans and a faded blue T-shirt, had her hair gathered up in some kind of clip at the back of her head, and her face was scrubbed clean of makeup, making the dark circles under her eyes stand out. He'd grabbed the chance and a soda and plopped down on the porch opposite her.

"I know," Regan said wearily. "Who else would have known about Donna at all? She wasn't here that long, and she wasn't going to be a permanent resident, even if she had been telling the truth."

Bitterness laced her voice. Regan clearly hadn't forgiven the woman for her fatal self-centeredness, and Alex doubted if she soon would.

His stomach knotted, and the soda he'd drunk seemed to be churning rather than bubbling. Regan had been rightfully enraged at Donna, and it hadn't escaped Alex that one of the main reasons for that fury was that Donna had lied. To her, and to all of the women of Rachel's House.

Just as he had been doing ever since he got here.

True, unlike Donna his reasons were benign, and his—and his mother's—intentions had been the best, but he wasn't sure how much weight that would carry with Regan.

"I still can't believe she did that," Regan said, staring out over the colorful garden as if she didn't see it at all anymore. "How could she lie like that?"

Oh, yes, there would be a price to pay, Alex thought. And he didn't relish the thought.

"Tunnel vision," he said. "All she saw was her tiny little corner. All she cared about was herself. They're out there."

"Yeah," Regan said, "and every time one of them pulls something like this, they damage all battered women."

"I'd say she damaged her husband more than anyone. Except maybe her son. I wouldn't want to have to explain to that boy when he's a little older."

Regan looked at him then, looking abashed. "You're right. And he didn't deserve that, nor did Ricky. Sometimes I have my own case of tunnel vision."

He saw Regan focus on something in the distance. Coming their way was the one person who could take down his house of cards with a word.

"I wonder if she has any news," Regan said, getting to her feet as Detective Garrison turned up the walkway to Rachel's House.

Alex thought it more likely she'd come to ask more questions they couldn't answer.

Or to blow him out of the water, he told himself grimly. He could only hope she would give him more time.

"Hello, Regan," the blonde said as she came up the steps. She glanced at Alex and he held his breath, waiting for her to call him "Mr. Court" in that pointed way she had before. After a moment, she only nodded at him and said, "Alex."

"Can I get you something?" Regan asked. "You look like I feel."

The smile she got for that was genuine, but weary. "Thanks, but I only stopped by to ask you for your sign-out sheets for the period of the last murder."

"I've got them inside," Regan said.

"I'll just sit here a moment, if you don't mind getting them now."

"Of course not."

As Regan turned to go inside, Alex braced himself. And sure enough, as soon as the door closed behind her, he was pinned by a pair of weary but still sharp eyes.

"You haven't told her."

It wasn't a question. "I just couldn't dump it on her right now. She's got enough to carry."

"I can't argue that." She studied him for a moment. "And is it going to matter to you if she finds out on her own, before you tell her? If she catches you in the lie herself?"

His jaw clenched, and he let out a compressed breath.

"I thought it might," she said before he could answer. Then she shrugged. "It's your risk. I won't burn you unless I feel I have to, for her sake."

"Thank you," he said, just as Regan came back out, papers in hand.

"I've been going over the copies I made of these," she said as she handed them to the detective, "comparing them to the times of the murders. No one person from Rachel's House has been unaccounted for for all of them."

"Except you," the detective said to Regan, "and if you did it, I'll turn in my badge."

Regan smiled at her. "Thanks. Not that I haven't muttered to myself that I'd like to wipe them all off the face of the planet."

"There's a real thick line between thinking and doing when it comes to murder. Most people don't cross it." She glanced at the pages before saying wryly, "We did consider the possibility of a conspiracy between all of you, but the theory didn't last long."

"Too hard for different people to duplicate a serial killer's signature so perfectly?" Alex asked.

Detective Garrison raised an eyebrow at him. "Have you been doing research, too?"

"Just something I read somewhere. Probably in one of the news stories about the Avenger."

She wrinkled her nose. "There are enough of those."

"I saw you went public asking for help," Alex said.

Something changed in the detective's face then, some darkness flickered in her eyes. But she only nodded. "When he's gotten away with it this many times, we have to take help where we can get it."

"Even from other investigators?"

At Regan's quiet question Garrison's head snapped around. And suddenly Alex remembered Officer McDonald, who'd responded to the office, joking about Detective Garrison and her ex-husband.

"Sorry if it's a sore spot," Regan said. "The officer who came to the office mentioned it in passing."

"Did he."

From her tone, Alex didn't care much for Mc-Donald's chances of escaping a blistering on when to keep his mouth shut.

"It's got to make an already hard job tougher," Regan said sympathetically.

"It has its moments," the woman answered, and Alex wondered what moment specifically she was thinking about when her expression momentarily softened.

"I've tried and tried to think of who it could be, who could have all the information," Regan said. "If you go just by that, then it *should* be me."

"Or Mrs. Tanaka."

Regan rolled her eyes. "If female serial killers are rare, then I'd guess females who start in their seventies must be the rarest."

She got a chuckle for that one. "There was one in Sacramento a while back, but you're right, that's a rare bird. But could be anybody who had the information go through their hands at any point. Or saw it accidentally. Somebody with a connection to the courts, other shelters, even us."

"But doesn't Donna's case narrow it down? There was no police report."

"Yes, it does. And it may be our break. She wasn't in the system very long and it may be easier to backtrack who would have known about her, and who her husband was."

"Do you think it's somebody who lives close by?" As soon as she said it Alex's mind leapt to Mr. Pilson.

"So far he's what we call geographically stable,

one who stays in one place. Of course, so far that's been where his victims are, too."

"You mean he might go farther?"

"He might. We just don't know. This is a tangled one," she admitted. "And you should know, Mr. Pilson is a pretty solid suspect. His lifestyle shows some red flags, and we picked up some possible evidence from his garage. He hasn't been arrested, but if some tests we're running come back positive . . ."

Regan shuddered. "I just can't believe that he could be the one." She broke off, and Alex put a soothing hand on her arm.

"It's always hard to believe," Lynne said. "But be careful around him. And by the way, you should probably also know Donna Grant confessed to everything. That she made up the abuse stories, lied to her family, even told her son his father had tried to kill him. All to make sure he wouldn't get custody and hopefully not even visitation."

Regan sighed. "I tried to tell her that was no guarantee, that even abusers sometimes get visitation. She wouldn't listen."

"She hadn't been abused, hadn't lived with the daily hammering home that you're a loser who will keep on losing," Garrison said. "She was sure it would all come out just like she wanted, and she'd get to humiliate him as he had her."

"And instead he's dead because of her. I hope she pays for that."

"I think she will. They haven't sorted out what all they're going to charge her with yet, but she's looking at serious trouble."

"Tell me something, Detective," Alex asked. "How is this, and the Wheeler killing, going to affect the killer?"

Regan gave him a quick glance, then turned back to the detective, as if she hadn't thought of this aspect of it.

"I can't say for sure. It may just roll off his back."

"Or?" Alex prodded.

"It may set him off. This is his personal quest. He may not like it being usurped by someone for their own ends."

"And he might not like being used?" Regan asked.

She nodded. "We think he's the visionary type of serial killer. For whatever reason, he's chosen this as his mission. He has to go through his ritual, to fulfill his vision in a very specific, particular way. Anything that interferes with that disrupts his vision and makes the killing for nothing. He doesn't get what he needs out of it."

"Just what we need," Alex said with a grimace. "A serial killer who's now even more crazed."

"That may be," the woman with the tired eyes said, "exactly what we've got."

CHAPTER 15

As she leaned back in her office chair, watching the light change as the afternoon ended and evening began, Regan began to relax. She had just returned from the hospital, after receiving the wonderful news that Mindy had come out of the coma. They still didn't know how much permanent damage had been done, but they were optimistic, and so was Rachel's House.

A sound from the kitchen drew her attention. Since all the residents were either at work or counseling just now, it had to be Mitch or Alex. Alex had been working on the sagging screen on the back kitchen door, so that must be what she'd heard.

But, she told herself, she should check anyway. She got to her feet and headed for the kitchen. It was Alex, screwdriver in hand. Which reminded her. "You haven't found any more little packages, have you?"

He finished tightening the screw he'd been working on. "No."

"Good," she said. "Then I feel like I did the right thing."

"By doing nothing?"

"You think I should have called the police or something?"

"I didn't say that. I know it would have been ugly. They probably would have wanted to search the house for more, and that would have been rough on everybody."

She relaxed, wondering why she'd worried. He might not have understood what went on at Rachel's House when he'd arrived, but he'd learned fast.

"It's going to be a nice night," he said.

"Yes."

"Night like this, I like to go down and watch the sunset over the ocean. I know the perfect place."

She smiled. "I haven't done that in years."

"Do it tonight. With me."

It sounded like an impulsive invitation, one he hadn't thought about, so she hesitated.

"You work too hard. And it's been quiet. Everything will be fine if you leave for a while. Maybe we can even get through the evening without any disaster calls."

If it had been an impulse, he didn't appear to regret it. Or want to back out.

"Give me an hour to clean up and get back here. We'll pick up some dinner and go watch the sun say good-bye."

She told herself she only agreed because she liked the way he said it, but as they drove west almost exactly an hour later, she knew it was much more.

She was surprised when he headed past the public beach parking lot and pulled off the road next to one of the few undeveloped tracts of land left along the coast, on a bluff overlooking the Pacific.

"It belongs to Court Corporation," he explained. "I've got a key to the gate, and they don't mind."

"Oh."

It felt isolated, but she told herself she was being silly. When he drove through the gate and out to a clearing on the bluff with a spectacular view up and down the coast, she knew he hadn't lied about this being the perfect place.

He turned the truck around and parked it heading back the way they'd come. He grabbed the bag of Chinese food they'd picked up and got out. He came around to her side and pulled her door open, then led the way to the back of the truck.

"Tailgate makes a decent table," he said, and proceeded to lower it and set out the meal. She couldn't help smiling; he was preparing like it was a Fourth of July fireworks show. He even pulled out a cushion that looked like it had escaped from a worn-out chaise longue, and put it crossways across the end of the tailgate so they both had a place to sit. She wanted more than anything for this evening to pass unmarred by the kind of interruptions that had ruined their last two times out.

"Something wrong?" he asked, and she realized she'd been lost in her musings.

"I was just wondering if I dare turn the cell phone off."

He grinned, and her heart did that little flip-flop he always seemed to cause. "The reception's lousy up here."

"Good," she said, grinning back at him.

He swallowed suddenly, and she wondered if he was feeling the same sort of nervousness as she was. She was glad of the distraction of eating, and surprised to realize she was starved. And more surprised to feel a sense of peace stealing over her. Eating in the outdoors, in this private place with the incredible view, wiped away the tension she'd been carrying for so long.

The display as the sun went down was nearly as good as the Fourth of July, Regan decided, as incredible shades of orange, pink, blue, and purple streaked the sky with color. A quiet, warming sort of joy began to build in her. She didn't know the source, but suspected it might just have something to do with the man who had thought to do this, the man who looked at her now and said softly, "Better than anything Hollywood can come up with."

She returned his gaze, and said just as softly, "Yes, it is. Thank you."

"I didn't have much to do with it."

"You knew I needed this."

He shrugged, but with a smile. "I knew it has brought me peace, coming up here. I thought it might work for you."

"It did."

It happened later, in the moonless dark, as they picked up the debris from their meal. Simple enough, both of them reaching for the same little white box, colliding, excusing . . .

There was a split second when she was looking into his eyes, when she saw the hunger burst free. And then he pulled her to him, and before she could take another breath his mouth was on hers.

As kisses went, at least in her experience, it was shattering. The memory of the brotherly kiss he'd given her that day vanished, burned away by the passionate heat of this one. His hunger fired hers and she was clinging to him, kissing him back with a fierceness that astonished her. With each passing second the heat built, grew, until she could barely breathe.

His hands slid down her back to her hips, then to the curve of her backside, pulling her harder against him. His tongue swept over her lips, and she met it with her own without hesitation. She couldn't get enough, couldn't taste enough, and somewhere in the back of her pleasure-fogged mind all her long-held cautions and reservations were seared to ash.

When he broke the kiss she whimpered. She heard him whisper her name, hoarsely, with a quiver of harsh need in his voice. An echoing need cramped inside her, and this time it was she who took his mouth, urgently, needily. And it was her hands that roved this time, first tangling in his hair, savoring the soft, heavy, silken feel of it, then slipping down his back to his waist, where she paused, the heat gathering before she boldly cupped his buttocks as he had hers.

She heard his hissed intake of breath, realized he was rock hard against her belly. She wanted to explore that hardness, wanted to touch it, stroke it as she had the rest of him, wanted to see his reaction, wanted to hear him groan aloud, wanted to feel him respond to her hands, her touch.

She wanted it all, she wanted it now, in a way she'd never wanted before in her life.

She felt his hand move once more, up her side until he was brushing the side of her breast. She moved, not pushing him away as she usually did with any man in the past, but shifting her body to give him access, aching to feel his hands on her in the same way she had ached to put hers on him. When his hand cupped her, lifting the soft flesh of her breast, she nearly gasped. When his thumb found and rubbed her nipple, she cried out at the spearing bolt of sensation that shot through her.

At last, with a groan that rang with reluctance, he pulled away. Regan stared at him, hating that he'd done it, while at the same time savoring the wild, hungry look of him, panting for breath, his face stark with urgency and need.

"I—" He stopped, swallowed heavily, then tried again. "I didn't bring you up here for this."

"I never thought you did," she said, feeling her heart still hammering in her chest. "But now that you have . . ."

He groaned again. "Don't look at me like that."

"Why not?"

"Because it makes me think about how private it is up here, and I'm already hanging on by a thread."

"Privacy is good," she whispered. And she couldn't deny that the thought of making love, out here in the open yet without the fear of being seen, was incredibly arousing.

But nothing was as arousing as the look on Alex's face, the gleam in his eyes, the tension evident in the cords of his neck. He wanted her, pure and simple, and it had been so long since any man had looked at her that way, it made her a little delirious.

She reached out to cup his face, as if she could save that look in her hands, as she wanted to save this entire, perfect evening. The back of a workman's pickup truck might seem like a tacky place to some, but to Regan, it was Alex's truck, Alex was with her, and that was all she needed.

"Do you have any idea," he asked hoarsely, "what you're doing to me?"

"I think I might," she answered, "if it's the same as what you're doing to me."

She leaned up to kiss him again, wanting the feel of his mouth more than she could remember wanting anything. When he stopped her, she frowned.

"Regan, wait, are you sure?"

"I'm sure."

"But you . . . don't know much about me—"

"I know enough."

"I don't want you to be sorry."

"I won't be."

And then she did kiss him, slowly, tentatively, liking the way it made him suck in his breath. Still he seemed to hesitate, seemed to fight the need.

"Regan, wait," he breathed, barely audible.

She weighed her innate wariness against the look she'd seen in his eyes. The fire won. She moved closer, her body seeking his heat. Her breasts brushed his chest, and she liked the feel of it so much she did it again, rubbing sinuously against him.

Alex groaned, low and harsh. And then, like a man whose final restraint had snapped, his arms came around her and slammed her tight against him. His mouth took hers, and she felt every bit of the hunger she'd seen in his face.

She couldn't be still. She'd never before felt this crazed need to move, to stroke, to touch, to feel his hands and mouth on her. And when his hands cupped her breasts once more, less gently this time, she squirmed to keep her body close yet give him room. Her nipples ached for his touch, and when he rubbed them she cried out against his mouth at the fire that burst loose.

Suddenly he moved, grasping her waist and lifting her to sit once more on the tailgate. She only knew he'd unbuttoned her blouse by the brush of balmy summer night air over her skin. He trailed a path of tiny nibbling kisses down from her throat to the swell of her breasts. When his hand slipped behind her to the clasp of her bra she moved to help him, wanting to be free of the binding lace. When she felt it give, she hastily pulled an arm free of strap and sleeve. She nearly lost her balance, and instinctively threw a hand back to catch herself. She heard Alex groan again, and only then realized how her position arched her back, as if she were offering her breasts up to him.

As it always was with Alex, the woman who once would have shyly retreated instead arched more, begging without words, asking for the touch she craved.

Alex muttered her name, his voice thick and deep. And then he took her offering, first one nipple, then the other. Fingers, then lips, and then the wet heat of his mouth, drawing deeply, pulling, until her flesh tightened into achingly tight, sensitive peaks. She let her head loll back as she focused on the feel of his hands and mouth at her breasts. And suddenly that wasn't enough, she wanted him naked, on top of her, in her. She wanted to be naked under him, on top of him, however he wanted it.

She reached for his shoulders, opening her legs to let him take a step forward between them. The moment she felt the swell of flesh behind his zipper pressed against her intimately, her hips moved. She couldn't help herself, she wanted, had to have more. And this time, when the urge struck her, she followed it, running her hands down his body until she was cupping him, stroking his rigid length.

"You do that once more," he said against her ear, in a voice barely recognizable as his, "and there's no turning back."

She hesitated, just long enough for him to know it was a certain, deliberate choice. And then she touched him again, slowly, as if memorizing every inch.

With an oath that sounded wrenched from him, Alex left her. She nearly cried out until she realized he had only gone to the cab of the truck. In moments he was back, a small foil packet in his hand.

"Boy Scout?" she asked, not really caring if he was always prepared, as long as he was prepared now.

"A friend of mine's idea of a hint."

"Remind me to thank him." Regan reached for him again.

It was awkward, uncomfortable, clumsy. It was also the most erotic, incredible thing that had ever happened to her. She didn't know or care how he got her out of her jeans, or himself out of his. She was only vaguely aware that he had pulled the longue cushion over, lifted her onto it, and himself after her.

He kissed her, long and deep, his tongue probing as his fingers probed between her legs, stroking through already damp curls until he reached the knot of nerve endings that made her cry out. When she felt the weight of him come down on her hips, only some still-functioning level of her pleasure-dazed mind was aware it was her making that pleading sound.

Her body, as if it had forgotten this act, resisted at first. But her response to him eased the rest of the way, and Regan gasped with shocked pleasure as Alex slid into her, thick and deep. She felt him shudder, heard a low, guttural sound break from him even as she moaned at the pleasure of that stretched, full sensation. She was barely aware that her fingers were digging into his back, barely aware of the strangeness of looking up and seeing the night sky over his shoulder.

He shifted his body, and the movement opened her to him farther. Before she had a chance to savor the new deliciousness, he was moving, driving into her with long, hard plunges that made her gasp and Alex groan each time he buried himself in her.

This, it seemed, her body had not forgotten. Or if it had, Alex was teaching it all over again, until the tension coiling within her became unbearable. His hands were everywhere, stroking, caressing, his mouth too, kissing, tasting, tracing the curve of her ear and the line of her neck. And always that pounding, that steady, deep hammering of his body into hers.

It caught her unaware, welling up so fast it swamped her. "Alex!"

Her body convulsed around his, and as she felt the pulses in her own inner flesh, she heard him call out her name. Then he drove deep one last time, shuddered against her, grinding his hips against hers as if he wanted to climb inside her.

And then nothing broke the quiet of the night but their own quickened breathing and the distant sound of traffic on the road out of sight below the cliff.

Alex knew he'd made a horrible mistake. He knew it, but he didn't care. Not now, not with Regan still lying soft and sated in his arms. Not after the way she'd come unraveled at his touch, not after the way her body had coaxed his to a climax more powerful than anything he'd ever felt before.

Later, he would have to deal with it. Later, he would think about how much more complicated this made things, how much more difficult it was going to be to tell her the truth, as he would eventually have to.

Later. Much later.

Before long he remembered an old saying that you might as well be hung for a sheep as a lamb, and reached for her again.

CHAPTER 16

"Regan?"

She looked up, fear spiking through her at the unusual note in Marita's voice. But the woman in the office doorway was staring down at some papers in her hand, something Regan guessed had come in the noon mail, given the manila envelope Marita also held. Regan got up and walked quickly over to her.

"What is it, Marita?"

The woman looked up then, her dark eyes full of conflicting emotions. "It's final. My divorce is final."

Congratulations, Regan thought, but the confusion in Marita's eyes kept her from saying it aloud. This woman had become a friend and a colleague in her nearly six months here at Rachel's House, and Regan knew that while it was what she wanted, it was also the final grieving for what could have been.

It also marked the arrival of the self-imposed deadline Marita had set. She'd said all along that when her divorce was final, it would be time to move on, begin a new life.

"I know it's bittersweet, Marita. But now you can start over. There's nothing tying you to him."

"I don't want to leave here," Marita admitted. "This has become my home."

"I don't want you to leave," Regan said. "I'll miss you terribly."

Marita's mouth twisted. "There's a 'however' attached to that, though, isn't there?"

Regan hugged her. "You know you can't stay forever. You can't keep hiding. You have to move on with your life."

"I know."

"And once you get out on your own, your outlook will change."

"Maybe."

"And someday, if you still want to come back, maybe I can convince Mrs. Court to make what you've been doing anyway a paying job."

Marita's eyes brightened. "You'd do that?"

"I would. But you might want to think about helping start your own Rachel's House, in a place that doesn't have one."

"I could never do that."

"You could, Marita. You've learned so much since you've been here. You might have to go to school and add some organizational and business skills, but you can do it."

"You think?" she asked.

"I know," Regan answered. "Don't let him keep holding you back even when he's not around anymore. You can do anything you want now. Anything."

Hope crept into Marita's eyes. And Regan knew as long as she could hold on to that hope, she had a chance.

Grimm opened the doors of the library that served as her office just as Alexander was coming in.

"Good morning, sir," Grimm said, and exited. Alexander stared after him, then turned to his mother.

"Did he just call me sir?"

"I believe so. Sit down, Alexander."

Still looking perplexed, her son took the indicated chair.

"All's quiet on the serial killer front."

"So I've gathered, but that's not what I asked you to come over for."

"Breakfast, then?" he asked, looking hopeful. "Or brunch," he amended with a glance at his watch. "Would you let me take you to brunch?"

"Brunch with my handsome son? I'd like that. It's been far too long." His surprise at her acceptance told her she had truly let things go for too long. "I'll call the Shores Grill, and have them save my regular table."

His change of expression stopped her in the act of reaching for the phone.

"Problem?"

"That's across the street from the Rachel's House off-site office."

"Yes, I know."

"Regan often goes over there on Saturday, to catch up."

"So?"

For the first time since he'd been about twelve, he squirmed in the chair. "She might see us together."

Now, this was interesting, she thought. "Really, Alexander, the timing it would take for that to happen is a bit of a stretch, isn't it?"

He sighed. "I guess."

"Besides, you said you were going to tell her the truth anyway, because the detective already knew. Haven't you?"

"No."

"Why?"

"I know I have to." He grimaced. "But I don't want her to know I've been lying to her."

There was obviously more to it than that. She'd suspected it even as he'd used the excuse of Detective Garrison having found him out. Now she was even more certain. She could see it in his eyes—when he wasn't dodging looking at her. Yes, very interesting, Lillian thought.

"Then why must she know? When this is over, you simply depart, your work finished, correct? It's not as if you make a habit of attending the Rachel's House fund-raisers or annual parties where you might see her again."

She thought he winced, but the expression was gone so quickly she couldn't be sure. "No, it's not." He stood up abruptly. "Let's just go, Mom. I'm hungry."

They took her Mercedes, although she let him

drive. She was still a traditionalist in that. Besides, she needed to make a couple of calls on the way to rearrange her schedule for this unforeseen engagement. And time to analyze her son's palpable tension when it came to the subject of Regan Keller.

As they pulled into the parking lot of the Shores Grill, she saw Alex glance over at the Rachel's House office. A white pickup and a battered gray sedan were parked in the adjacent lot, but not Regan's car, and he seemed to relax.

Curiouser and curiouser, Lillian thought, and smiled inwardly. She couldn't deny she'd thought more than once that Regan, with her courage and determination, might just be a match for her quicksilver son.

Not until they had eaten, the maître d' had quit hovering, and she was sipping at a last flute of champagne did she return to the subject of Regan.

"I need to ask you something, Alexander."

"Yes?"

Just then something caught her eye. She looked, and with a smile said, "It appears you were right."

"I was?"

"Regan just arrived."

She thought he swore, but it was so low she couldn't be sure. He sneaked a look as Regan apparently gathered up some things from the seat beside her. Then he jerked his head back, staring at the bit of chocolate and crust left on his plate.

Lillian opened her mouth to tease him, then shut it again, frowning as she looked once more across the street.

"Alexander," she began.

"Don't rag on me about her, Mom, all right?"

"No, listen. There's something odd. A man was sitting in that gray car, watching as she drove in. And now, just as Regan got out, so did he."

His head snapped around to look.

"I don't like the look of him," Lillian said.

"Neither do I," he muttered.

Alexander sprang to his feet. He spun on his heel and left the restaurant at a run. Lillian quickly signed the tab and got up herself. In that few seconds, her premonition turned into frightening reality.

The man from the gray car had Regan backed up against the wall of the office building, his hands at her throat.

Alex was halfway across the street when he saw Regan jerk her knee upward. She missed the intended target, but threw the man off balance. He ran harder as Regan ignored the hands still at her throat and jabbed at her attacker's face quickly, sharply, with something in her hand.

The man screamed and backed up. Alex launched himself, aiming with a hard, driving fist for the face Regan had already bloodied. The man went down. The knife clattered on the cement, inches from Regan's feet. She kicked it out of reach.

"Son of a bitch!" the man said, rolling to his knees.

"Stay down," Alex advised him, "or I'll make sure you *can't* get up."

"Get the hell out of my way! What do you want to help this bitch for anyway?"

"Keep your mouth shut, too, or the same goes."

Staying very aware of her attacker, he turned to Regan anxiously. "Are you all right?"

She nodded, but he could see the red marks on her slender neck. And in that moment he again understood, very clearly, what might make a man want to kill.

"I could have handled it," she said.

He waited a moment until he thought he could mask the fury he was feeling. "I can see that. You had him on the run."

"Like hell," the man spat out.

"You're the one bleeding," Alex pointed out.

The string of curses that erupted then were nothing Alex hadn't heard before, but never all at once. He ignored them.

"Who is he?" he asked Regan.

"Daryl Bowers. Marita's ex-husband, as of today."

"Thanks to you, bitch! She never would have gone through with the divorce if you hadn't encouraged her, going to court with her and pushing her to do it."

"As of today?" Alex asked. "Maybe that's what set him off." He glanced at the man who, despite his bluster, was still on his knees, watching Alex warily. "Was that it, moron? You get your good-riddance papers today?"

The same curses, in revised order, came again. "Papers don't mean a damn thing. She's still mine. She always will be. I own that bitch!"

"I think I've had about enough of your mouth. Why don't you take a swing at me, so I can tie you in a knot around that pole there? Oh, I forgot, you only beat up women."

The man glared at him. Alex laughed, and Daryl Bowers reddened furiously.

"I called 911. The police are on their way."

Alex's heart sank as he heard his mother's voice. He saw Regan's eyes widen in surprise. "Mrs. Court?"

"Good work, dear, I saw you fight him off."

Regan looked at the car keys in her hand, that she had apparently used on Bowers' face. Then she looked back at Lillian Court, still surprised to see her.

"Alex helped," she said. "I'm not sure I could have held him off if he'd come after me again." Her free hand came up to touch her throat.

"You're sure you're all right?" Alex touched her cheek, realizing nothing mattered except that she wasn't hurt.

"I think so."

"They're here," his mother said, and went to flag down the approaching officers.

By the time Bowers was stuffed into the back of the police unit, still shouting, Alex thought he just might get by with a tale of coincidence. Right place, right time. It might work.

His mother finished giving her statement to the officers and then hurried back to Regan. "I asked them to keep a closer eye on the place from now on. Are you sure you don't need to have the paramedics take a look at you?"

"No, I'm fine, really." Regan's fingers were still rubbing her throat gently, but Alex could see the questions growing as she looked from him to his mother and back again.

"You should at least sit down for a while, rest while you get over the shock," Alex said.

"I will," she said. "I am a little shaky." She managed a smile, but it was as shaky as she said she felt.

"I'm not surprised." His mother patted Regan's arm. "It's been quite a month here."

"If Alex hadn't been here, both times . . ."

Here it comes, Alex thought when her voice trailed away.

"Why *were* you here?" Regan's gaze flicked to his mother as if she'd like to ask her the same thing, but didn't dare.

His mother turned to him, not saying a word. She was going to leave it to him, and would go along with whatever he chose. But he knew deep down that he had only one choice.

"I'll explain it all," he promised with a glance at his mother, "if you'll just sit down somewhere. You're shaking."

She looked around, a little puzzled, as if she wasn't quite sure where he wanted her to sit, short of on the ground.

"Let's go to the house," his mother said. "It's close, and she won't be bothered."

Alex hesitated, then nodded, acknowledging what he'd just agreed to, taking Regan into the Court world. His world. "I'll drive her over in her car so she has it."

He wasn't quite sure she'd taken it all in, because she seemed dazed until they turned into the exclusive hilltop neighborhood. Then she began to look around as he followed his mother's car through the automatic gate she'd opened.

They drove past the carriage house and up the curving drive to the main house. They hustled Regan inside and set her down in the cozy study. She refused a drink of anything, and Alex saw her looking around with interest. This was one of his favorite rooms, homey and warm, but he also knew Regan hadn't missed the formal elegance of the rest of the house they'd walked through. He wondered what she was thinking.

"You're going to tell her?" his mother whispered to him.

"I have to. I can't go on like this." He didn't tell her why it might well be too late. That telling Regan she'd spent an incredible, passionate night with a man who wasn't who she thought he was might well destroy what was between them before it ever had a chance to live.

"I'll leave you to it, then. But not before I do what I can to help." Before he could react to that, she was sitting on the arm of Regan's chair. "Regan, Alexander has something to tell you, but before he does I have something to say."

Regan seemed to sense the seriousness of his mother's words, and gave her her full attention.

"I want you to remember, no matter how you feel, no matter how angry you might be, that none of this was his idea. It was mine. He never would have done it, nor hidden his actions from you, had I not ordered him to."

Regan looked first puzzled, then bewildered as his mother left them alone.

"Alex, what is she talking about?"

He took a deep breath, and plunged in. "She's talking about being so worried about all of you at Rachel's House that she did something to make sure you weren't harassed over these murders."

"Did what?"

"Sent someone to watch over you."

"Watch over—" She stopped short, her eyes widening. "You?" she whispered. "She sent you?"

He explained that he was the troubleshooter for Court Corporation, called in to protect them for the duration of this terror, and how what had begun as a job had become something much more personal. How it had come to be something he hated, because it meant deceiving her. He told her everything, except the one last thing he suspected was going to be the worst.

"So it was all a front? A . . . a cover?" She looked stunned, but he knew anger had to be right around the corner.

"For good reason. I told you, she didn't want you on edge or nervous any more than you already were."

Her hands knotted in her lap. "And the talks, the dinners, they were lies, too? To . . . what, take my mind off it? 'Romance her a little and she'll forget all her troubles,' is that what that was? Is that—" Her voice broke. "Is that what the sunset was?"

Color flooded her face, and he knew she was remembering much more than that sunset. She was remembering everything that had followed. He crouched down before her. "God, no, Regan. That was never a lie. That was the most real thing that's ever happened to me in my life."

She lowered her eyes, and he put his hands over her knotted ones. Only then did he feel the tremors going through her, like tiny quakes before an eruption. An eruption he knew was coming. He'd come to know Regan Keller would tolerate many things, but being consistently lied to was not one of them.

"I know I should have stopped. I tried. Remember? But I know that's not enough. I should never have let it happen, not with this"—he gestured vaguely at the house—"between us. I should have told you the moment I realized I wasn't going to be able to stop, the moment I knew just how much I wanted you."

He paused, took a deep breath, summoning up every bit of courage he had to go on. And it took every ounce of it.

"She doesn't know how far I let it go. If she did, I don't know if she could forgive me, either."

"Mrs. Court?"

With the feeling he was stepping off a cliff, knowing what this was going to do, he took a last deep breath and answered.

"My mother."

She stared at him. "What?"

"My mother. Lillian Court. My real name is Alexander Edward Court."

The eruption hit.

CHAPTER 17

"Six murders in less than three months. We've eliminated one as a copycat—nice work, Nick—but five we can accredit with some certainty to the same killer. Same MO, same weapon, same posing of the victim postmortem. But he's smart, and careful, and clean, and he's not doing a damn thing to help us."

Lynne studied the paper clip she'd grabbed to give her hands something to do and her eyes something to watch as Drew spoke. Ben Durwin, Captain Greer, and Nick Kelso were all listening intently.

Nick was back on this case after his triumphant, single-handed resolution of the copycat murder. Which, Lynne realized, put him in a very strong position, not only in detectives, but with the department. And made what she knew about him all the harder to deal with, all the harder for anyone to believe.

Except maybe another woman, she thought. Another woman might see in Nick's zeal to prove that

Priscilla Wheeler had had her abusive husband murdered just another side of his zeal to talk battered women out of taking action.

So what was he, a closet misogynist? Did that charming, flirtatious facade hide a dark side? Had the sudden defection of his fiancée embittered him so much he took it out on all women? No, that made no sense. Most of those cases he'd kissed off had been before she'd left him. So why?

Not that the why mattered. It was what he'd been doing that had to be dealt with. And she couldn't help wondering, with that sinking feeling in the pit of her stomach all over again, if any of those women he'd talked out of taking action had paid the ultimate price for staying.

"—each of the crime-scene diagrams." Lynne suddenly tuned back in as her ex-husband began to post copies on the bulletin board they'd been working with. "There's nothing new to you here. And if we sit back waiting for this guy to make a mistake and leave us a big fat clue, I think we're kidding ourselves."

"He's never gone this long between kills since the first one," Durwin said. "What if he's stopped?"

Lynne knew the answer, but she wasn't about to tread on Drew's show.

"Serial killers," Drew said, "*never* stop on their own."

"Even when they make a mistake, like this last one?"

"It may take him a while to get over that disruption in his vision. Or it may take something particularly strong to motivate him. But he will kill again, they always do. They may move out of the area, they may get arrested for something else and go to jail, they may be taken out of action due to illness or some other incapacitation, they may die. The urge, that thing that drives them, may abate for a while, but once they start, sooner or later they'll kill again."

"What's your recommendation?" Captain Greer asked.

"With unlimited manpower, I'd say put a surveillance on every possible victim, every batterer connected to Rachel's House."

Durwin let out a low whistle. "That's how many?" he asked, with a glance at Lynne.

"There have been nearly three hundred residents since Rachel's House opened," she said, glad she had tuned back in time to keep from embarrassing herself. Especially in front of Drew. "Of those, roughly half have been relocated out of state and hopefully out of reach, or their abusers have relocated."

"That still leaves a hundred and fifty or so," Greer said. "That's more than we can possibly put full surveillance on, even if we call in help from the entire county."

"It might not be necessary," Lynne said. "The killings have only involved men connected to the more recent residents. The first, the victim's wife had been at Rachel's House only two years ago. For all the good it did her," she couldn't help adding, remember too well how the young woman who had tried so hard to escape her brutal husband had ended up literally crucified on her own living-room floor.

"Sometimes them leaving is the spark that sets a normal guy off," Nick said.

A normal *guy*? Lynne's head snapped around to look at the big, good-looking blond. Was nobody going to call him on this? Did nobody else see it?

No sooner did she think it than Drew spoke. "I'm sure you didn't mean to infer that battered women are in some way to blame for their own abuse." Nick flushed and, point made, Drew left it there. "Let's move on. If we do as Detective Garrison suggests and limit this to abusers of women who have been in Rachel's House for the past two years, how many are we talking about?"

Trying to ignore how odd it was to hear Investigator Garrison refer to Detective Garrison in such clipped tones, Lynne did some quick figuring. "Fifty to sixty."

"A more manageable number," Greer said, "but still not easy."

"So it looks like the options are, we call for help, rotate surveillance, and hope we're in the right place at the right time, or we try to narrow it down to who's likely next and focus on them," Durwin said.

Drew nodded. "If it was any other kind of case, I'd say we had one more option."

"Such as?" Greer asked.

"Bait." At Greer's frown, he elaborated, "Pick one of the guys who had somebody in Rachel's House, have him purposely go after her again, and then set up on him and wait."

"But?"

Drew shrugged. "These guys are cowards. I doubt if any of them have the guts to set themselves up to lure out a real killer. If they did, they wouldn't be beating up women and kids in the first place."

Lynne looked up, wanting to give Drew a silent thank-you for that, and for putting Nick in his place. As she did, she caught a glimpse of Nick's face, and the muscle jumping along his jawline.

"We'll hold that as a last resort," Greer directed. "For now, where would you start? With those who live closest to the area of the previous killings?"

Drew nodded. "As good a place as any to start. We'll need the geographic data."

"I've got it," Durwin said.

"And," Drew added, "you might want to consider calling the FBI for an ERT on the next one. I've worked with the San Francisco team before. They're the best."

None of them commented on his use of the words "the next one"; they all knew it was more than likely there would be another killing before they got this guy. Instead they all looked at Greer, knowing that calling in the FBI's Evidence Response Team was the first step toward giving up control of your situation. But since they didn't have control of it in the first place, it seemed a moot point. Greer seemed to agree, nodding decisively.

"You work it out. I want a plan by the end of the day, people. We're looking pretty stupid here, and I don't like it."

Lynne tossed her mangled paper clip in the

wastebasket, stood up, and started toward the door, as did Durwin. Nick, apparently still feeling put upon, went the other way, toward the door to the parking facility. Drew had been cornered by Greer, she noticed thankfully, and felt a sense of escape as she left the room.

"That must be tough on you," Durwin said when they were clear of the briefing room.

"What?"

"Sitting there with your ex."

Startled, she gave the older man a sideways look. "I've been through worse."

He said nothing more until they turned the corner outside the detective division office. "Lynne."

She stopped, startled. He almost never used her first name.

"Look . . ." He stopped, looking uncomfortable, then started again. "I worked an undercover job, back when I was at LAPD. It went on longer than anyone expected, and I kept getting in deeper. And the longer it went, the harder it got to remember who I really was. It . . . seeps into you, the dirt, the crap, the way of life. You start out having to learn how they think, and you end up fighting not to think the same way."

Lynne hoped she wasn't staring, but this was more than Ben Durwin had said to her at one time in the entire ten years she'd known him.

"My point is," he said, his obvious discomfort growing, "that you can lose yourself, lose touch with everything that's real and important when you're under like that." He hesitated before adding, "Like Drew was."

Lynne's breath died in her throat. Was he defending Drew to her? He'd barely known her back then, and she hadn't been aware he knew Drew at all.

"Look, I don't know what happened between you two, I just wanted to say, my wife and I, we had a hard time after that. She was alone too long, and I was so out of touch with our life that it took months for me to get back to normal, and even longer for us to get it back together."

She wanted to say there was more to their situation than that, wanted to burst out that she hadn't just been alone too long, she'd been left to deal with a tragedy no one should have to handle by themselves, but it was obvious that this had taken a great deal of effort on his part.

"Thanks, Ben," she said softly instead.

He colored slightly. "I'm not much for talking like this, to her or anybody. I know I'm short-tempered and blunt, but she loves me anyway. God knows why."

He started to walk into the detective office, then stopped in the doorway and looked back at her.

"He's still crazy about you, you know."

Without waiting for her to answer, he continued inside, leaving Lynne standing in the hallway.

"My God, Regan, I am so sorry."

Regan shook her head. "It wasn't your fault, Marita, any more than anything else he's ever done has been your fault."

"But for him to go after *you!*"

They were all fussing over her, and had been ever since she'd come back to Rachel's House. Detective Garrison had called Marita as soon as she'd heard about Daryl's arrest, and by the time Regan had returned from the aimless driving she'd been doing after she'd left the Court home, everybody who'd been home knew what had happened.

Thankfully, they were chalking her emotional state up to the frightening encounter with Daryl Bowers, and she was more than happy to let them think that. But in fact, that seemed to pale next to the reality she'd just been hit with.

She'd thought all along that Alex Edwards wasn't a case of what you see is what you get. She'd wondered when he'd handled the man with the knife like a pro, and wondered more when he'd seemed to be scrounging up reasons to stretch out his time at Rachel's House. But she'd let her ego get in the way, let herself think he'd been brave to protect her, that he'd stayed because of her.

And now she knew just how right—and how wrong—she'd been. He'd been lying to her from day one.

The back door opened, tearing her out of her miserable reverie. There were footsteps in the kitchen, and then Laura came into the living room.

"Hi, everybody, what's up? Are you all— Regan, what happened to you?"

"I had a little unpleasant encounter," she answered. Marita was avoiding her gaze, and she knew the woman was ashamed, still thinking she was somehow to blame.

"My God, your neck, you're going to bruise," Laura said, kneeling down and looking at her with eyes too used to seeing such marks. And then anger inflamed her normally placid expression. "Damn him, did Alex do this to you?"

Alex? Hurt her?

"No," she said, her voice a little harsh, whether from her madly tangled emotions or the bruises around her throat she wasn't sure.

"It was Daryl," Marita said bitterly. "The divorce was final today. He couldn't find me to beat up, so he waited at the main office and took it out on Regan."

"Regan? He hurt Regan?"

They hadn't even heard Mitch come in, but when he hurried over to them they made room for him beside her chair.

"I'm okay, Mitch, really."

"Are you sure?"

His warm brown eyes were so troubled that Regan reached out to give his arm a reassuring squeeze. "I'm fine. It was ugly, but it's over. He's in jail where he belongs."

"For now," Marita said, her voice still tight with bitterness. Regan understood; she'd been trying to break free from this man for nearly two years, and still he haunted her.

"Maybe they'll keep him locked up this time," Laura said.

Marita laughed, and it wasn't a cheerful sound. "Like they did when he beat up my mother, trying to get her to tell him where I was?"

Mitch stared up at Marita from where he still crouched at Regan's side. "He beat up your mother?"

She nodded. "He barely got his wrist slapped for

that one. My dad, he beats her like Daryl beat me. He beat her when she wanted to help me. Dad told her he wouldn't allow her to testify, that I'd had it coming, what Daryl did to me."

"Marita," Regan said firmly, "that was not your fault, and this was not your fault. There's only one person to blame here, and that's Daryl."

It took her a lot of time and effort she could ill afford to calm them. They were more shaken by her bruises than they had ever been about their own much worse injuries.

"Because it's you," Laura explained. "You're sort of a symbol to us, that there's another kind of life. If our lives spill over and hurt you . . ." She shook her head, but her eyes were so troubled Regan didn't push for anything more.

By the time Regan was able to retreat to her room she was truly exhausted. Yet when she lay down on the bed, her mind continued to race like a mouse on a wheel.

Laura's assumption that it had been Alex who had hurt her had rattled her. Her instant leap to his defense had rattled her even more. She knew she would get no rest until she faced this, so she quit fighting and let the painful memories, both good and bad, flow in like a stream of acid-laced honey.

He'd insisted that everything he'd told her was true, it just wasn't all of the truth. But that didn't help much. It just made her rocket back and forth from a simmering anger to a wrenching ache in her chest, going from rage through shock to heartache and then back again.

Lillian Court's son. The woman she owed everything to, who had given her the chance to build Rachel's House. Given her the chance even though she had nothing to recommend her but a brand-new college degree that wasn't even in a related field, and a passion that was heartfelt and bone deep, born on the day she'd found Rachel's body arranged carefully inside her front door.

Although she hadn't realized it then, hadn't realized anything beyond her horror, shock, and pain, her entire life had changed in that instant. Gone was the plan to work at an upscale advertising firm until she was ready to strike out on her own. Gone was the dream of using her inheritance from her father to build her own business with the clients she intended to make sure found her indispensable. Gone was the ten-year goal of being a recognized name in her chosen field.

In their place, fueled by a steady, burning outrage, was one single thing—the determination to fight back. To save as many as she could from this epidemic that had stolen her father and her best friend.

She'd done that, with Rachel's House. But she couldn't even have started if not for Lillian Court.

I want you to remember, no matter how you feel, no matter how angry you might be, that none of this was his idea. It was mine. He never would have done it, nor hidden his actions from you, had I not ordered him to.

The words of the woman who'd become a mentor to her echoed in her mind. The woman she'd come to admire, respect, and even love as they shared their vision of how to fight this cancer that ruined so many lives.

The woman who had sent her son to protect the residents of the place she'd put her considerable standing behind.

How stupid can I be? she wondered. Stupid that it had never occurred to her that he'd shown up after the third killing to *watch* them. It should have at least occurred to her that he might be an undercover cop or something. But she'd gotten so tangled up in her emotions about him that her brain seemed to have shut off.

So was it Alex's fault she'd gotten silly over him? Was it even a surprise, given she'd had so little social life in the past eight years? Did she even have any right to be angry at him?

She didn't know. She only knew she felt shattered, lost, in a way she hadn't known since she'd opened Rachel's House.

And it didn't help any that when she at last drifted off, she dreamed of sunsets and Alex.

"You need an interview room, Detective?"

Nick Kelso shook his head at the jailer. "No. I'm just going to go take a look at Bowers."

"Need the recorder on?"

"No. I won't be there that long."

"Cell three," the man said, gesturing to the right as if people had trouble finding their way in the small, four-cell jail. Kelso nodded and walked down the cool, green-walled hallway. He noted that the cell before Daryl Bowers was empty, and after his cell came the doorway to the covered sally port where units pulled in with prisoners. He turned his back to the security cameras without looking up at them.

The man in the cell pointedly ignored him. Kelso leaned a shoulder against the bars and waited. Silently. At last the man looked up.

"Who the hell are you?" he said, sounding surly.

"Detective Kelso. Just wanted to meet the guy who got caught in the middle of this mess."

Bowers eyed him warily. "Look, all I wanted to do was make them tell me where my wife is. I got a right."

"A guy did have the right, once. Nowadays . . ." Kelso shrugged.

Bowers swore under his breath.

"I know," Kelso said. "Doesn't seem right or fair, does it?"

An expression of suspicion spread over Bowers' face. "What are you trying to pull?"

Kelso shrugged. "Me? Not a thing. Just came by because I know the feeling, man."

"What feeling?"

"That everybody else is in your way, when all you want to do is get your life back."

Bowers blinked. "Yeah. That's all I wanted."

"I get you. Women today . . ." He shrugged again.

Bowers swore again, but this time his tone was of a man sharing a gripe with someone who understands.

"Well, at least you won't have to spend much time in here because of her," Kelso said.

"How you figure?"

"Bail. Piece of cake for somebody with only one prior. That ought to fry her."

Bowers looked pleased at that thought, but then grimaced. "I don't have that kind of cash."

"Bet you know somebody who does, though. Somebody you could call, they have to let you call for that. Maybe somebody who feels like you do?"

"Nah, I don't . . ."

Bowers' voice trailed away, and his brow furrowed as if he'd just had a thought.

"Maybe. Yeah, maybe."

"Relative?"

"Nah. Well, sort of."

"Who? Maybe I can help."

Bowers hesitated, then told Kelso who he was thinking of.

Kelso laughed out loud.

Lillian watched her son pace. "Give her time, Alexander."

Alex grimaced. "I don't know. I've never seen her so angry."

"She had reason to be, I'm afraid. You should have told her the moment you began to get personally involved."

"I know, I know, it's my own fault. I should never have let it go so far."

"Just how far did it go?"

To her amazement, her self-contained son blushed. And then, tiredly, he said, "Too far. Not far enough."

"I see." And she thought she did. "She's not an

unfair woman, or a vindictive one. Give her time to work through it."

Distractedly, he shoved his fingers through his already tousled hair. "How much time?"

Despite her worry over the whole situation, Lillian stifled a smile. "As much as it takes."

"Gee, thanks," Alexander said wryly.

"Do you want me to speak to her?"

"I've already messed up enough, without hiding behind you, thank you."

"Very wise," she said, glad he saw it that way. "And don't forget, there's more than just a deception for her to deal with."

"More?"

"She not only has to deal with the fact that you're not who she thought, she also has to deal with who you really are. For many people, that's not easy."

Alex groaned, and Lillian knew he hadn't thought about that aspect yet. "And she's the kind of person who's just as likely to find it a drawback as an advantage.

"I'll arrange for someone else to keep watch for now, if you like."

He grimaced again, as if he didn't trust the safety of Rachel's House to anyone else. Lillian smiled to herself.

"For now," he muttered, sounding unhappy.

"Lynne, it's me."

"Another one?" she asked. It was the only reason she could think of for him to be calling her at three in the morning.

"No," Drew answered. "But I had an idea."

"What's the idea that couldn't wait?" Her tiredness put a snap in her voice.

"Sorry, I know it's late, but if I'm right, we'll have to be ready to hit the ground running."

She sat up, shoving her hair out of her eyes and flipping on the bedside lamp. This was business, the business of catching a murderer, and nobody was better at it than Drew Garrison.

"Move on what?"

"You said the woman who runs Rachel's House was attacked this morning."

"Regan Keller, yes. The suspect's in custody."

"And he's the husband of one of the residents?"

"Ex-husband now. Apparently getting the final divorce papers set him off." Her mouth quirked. "Most guys just get drunk."

"That's what I did," he said, and Lynne's breath stopped at this uncharacteristic intrusion of the personal. "Fortunately, I got too drunk to do what else I'd intended, which was drive off a cliff. Or perhaps unfortunately."

The idea that he had reacted that strongly shook her; whenever they'd encountered each other during the painful process, he'd seemed calm, accommodating, almost uncaring.

Her stomach knotted, and that kept the edge in her voice. "What's the idea?"

For a moment he didn't answer, but when he finally spoke there was no sign of reaction to her tone. "If our killer is going after anybody who makes a move against the women of Rachel's

House, what's he going to do about somebody who goes after the woman who runs the place?"

Lynne went still. "You mean Regan? That he might go after the guy who attacked her?"

"We already know our killer is tied in some way to the place. It might be enough that Bowers' ex-wife is there. He might see this as an attack on her as well."

"He did go after Regan because he couldn't get to Marita."

"It could even be more convoluted. If in his mind it's all of Rachel's House he's defending—"

"Then he might feel he has to defend Regan, too?"

"I know she hasn't been abused like the others, but she's part of Rachel's House, a big part, right?"

"She's the rock it's built on," Lynne said.

"Then he might feel he has to protect her most of all. It might even be enough to get him over having killed an innocent man last time."

It made sense. "You want to set up on Bowers?"

"My gut says it's our best shot."

His gut when it came to murder, as she knew perhaps better than anyone, was right a lot more often than wrong. "You call Greer yet?" she asked.

"No, I wanted to run it by you first."

The obvious question was why he'd called her when technically this was Durwin's case. But she wasn't sure she wanted to know the answer to that, so she didn't ask.

"I want you to work it with me."

Sit trapped with him in a surveillance vehicle for hours on end? Nothing to do but talk or maintain a stony silence that would only feed the already palpable tension between them? Not her idea of a top ten way to spend her time.

"You'd probably be better off with Ben, or even Nick."

She winced as that "even" slipped out, waited for him to pounce on it. But he didn't.

"Probably," he agreed, "but I want you."

She shivered, hating those words, even out of context. But it wasn't like him to manipulate her. Maybe he didn't realize. When he got on a scent, everything else fell by the wayside.

"Lynne?"

With an effort she pulled herself together, accepting the inevitable. "I was just thinking . . . first we'd better call the jail and make sure they'll let us know if he bails out."

"I already did. They said he hasn't called anybody."

"Nobody cares, maybe. His ex-wife sure doesn't."

"Good for her. So are you with me?"

Like I have a choice, she thought. "I—"

"Hang on, my pager just went off."

She heard a rustling, and for the first time thought to wonder where he was. The last she'd heard, from a fellow cop who'd run into him and couldn't resist telling her, was that he had an apartment very near their old house. Before she could dwell on that, he was back.

"The jail. Only reason they'd call me is if he's bailing."

Resigned, Lynne said, "I'll meet you at the station."

"I'll pick you up. You're on the way anyway."

"All right. I'll meet you out front."

"Ten minutes. I'll call the jail on the way."

He hung up without saying good-bye.

She splashed water on her face, then dressed hurriedly. Nights like this had trained her to keep her hair and makeup simple, and she was ready quickly.

She had been outside less than a minute when a standard-issue plain unit pulled up. The minute she got in and closed the door, he hit the accelerator hard.

"He's already gone." Anger rang in his voice.

"What?"

"The jailer said they tried to call me three times before they finally thought of my pager. Idiots."

"You need call waiting," she said before she thought.

"You're the techno-holic, not me," he snapped.

It wasn't true, she wasn't a techno-holic as much as he was a technophobe. She just tried to keep up, while he regarded things like call waiting as just one more way to be found when he didn't want to be. He'd resisted the pager until the sheriff's office had mandated them for detectives.

But she should have known better than to say anything. "Who bailed him out?"

"Some guy named Yantz. They said Bowers seemed surprised to see him, and more surprised he was bailing him out."

"Yantz," Lynne muttered.

"You know him?"

She shook her head. "I don't think so, but the name rings a bell. Wait a sec."

She dug into her purse for the dog-eared notebook she carried, thinking that that alone proved she wasn't a techno-holic. She didn't trust any of the new handheld electronic personal organizers to hold crucial information on an investigation. If it went down, or any data was lost, it could jeopardize an entire case. But she wisely didn't say it.

"I remember writing that name, fairly recently, but I don't remember why, or even if it was this case, but I—"

She stopped, staring at the page she'd just flipped to.

"You found it?"

She nodded slowly.

"Who is he?"

Her mouth tightening, she looked at him. "Marita's father."

CHAPTER 18

He'd made it nearly twenty-four hours.

Alex paced the living room of the carriage house, passing time and again through the shaft of morning light.

When the phone rang he whirled. His mind leapt to Regan, even knowing she didn't have this number. He took a steadying breath before answering, and heard the voice of his mother.

"Alexander, I only have a moment, but I thought you might want to know that Bowers was bailed out late last night."

"Was bailed out? As in somebody else posted it?"

"Yes." His mother's voice told him she wasn't happy. "His now ex-wife's father."

"What?" Alex exclaimed. "Marita's father bailed out her abusive husband after he attacked Regan?"

"That's what I was told. I thought perhaps you might want to let Regan know."

"I thought you said I should stay away."

"I didn't mean forever, dear. Now I have to go. I'll talk to you later. I should be home by noon."

She hung up, and for a long moment he stood there with his hand on the receiver, wondering if he should call Regan or simply show up at Rachel's House. Just show up, he decided. It would be harder for her to blow him off in front of everybody.

When he got there a few minutes later, Mitch was just unloading his tools from the back of his mini-truck. He stopped when he saw Alex, shoved some gear back into a slot in the truck bed, and walked toward him.

"I heard what you did, helping Regan."

"I'm just glad I was there," Alex said.

Mitch nodded. "Some people wouldn't help, they'd just stand by and watch. You didn't."

"Couldn't," Alex said. "To be honest, for the first time I really, honestly understood the Avenger. I wanted to strangle the guy myself."

Mitch just looked at him for a moment, then slowly nodded. "I'm glad you were there, too." He grinned suddenly, warmly. "Even the Avenger can't be everywhere, I guess."

Alex laughed. "Guess not. Is she here? Regan?"

"I think so. I haven't seen her leave for the office yet." Mitch grimaced. "Not that she'd want to go back there."

"She shouldn't," Alex agreed, "but she will."

He started up the walk. Mitch followed, and laid out a pair of snips and a bag for clippings on the front porch. Alex stuck his head in the door first, wondering if perhaps he should have brought a hat to put on a stick and poke it in, to see if anyone shot at it.

The caution was unnecessary. Regan wasn't even watching the door. She and Laura were huddled around Marita, who was sitting in the big chair with her feet curled up beneath her and looking more upset than he could remember seeing her.

"How could they let him go so fast?" she was saying, her voice strained.

"Thanks to our justice system, he's only been arrested once and got off with a fine, so bail was probably low." Regan didn't sound angry, merely tired. She'd probably seen this once too often.

Marita looked up and saw him, and waved him over. "Come join the misery party, Alex."

Regan looked at him, but didn't speak. Feeling as if he were crossing a minefield, he made his way across the room.

"I see you heard about your ex getting out last night," he said.

"Yeah," Marita said, her tone morose.

"I'm sorry," Alex said, meaning it. "If I were you, I wouldn't know who to be maddest at, him or your father."

Marita blinked. "My father?"

Uh-oh, Alex thought.

"What about my father?"

"I . . ." He looked at Regan. Whatever anger she was still feeling toward him, it apparently wasn't strong enough to leave him dangling.

"Detective Garrison called to warn us he had bailed out," she said, "but that's all she said. What does Marita's father have to do with it?"

Alex wished he'd kept his mouth shut, but knew it was too late now. He started to speak, but stopped as a gasp from Marita told him she'd figured it out.

"He did it? My *father* bailed him out?"

"I'm sorry, Marita. When you said you knew about the bail out, I thought you knew that, too."

"That son of a bitch!"

From the normally steady-tempered Marita the curse seemed extraordinarily vehement. She jumped to her feet and ran for the stairway. Laura followed close behind.

Regan stayed. She sat down in the chair Marita had vacated and simply looked at him.

Here we go, Alex thought.

"I really thought she already knew," he said, knowing he was stalling, and wishing he'd spent more time thinking about exactly what he was going to say.

"It's best she does know."

He wondered if that was also aimed at him. He walked the length of the living room, then came back. Regan didn't speak. Finally, he sat down on the edge of the coffee table in front of her.

"I'm sorry, Regan. I never meant to hurt you." He ran his fingers through his hair. "I've never done this before."

"Done what? I know you've apologized before."

"What I meant was I've never gotten personally involved with anyone on a job before."

"Is that what we are? Personally involved?"

"I thought so." He took a breath. "I hope so."

That seemed to startle her, and she glanced up. He pressed his case.

"Everything I said to you was the truth. As much of the truth as I was free to say. This started out as a job for my mother, but it changed, it changed in a hurry."

"I understand why she did it. I even understand why she didn't want me to know. But . . ."

He grimaced. "She's not very happy with me either."

"But she asked you to come here."

"To protect you, not to hurt you."

"It's a bit late for that."

"Regan, please. You've got to believe that I was going to tell you. And then that whole thing with Donna and her son happened, and I just couldn't add that to your load."

She lowered her eyes again. "I'd like to believe that."

"Ask my mother. I told her I was going to tell you, that I had no choice anymore."

"No choice?"

"Because I couldn't keep lying to you, even lies of omission."

She let out a long, sighing breath. He leaned forward, reached out to her, then drew his hands back, not sure his touch would be welcomed.

"It's your call, Regan. I don't blame you for being mad at me. I should have told you before we . . ." He grimaced, then plunged on. "There's no excuse for that. But you've always been good at putting yourself in another's shoes. I hope you'll try mine, and realize I was between a rock and a hard place."

After a long, silent moment, Regan raised her eyes, meeting his gaze at last.

"Is your mother the rock or the hard place?"

He blinked. And then he caught the slightest glint of humor in her eyes. Not enough to relieve him, but enough to give him hope.

*　　*　　*

"Where the hell could he be?" Drew muttered.

"I wish I knew," Lynne answered.

They'd gone straight to Bowers' apartment, but no one was there and the vehicle registered to him sat empty and cold. Thinking he might have gone home with Marita's father, they raced there, arriving just as the man pulled into his driveway and got out of his car—alone. They'd gone back to Bowers' small, dreary house and been there ever since. Now it had been daylight for an hour.

"We could go ask Yantz where he dropped him," Drew said, in that distracted tone that she knew meant he was just turning options over in his mind.

"No, you were right about that one. He'd probably tip Bowers off that the cops were asking about him, and he'd run."

"We're trying to save his ass, damn it."

"He doesn't know that. I'm not sure he'd believe it if we told him."

Drew shook his head in frustration. "It's pointless for us to sit and wait for him to come back. A uniform could do that."

"What else can we do? We don't know what he'd do, where he might go . . ."

Drew looked at her as her voice trailed away. "What?"

"Maybe," she said, digging her cell phone out of her purse. "Just maybe."

"What?"

She waved him quiet as she dialed the number she by now knew by heart. It rang only once before a voice she didn't immediately recognize answered with a cautious hello.

"May I speak to Marita, please?"

"I don't know . . . Who's this?"

Laura, Lynne decided. "Is this Laura? This is Detective Garrison."

"Oh."

There was a whispered exchange with someone else in the background. Lynne tried to rein in her patience, knowing these women had every reason to be cautious. A rustling sound and then Marita's voice, rather stiff.

"Detective? Regan's busy. We don't want to interrupt her just now."

"Is there a problem?"

"She's with Alex. I think it's one of those heavy kind of talks."

About time, Lynne thought, guessing at what they must be talking about. "That's all right. It's really you I wanted to talk to."

"It's all right, I already know."

"Know what?"

"About my father bailing Daryl out."

Lynne winced. "I was hoping you wouldn't have to find that out."

"I appreciate your concern, Detective, but I'd prefer to know. It keeps me strong."

"I hadn't thought of it that way. But that's not what I called for."

"Oh?"

"I need to ask you something about Daryl."

"What?" Marita asked, sounding very wary.

"I need to know where he'd likely go to celebrate getting out of jail."

She didn't hesitate. "The Alley. Bar over on Thirty-second Street. It's where he always goes."

"Even at seven in the morning?"

"Especially at seven in the morning."

"Thanks, Marita."

She disconnected and looked at Drew. "The Alley," she said.

A familiar smile curved his mouth. "Nice work, Detective Garrison."

"Just drive, Investigator Garrison."

The old joking exchange made them both uncomfortable enough to avoid each other's eyes for a while. When they arrived, Drew eyed the dingy-looking hole in the wall. The Alley also masqueraded as a restaurant in order to be able to open up early for its loyal clientele who had to have a shooter with their eggs in the morning. Closing between two and four a.m. was their flick of acknowledgment to state law.

"I'll go in," Drew said. "Nobody will know me. They might have seen you around."

She doubted that was the real reason, but she accepted it. "I'll watch the outside. Pull over there so I can see the back door, too."

He took the order without comment, and backed the car into a vacant slot on the street opposite the bar, so she could pull right out if she had to.

She didn't. In a few minutes Drew was back, sliding into the passenger seat she'd vacated.

"I don't know how anybody can face pancakes and beer at seven in the morning," he said, his lip curling.

"Not on the pancakes, I hope?"

"I didn't look that close. I didn't want to know. Anyway, he was there earlier, after they reopened at four, but he left."

She started the car. "Shall we cruise between here and his place?"

Drew nodded. "Maybe we'll find his drunk butt staggering down the road."

They didn't.

Without a word Lynne turned and started back, this time going up and down the side streets and alleys. The neighborhood changed from houses like Bowers' run-down place to a mixture of tidier houses and the occasional small storefront or strip mall, and then into the mostly commercial area that housed The Alley and a few other low-rent but high-volume businesses.

Prodded by instinct, Lynne turned down the alley for which the bar was named. As they reached the next street, she saw across it a small business complex, newer, with a large parking area to the rear. At this hour it was mostly deserted.

"It's the right kind of place," he said. "Commercial, empty at this hour, paved area out of sight from the street."

"I know," she murmured as she nosed the car toward the back of the building.

Drew spotted him as soon as they cleared the big Dumpster. He was on his knees like all the others, placed like some bloody, prayerful supplicant neatly in the center of, Lynne noticed with a grim spurt of black humor, a blue handicapped parking symbol.

There was little doubt he was dead, but she knew they had to check.

"Best only one of us goes," Drew said.

She nodded. The less they messed with the crime scene the better. And he was the expert, she couldn't argue with that. She opened the trunk of the car and got out a chalk marker. She handed it to him, then handed him a pair of disposable latex gloves.

"You want me to call it in?"

"Yes." He pulled on the gloves. "And start taking photos, all you can without tromping through the middle. If by some crazy chance he's not dead, we're going to have to call for paramedics, and you know what they do to a crime scene."

She nodded and reached for both the instant and the 35mm camera also in the trunk.

Drew walked along the edge of the parking lot until he was opposite the body. It would give him, she realized, the shortest path, causing the least disturbance of the scene. He bent and marked where he started with the chalk, then walked carefully toward the body, stopping to mark his path with the chalk to indicate to CSI where he'd been.

He knelt next to the body, reached out with one hand, and probed for a carotid pulse. He peered more closely, then stood up.

"He's gone?" she asked.

"Yes," Drew said grimly. Then he looked at her. "And he's still warm. I'd guess only three or four degrees lost. And no rigor yet."

Lynne swore softly. Three or four degrees. No rigor mortis.

They'd only missed the Avenger by hours.

CHAPTER 19

"I'll go with you."

"You don't need to."

"Yes, I do."

Regan turned, hands on hips, and glared at Alex. "What are the chances something like that would happen again the very next day?"

"Probably the same as it happening at all. I'm going with you."

She knew, and she guessed Alex knew, his going with her wasn't what had them snapping at each other. It was only the excuse. But it was easier than facing the real reason, especially when it was still so raw.

"I have work to get done. Two days' worth now. What are you going to do, just sit there?"

A light tapping drew their attention. Marita stood at the edge of the living room, looking uncertain. "I don't want to interrupt. I know you're having a personal discussion."

"Not anymore," Regan said. "I'm just telling him I don't need a bodyguard just to go back to the office."

Marita glanced from Regan's face to Alex's set jaw. "You stick to your guns, Alex," she said. "You go with her, so we don't have to worry."

"Exactly my point," Alex said, sounding more than happy with Marita's support. "Well, one of them, anyway."

Short of shouting that even if she needed a body-guard she didn't want *him*, there wasn't much Regan could do. She wanted more time, time alone, to think about what had happened. But at the same time she wasn't sure it would change anything.

"Fine," she said, giving up with what grace she could muster. "But I need to take my car. There are some office supplies in it I need to unload."

"Fine."

Regan turned to Marita. "Are you all right?"

"I will be. It was a good reminder that they're birds of a feather, I guess."

"I'm sorry," Regan said. "But you're right. It just proves all over again that you made the right decision."

"I know. Have you?"

Regan's brow furrowed. "Have I what?"

Marita's dark eyes flicked to Alex. "Made the right decision."

She managed not to blush. Barely. "I haven't made any decision. Yet."

Marita nodded, turned to go, then stopped and looked back. "Whatever you're mad about, girl, you compare it to the real world before you decide."

Wisdom, Regan thought as she slid into the driver's seat and waited for Alex to settle in and fasten his seat belt. Marita had always been wise, for everybody else. What she'd been through this morning had only added another layer.

Regan resisted the urge to look at Alex. She knew now that everything he had told her had indeed been the truth. His mother, his father, it was all true. Did a lie of omission for a good cause taint all that?

No, she admitted, but she'd realized that the first night after she'd found out. It wasn't that she was mad about at all.

What she was mad about was that his lie did taint what had happened between them. No matter how much she might want to believe that had they met under other circumstances they might still have been attracted, she couldn't. He was a Court, the crown prince of a family empire that was deserving of the name. She was plain Regan Keller, daughter of a cop.

Then again, he'd worked hard in his role as Alex the roofer, and in the other work he'd been doing at Rachel's House. But she couldn't quite brush off the question in the back of her mind. Was he just a spoiled rich boy, used to getting what—and who— he wanted?

"Where'd you learn construction?" she asked, at this point not really caring if the question seemed abrupt.

"My parents were big on learning from the ground up," he answered without hesitation. "I started when I was thirteen, working on one of Dad's development projects after school and weekends. At the literal bottom, lugging lumber, picking up nails, cleaning up after the crew finished for the day. By the time the project was done two years later, I was a decent carpenter."

They lapsed back into silence. She was grateful he didn't take the question as license to chat. She drove on for a while before asking, "What do you normally do for Court Corporation?"

"I'm a troubleshooter. Wherever there's a problem my mother wants close attention paid to, she sends me."

"Do you often have to lie?" She kept her voice carefully neutral.

"Yes," he said, again unhesitatingly. "Many times it's the only way to get the job done, so I do what I have to do." But then he added, "It never bothered me much. Until now. I found out I really hated lying to you. To everyone at Rachel's House, because they've had enough lies in their lives, but especially to you. It took me a while to figure out why."

She knew she wasn't ready to hear that why.

"I can't deny it makes me nervous that you're so good at it," she finally said.

He didn't look away. "You mean lying?" he asked evenly.

She appreciated his honesty. "And keeping up a facade. You must be very . . . adaptable."

"Comes with the territory. It's an unusual job. You have to be a secret agent, a company rep, a cop, a diplomat, a businessman, all in one. I've spent the night spying, then had to put on a suit and tie for a business meeting the next morning."

She was fascinated despite herself. "And you've done this all over the world?"

"I came here from Jakarta. Last month it was

Australia, and Singapore. Before that it was Europe."

He changed the subject abruptly. "I'm so sorry it happened this way, Regan. Except for one thing."

"One thing?"

"You've given me something no one else ever has." She gave him a look that made him wince. "I didn't mean sex. Although it was the most earth-shattering I've ever had."

She would *not* blush. "Then what did you mean?"

"An honest relationship."

"Honest?" she asked, incredulous.

"Yeah, I know, but listen. You didn't have any idea who I was, or who my family was. For the first time in my life, the fact that I was a Court didn't have a thing to do with the way a woman looked at me."

She glanced at him, startled. She had never thought about such a thing.

"That's what I thought," he said. "Your mind just doesn't work that way. You would have treated me the same even if you had known who I was. But I wouldn't have known that. Not like I do now."

It was a compelling argument, and one she had no answer for.

"My feelings for you are real, Regan. I just realized them a little quicker than I would have, because I had to figure out why it was bothering me so much to lie to you."

"I see." It was all she could think of to say.

"So," Alex said, "if you're going to tell me I read you all wrong, that you don't feel the same, that there's nothing between us to fight for, tell me now, before I make an even bigger fool of myself."

"I . . ."

Her cell phone rang, and for once she was glad. It saved her from answering.

"Regan?" Marita said, speaking before she even had a chance to say hello.

"Yes, Ma—"

"Can you come back? Now?"

She went very still at the abruptness of the request.

"What's wrong? Is somebody hurt?"

"We're fine. Detective Garrison is here. Come back, please."

"On my way," she said, and Marita hung up without saying good-bye, either.

She looked at Alex, already on his feet, watching her.

"I don't know," she said. "But we have to go back. Now."

Lynne heard the sound of a car pulling up out front. Regan had apparently forgone the usual security measure of parking at some distance. And Alex Court was with her, she noted as Regan came up the walkway at a run. She stood up.

"Marita?" Regan called as she opened the door.

"She's upstairs," Lynne said. "Laura is with her."

"What's wrong?" Regan hurried over while Alex pulled the door closed. "What happened?"

"Why don't you sit down?" Lynne suggested.

"Just tell me."

Lynne gave in. "We founder the Avenger's sixth this morning."

Regan sank down on the sofa. She closed her eyes and breathed out a soft "God."

Alex sat down beside her, close, Lynne noticed, but not touching. Then Regan's eyes snapped open. "Marita? It was Daryl?"

Quick, Lynne thought. "Yes."

Regan shivered violently. Alex put his arm around her then, and she leaned slightly into him.

"I was really hoping he'd stop," Regan whispered. "After the innocent one."

Lynne didn't bother to explain they never stopped of their own will. It didn't matter now anyway.

"Is Marita all right?" Regan asked.

"She's . . . ambivalent, I think," Lynne said. "I would guess she thought she'd be gladder than she is."

"I don't understand. He didn't hurt Marita. All the others have been when somebody was hurt or damaged in some way."

"We think there may be more to it this time, Regan."

"More to it? What—"

She broke off, and Lynne thought if she hadn't figured it out already, she was close. Regan Keller was a very bright woman.

"Would you excuse us, Mr.—Alex?"

"I'm staying," he said shortly.

Lynne's brows rose.

"This is my family's business." Lynne glanced at Regan, then back to him questioningly. "She knows," he said.

"Good."

Regan frowned, registering that Lynne had already known who Alex was, but she clearly decided that could wait.

"Are you saying," she asked, "that you think this time it has something to do with me? Because of what Daryl did to me?"

Lynne nodded. "We think that may have been enough to set the killer off again, despite the mistake he made last time. That hurting you, in the killer's mind, is the worst thing yet, because you *are* Rachel's House."

She shivered again.

"I've got to ask you again, Regan. Does anyone, anyone at all, come to mind?"

She laughed, a harsh, humorless sound. "The only people I can think of capable of killing like this are the ones being killed."

"Then don't think of that. They won't seem capable of it. They're generally charming and affable. Think of anybody who might feel strongly enough about Rachel's House and you to defend you."

Lynne saw Regan's gaze flick to Alex. He winced.

"He's already accounted for his time to us for at least three of the murders," Lynne said quickly. "And his alibis all checked out."

Regan said nothing more about it, nor did Alex.

"I need to go see Marita."

"All right," Lynne said. "Just be careful, Regan. We don't know what he's thinking, and now he's focused on you as well as the others."

Regan nodded and stood up. Then, troubled, "Does she blame me? Think I got him killed?"

Lynne blinked, surprised at the question. "I don't

think so. She certainly didn't indicate anything like that."

Regan took a long, considering look at Alex, then left them to go upstairs to Marita.

"I'm glad you finally told her," Lynne said to Alex.

"I didn't have much choice. I couldn't go on like that. Even if she did feel a bit . . . duped when I told her."

"You're still with her, though."

"She's still deciding."

Lynne grinned. "Good for her."

Alex's mouth twisted wryly. "Thanks a lot."

A few minutes later, as Lynne walked back to her car from Rachel's House, her cell phone rang.

The caller ID registered the number of Drew's cell. He must be done with Yantz. They'd agreed she would come here to break the news to Marita and Regan, while he went to talk to the man who had bailed out their latest victim. Under less urgent circumstances, she would have liked to make the man answer to a woman, but time was more important than blows for the sisterhood just now.

"Garrison," she said into the phone.

"Lynnie, we finally caught a break."

She stopped dead on the sidewalk, ignoring his use of the pet name. "What?"

"Yantz said he only knew Bowers was in jail because he got a phone call that he was in the slam because of his daughter again, and Yantz might want to bail him out."

"So Bowers did make a call?"

"No. I double-checked."

"Then who called him?"

"That's just it. It was an anonymous call. A male voice."

Her breath caught. "You think . . . ?"

"Yeah, I do. It was the killer."

CHAPTER 20

"Marty is our best suspect. He's got motive, and a temper. He fits the profile mostly, but he just doesn't feel right," Drew said as he paced.

"What about that discrepancy in his story?" Ben asked.

"We can't prove his version isn't true, and a time gap isn't enough to book him on. I'm more concerned about the traveling aspect. With a geographically stable killer, I'd expect him to stay in one place."

"That phone call to Yantz," Durwin began.

"Came from a pay phone just about dead center of all the Avenger killings," Drew said. "At that hour, not likely we'll turn up any witnesses."

"Marty's beef was over his sister," Lynne said. "I just don't read him as a guy who would become a crusader for all battered women."

"Murderer, you mean," Nick said.

Lynne shot him a sideways glance, but didn't let it linger for fear he'd read too much into it. She thought he might already be suspicious. She'd caught him at her desk once, and afterward had found some of her files disturbed.

"Maybe we need to go back to square one," Durwin said.

"Good idea, Ben," Drew said. "In a large percentage of cases, the killer turns out to be somebody police talked to early on."

"So we go back and talk to everybody again?" Nick asked, sounding weary. "Mrs. Tanaka from the office, the deliverymen, the gardener, the families of the women?"

"Until we get the full crime-scene report back from the feds, not much else we can do," Drew said. "Unless anybody's got any better ideas."

"What about Gene Pilson?" Lynne asked. "I got a call back from Cincinnati. No abuse, but some other red flags. A real loner, the quiet type, no friends, that kind of thing."

"Good," Drew said. "He's looking better and better. Let's concentrate there, too."

"Maybe we should look harder at the idea of it being one of those women," Nick said. "I know it's rare, but if you were going to have a female serial killer, it'd be a woman like that."

It was all Lynne could do to bite back a scathing retort.

"You mean a woman who, thanks to a man, has a very good reason to hate men in general?" Drew asked, and Lynne guessed she was the only one not fooled by his innocent expression.

Nick looked slightly uncomfortable, but said only, "Yeah."

"What about that guy who was working at the

shelter?" Durwin asked. "The one who hadn't been there long."

"I think you can eliminate that possibility," Lynne said. "Turns out he was sent in by the Court Corporation, the main backers of the shelter, to keep the women safe."

"From what?" Nick asked. "It's the guys who are getting offed."

"From any cops," Lynne said, at last unable to help the bite in her tone, "who can't seem to remember that the women are victims, too."

Something flashed in Nick's eyes, something quick and dark.

Ben Durwin coughed and spoke quickly. "Any idea when we'll get the reports back from the feds?"

"It'll be a couple of days. I've got the prelims, though. They found one of the fibers we recovered visually matches the one our guys found on victim three. They managed to lift an impression of a smudge print that's similar to the other one we found, so they may be able to narrow down what made the mark. And they found some dirt."

"Dirt?" Lynne asked, remembering the crime scene and its endless asphalt.

"A tiny sample, maybe not even enough to analyze," Drew cautioned. "And although it was close to the body, it could be entirely unrelated. Anybody could have left it at any time, walking across that parking lot."

With that caution they headed out, each to do repeat interviews with the people they'd done before, except Nick took over the volunteer staff from the Rachel's House office at Drew's direction.

"Lynne, can I see you a moment?" Drew asked.

She turned back to see him already headed into Captain Greer's empty office. The captain was in with the chief, no doubt getting chewed on for the lack of progress.

When he shut the door behind them, she knew she wasn't going to like this, whatever it was.

"What's going on with you and Kelso?"

"You mean besides that he's got a stinking attitude toward battered women?"

"Yes, besides that."

"Isn't that enough?"

"Not for you. You've been in the job too long to go off when a guy pulls out his chauvinist pigness."

And you know me too well, Lynne thought.

"You sure you want this now? It's nothing that directly affects this case," she began, then stopped. She suddenly wasn't so sure of that anymore. Could his attitude affect Nick's handling of this case as it had those others?

Her face must have changed, because Drew said softly, "What is it, Lynne? It's obviously eating you up."

She hesitated, then realized there was probably no one better to tell. Drew would give her an honest reaction, and could probably tell her how to handle it better than anybody.

"I'll tell you," she said, "because I need someone an emotional step back from this. But that's all I want. I'll handle it myself."

"All right."

She poured it out then, what she'd found in going through the domestic-violence crime reports. And how he'd seemed so eager to make sure potential targets were warned, as if it were more important than focusing on the killer himself, as if he didn't trust anyone else to do it. Then she told him of the other occasions when he'd made comments like he had today, things that taken alone might be ignored as just mouthing off, but put together with everything took on an entirely different connotation.

Drew listened without speaking until she was done. And even then he said nothing as he paced the office, but she could almost see his mind working. Finally, he stopped and turned to face her. "What are you thinking?"

"I just thought he might not be going at this without bias, as he should."

"More likely he'd be going at it harder, don't you think? If he feels that way, he'd probably want this guy who's killing his like-minded brethren wrapped up as soon as possible."

She hadn't thought of it quite that way. She sighed. "You're probably right."

Drew looked thoughtful. "Didn't he get himself in some hot water once, over a public fight in a restaurant with his girlfriend?"

Lynne frowned. "I'm not sure."

"I think it was in our territory, one of the big hotels near the airport."

"Then I might not have heard. I do know she dumped him pretty unceremoniously. A vanish in the middle of the night kind of thing. Pretty humiliating."

"Very, for a guy like Kelso. Remember her name?"

Lynne thought for a moment. "Tanya, I think."

"Anybody heard from her since then?"

"I don't know. I think one of the records clerks was a friend of hers, though. I could ask. Why?"

"Just thinking."

Drew was never "just thinking," but Lynne knew that if he wasn't inclined to share those thoughts yet, nothing would make him.

Her cell phone rang, and she tugged it out. "Garrison."

"You owe me," the female voice said.

"Helen? What have you got?"

"The correct answer is 'Thank you so much, Helen, you're right, I owe you big time.'"

"You're right, you're right, but not now."

The crime-scene technician gave in. "You've got blood." Lynne's heart leapt; Helen had promised to get to the testing on the swords as soon as she could, but as backed up as the lab always was, Lynne hadn't expected results already. "However," she added, "that's all I can tell you. The sample is too small and too old, not to mention contaminated with some kind of cleaner or detergent, for me to tell much except that it's human and *maybe* type O."

Naturally, Lynne thought. The type of at least three of the victims, but also the most common blood type in the world.

"But there are limits to what I can do here. State

might be able to pull up some DNA for you. If not, then there's always the feds. Shall I send it on?"

"Yes, please," Lynne said. "And thanks, Helen. Really."

By the time she hung up she was already on her feet. Drew was looking at her curiously, waiting.

"There was human blood on the swords. We need to go pick up Gene Pilson."

Pilson seemed stunned. If Lynne hadn't seen that kind of reaction before, in suspects as guilty as sin, she might have been convinced.

The thin, balding man barely protested when she and Durwin went to his tiny office and took him into custody, just kept repeating "I never, I never," as if he were stuck on those words and couldn't get past them. Then he lapsed into silence until they reached the station. In fact, he stayed silent, as if numbed, only shaking his head no at every point they made. The time cards that showed he was not working at the times of any of the murders—although the long lunch break was questionable, they didn't mention that. His statements about the murders, which they'd been able to corroborate with coworkers, saving them from having to use Regan's statements. His access to Rachel's House, and knowledge about its occupants and their situations. But he stayed silent, until they confronted him with the blood evidence.

"Of course there's human blood on them! They're Japanese ceremonial swords. They've been used."

That was a curve they hadn't expected. "How long have you owned them?"

"Just over a year. I bought them at an antiques show." He drew himself up. "I'm interested in Asian culture. Is that a crime now?"

Was it possible, Lynne wondered, that the blood Helen had found could have been there that long? Maybe. She'd said it was old.

They continued the questioning but got nowhere. Lynne couldn't decide if he was playing it smart, or was truly bewildered. Finally, Durwin signaled her that it was time to withdraw and let him stew for a while.

As they were leaving Pilson finally spoke. "They don't think I did it, do they? The ladies at Rachel's House? They didn't tell you they suspect me?"

His voice was so plaintive Lynne thought his feelings might really be hurt by the idea. Since low self-esteem was another hallmark of a murderer, she wondered if this was a sign. Deciding not to answer, she merely looked at him, shook her head sadly, and left him there.

"Let Drew go at him," she suggested, and to her surprise, Durwin agreed without protest.

"I'll page him," her partner said.

"I'm heading back out to Rachel's House," she said. "I want to talk to them some more about our friend here."

She knew they wouldn't like being interviewed yet again, but sometimes dogged perseverance was the only thing that broke a case. Regan was holding up well, although Lynne suspected she would never let herself be beaten. Marita was still taking

n the shock that her war was over. There were only
wo other residents now; they'd lost another, Regan
aid. Trish had caved when her husband had hired
 notorious divorce attorney, saying he would
nake sure neither she nor her family had anything
eft when he was done with them. Sometimes even
he support of places like Rachel's House wasn't
nough.

When she was done, she'd turned up nothing
new, but not from lack of trying. The women were
ll shocked that Mr. Pilson had been arrested, and
ynne felt terrible, as if she'd added to their burden
by telling them. And she wasn't confident enough
of the circumstantial evidence they had to tell them
t was all over.

Regan walked her outside, and Marita came with
hem, saying she still couldn't quite believe she was
ree to keep right on walking if she wanted to.

"Believe it," Regan said, putting her arm around
Marita's shoulders.

"Yes, believe it," the gardener—Mitch, Lynne remembered—said from the bottom of the porch
steps. He stepped up to Marita and handed her a
uscious buttery yellow rose. "To freedom."

"Aw, Mitch, you sweetie," Marita drawled. "A
yellow rose. How'd you know I'm from Texas?"

The man looked startled. "I . . ."

Marita laughed, Regan laughed with her, and
ynne smiled herself at the joyous sound. Mitch
oined in, and Lynne wondered how long it had
been since this place had heard such laughter.

"Hey, Mitch, if Regan and Alex end up getting

married, are you going to do the flowers?" Marit;
asked.

"Married?" Mitch looked stunned. Rega▸
blushed.

"So, you two have worked out your . . . differ
ences?" Lynne asked.

"Not yet," Regan said, sliding a look at Marit;
that only made her grin. It did Lynne's heart goo(
to see the woman strong enough to tease, and sh◂
suspected Regan's annoyance was mostly feigned
too.

"Mitch," Lynne said, "Detective Durwin wil
probably be wanting to talk to you again, too
We're going through everybody all over again."

"Anything I can do to help. Should I call him? O▸
just wait here?"

"I'll let him know you're waiting," Lynne said
"He'll be in touch."

At the man's nod, Lynne said a final good-bye t(
the two women and headed back to the station
When she got there, Drew was seated at her desk
And he did not look happy.

"Now what?" she asked, almost afraid to hea▸
the answer.

"Come with me," he said. "Outside."

He led her out to a grassy area next to the publi◂
parking lot. Now she was sure she didn't want t(
hear this, if he wouldn't even risk saying it insid◂
her own station.

"What?" she asked when he finally stopped.

"I did a little checking while you were gone."

"On?"

"Kelso's girlfriend."

"Tanya? And?"

"I asked around here, including her friend in records, and she supposedly dumped him three months ago."

"That sounds about right."

"The consensus was she'd gone off to New York. Friends and family got E-mails from her, but after about six weeks they stopped coming."

"And?"

"No one's heard from her since."

Lynne frowned. "Have they tried to contact her?"

"Supposedly she was staying with friends in the city, different ones, until she found her own place. Told them she didn't want to tie up their phones so she'd contact them."

"Makes sense, I guess."

"Yeah. Except that nobody had any idea she even knew anyone in New York. And the names she gave in the E-mails were always very common, impossible to track down in a city that size."

"Where are you heading with this, Drew?"

He let out a breath. "After that, I called her family."

Lynne went very still. Asking around the department was one thing, involving civilians was something else.

"She didn't call them, either. Still the E-mail route. But eventually even those stopped." He rubbed his hand over his jaw before going on, almost reluctantly. "They filed a missing persons report on her a month ago. Nothing's turned up."

"In New York City, I'm not surprised."

"They also hired a private investigator. He found she bought a plane ticket on-line, with her credit card, the day before the flight."

"Didn't she have a car she would want to take with her?"

"Not anymore." He sounded grim. "Her mother says Nick made her sell it, that he said they didn't need two cars."

Lynne's breath caught. It was a typical ploy of a controlling male, limiting her mobility.

"Yeah," Drew said.

"Drew . . . what are you saying? That you think he killed her?"

"I don't know. I just know that she vanished. No one's seen her since the night she supposedly left."

"But the E-mails," Lynne began, then realized the flaw in that. "Which are easy to fake."

"Especially if he had access to her password, and if he's that kind, you know he did."

Slowly she nodded. "And he would know enough about her to make them sound real. God, do you realize what kind of premeditation and mentality that means? Six weeks of sending E-mails to the family of a woman you've murdered?"

His expression told her he'd already thought of all that. "And something else, Lynnie."

"What?"

"If she dumped him three months ago—or if he killed her then—that was just before the other murders started."

Lynne sucked in a breath, her eyes widening.

"And he had access, or could get it, to the files," Drew added. "He knew what was happening now as far as the Rachel's House connection, because he got himself put on the case. He'd be as careful as our killer is, more in fact, because he knows how CSI works. And he would have known Bowers was in jail, could have called Yantz to bail him out so he could follow and later get to him."

"But . . . why would he kill abusers if he is one?"

"I don't know," Drew said again. "Unless he was horrified by what he'd done to her. And by killing other abusers he's trying to atone."

"You mean he's killing the others out of guilt?"

"Or a suppressed urge to kill the killer he can't kill."

"You mean . . . himself?"

Drew nodded.

"My God," she whispered.

CHAPTER 21

She should have gone with Marita, Regan thought as she left the hospital. That first step back to a normal life was scary, and she shouldn't have had to take it alone. But she'd insisted she wanted to, and Regan hadn't argued with her, knowing this new forcefulness was fragile. Fortunately, the company she was interviewing with was a subsidiary of Court Corporation that often took on the graduates of Rachel's House, so Marita had a good chance.

Reaching her car, Regan tossed her purse on the seat and tugged off her jacket, even its light weight too much on this nearly ninety-degree day.

Maybe I'll go by and pick Marita up after she's finished, she thought as she got in and started the engine. *Take her to lunch.*

Regan smiled, wondering if Marita even realized she could do that now, go out to lunch anywhere she wanted, without ever having to look over her shoulder.

Thanks to a serial killer.

With a sigh, Regan shook her head and focused

on driving. She'd been battling that dichotomy for so long now it seemed to have dulled the brain cells that had to deal with it. It didn't seem right to be glad of anyone's death, but she couldn't deny she was very glad Marita no longer had to live in hiding, no longer had to be the one constantly on guard, when in fact she was the victim.

They're the victims, but they're the ones who have to hide.

Alex's words came back to her, words that had told her he really did understand.

Alex.

She was having a hard time getting past the fact that while she'd fallen hard for Alex the roofer, she had no idea how she felt about Alexander Edward Court. The only thing she was sure of was that whatever she felt, she felt it strongly. You didn't hurt this much about somebody you didn't care about.

She wrenched her mind off that path and tried to concentrate on the good news that Mindy would be released from the hospital soon. She was going to need serious care for a while, and she'd lost what little hearing she had left in the one ear, but the doctors were optimistic about the rest.

Of course, when she got out, she would learn what they'd managed to keep from her so far, that her brother was a prime suspect in Joel's death, and although Detective Garrison was careful not to say so, Regan guessed he might be a suspect in the rest of the murders as well. And she was afraid that it seemed more logical to her than quiet Mr. Pilson. And that wasn't going to do Mindy any good.

Regan had always liked Marty, liked how he'd tried to stand up to Joel for Mindy, and their abusive father before, and how protective he was of her now. But if that protectiveness had turned violent . . .

She felt a creeping weariness overtaking her, bringing with it a longing for simplicity, for a time when life hadn't been so fraught with ugliness and danger. Mrs. Court kept telling her she needed a vacation, which she had always declined. But for the first time the idea had some serious appeal.

For the first time in her life, she wanted to stop fighting. She wanted to run away.

Lynne glanced in her mirror again. This old, forgotten ridge-top road was getting more use than she'd thought. And whoever was driving that beat-up old sedan was darn lucky she had more urgent things to do right now, because the way he was tailgating her, when they were the only two cars here, was enough to tempt her into writing her first traffic citation in years.

She'd done her re-interview with Mrs. Tanaka first, since she lived up here in the hills and far enough out of town that Lynne had had to warn the detective secretary that if anything came up she was at least half an hour away. Now she was taking the shortcut back, the road that ran along the top of the hills before dropping back down toward the coast.

She ran through her mental list. Next, she would head toward the county crime lab. The toxicology reports on the last victim should be in soon, and al-

though she didn't expect anything more than a
high blood alcohol, you never knew.

Then—

A sudden thump snapped her head back. The
steering wheel jerked beneath her hands. She
fought it, sparing only a fraction of a second to
glance in the rearview mirror. The sedan was there,
rammed up into her left rear bumper. She could
hear the whine of its engine as it tried to push her
toward the shoulder.

Toward the drop, she realized. They'd topped the
ridge now, and while not steep enough to be called
a cliff, it would be a long, nasty, and possibly fatal
ride.

Braking would only make things worse, lessen-
ing her already scant control. So instead she hit the
accelerator, her jaw clenching as she put some distance between them.

The sedan sped up, clearly intent on hitting her
again. She jammed the gas pedal down, her mind
racing. Calling on old skills, she began to swerve,
right, then left, in varying arcs and speeds, making
it more difficult for him to judge where she would
be.

She couldn't divert her attention long enough to
use her cell or even reach for her radio to call for
help, not that it would work up here anyway. She
could probably get away from him, maybe pull off
a one-eighty skid turn and give herself some mar-
gin, but the road was so narrow she wasn't thrilled
with the idea.

Then the obvious hit her. The average person,
trying to drive somebody off the road, tended to

sideswipe, pulling up even and then using the length of their car to push their quarry.

This had been something else entirely. Poorly executed and ineffective, but still, it was a fishtail maneuver. Or as they'd put it so long ago in driving school, a tactical vehicle intervention.

She ignored the sick churning in her gut. What it was, even who it was, didn't matter at this moment. They were all alone on the road.

She strained to remember the layout of the next few miles of this road she hadn't used in a long time. She picked her spot, and set about luring her attacker in close. She watched the mirror, no longer able to deny who she saw.

She wasn't going to let him win. If she died, he could get away with it. All of it. She'd be damned if she'd let him. She would do whatever she had to. Including using his own arrogance against him.

They reached the curve she'd been waiting for. She slowed, letting him creep in closer. She guessed this was where he'd want to make his move. The drop here was steep. So she edged toward the outside shoulder, slowing even more, tempting him, urging him to try. And he took the bait, edging in.

"That's it, come on, I'm just a stupid woman, you can take me out," she muttered. This was the perfect place, and if he didn't try again now, she didn't know—

He hit the gas, and the coupe sped forward.

She counted in her head. Beat, beat, beat, *now!*

She slammed the accelerator to the floor. She cut hard left. The instant she was clear of the sedan she hit the brakes, just long enough for the sedan to shoot by her. She was behind him now. Whispering a thank-you to the inventor of antilock brakes, she hit the gas again, just as hard. She couldn't give him one extra second to think. She had to do it while he was still moving fast. The instant she was in position, her right front bumper between his left front and the left rear wheel, she cut right. Contact. Nudge.

It worked. Tactical vehicle intervention, textbook style.

She watched as the sedan spun. Once, twice, into the third revolution. A dust cloud rose as the wheels tried to dig into the dirt shoulder. And then he was gone, over the shoulder and into the ravine he'd tried to put her in. She'd beat him behind the wheel before, and she'd just done it again.

She drove to the shoulder. Stopped. Set the brake. Shaking, she sat there, unable to move. Like a videtape on endless rewind and play, it ran over and over in her head. She had hoped it was all a mistake, that they'd been wrong.

But they hadn't been. She knew that now.

Because Nick Kelso had just tried to kill her.

Alex walked up the sidewalk toward Rachel's House, lost in thought. He should have realized a lot earlier what a lie would mean to Regan. She spent her energy endlessly on picking up the pieces left by the biggest liars in the world. It was only natural that finding out he'd been at Rachel's House under false pretenses would have hit a very hot button for her.

He saw Mitch's truck out front, with its rack of

tools, though the gardener wasn't in sight. But Marita was, coming out the door, dressed in a snappy business suit that looked like something his mother would wear.

"You looking for Regan?"

"Yes, I was. Wow, you look great."

She beamed. "Thanks. I have a job interview."

"Congratulations." Something gave him a mental nudge, but he focused on Marita, guessing that this was a huge step for her. "You'll stun them with your brilliance."

She laughed. "I'll settle for impressing them enough to hire me. Anyway, Regan went to the hospital to see Mindy. But she should be back here soon if you want to wait inside," she said, her hand still on the door. "Belinda's off at work, and Laura had to go to the doctor, so I was going to lock up."

"Leave it if you want. I've got some work to finish, so I'll be here until Regan gets here."

"All right. I'd better get to my bus."

He knew they were required to take a bus from a stop at least one stop away from Rachel's House. He again ignored whatever was tickling at his memory and offered, "You want a ride? I could take you."

She shook her head. "No. I've got it all mapped out. But thank you, Alex."

She pulled the door shut but didn't lock it. She went past him and down the steps, then stopped and looked back.

"She'll get over it," she said.

Alex didn't pretend not to understand. "I hope so."

"You're awful nice, for a rich guy." He winced. Marita laughed. "Isn't it nice you knew Regan liked you even when she didn't know you were rich?"

He went to work, dragging out the ladder to set it up against the front eave. He started up to retrieve the hammer he'd forgotten and left up near the chimney, thinking while everybody was gone would be a good time to tackle that window in the living room that stuck in the track every time you tried to open it. Then after that he could—

It hit him then, what had been nagging at him. He turned, but couldn't see far enough from this angle. He went back down the ladder and walked out toward the street. With every step he grew more certain he was right. Could the murder weapon have been right here in plain sight all along? It seemed impossible, but what better way to hide it than not hide it at all?

A sound behind him made him spin around. No one was there, and he chided himself for overreacting. It was then that he realized his ability to stay cool under fire seemed to have deserted him. He was never this jumpy. Admittedly he'd never dealt with a serial killer before, but he'd handled some pretty nasty characters. So why was he losing it now?

Never mind, he told himself. He had to do something. He'd call Detective Garrison. Maybe she could get here before Regan did. He didn't want Regan anywhere around this, if he was right.

He yanked out his cell phone. Then he remembered Regan had Detective Garrison's card on her desk. He'd have better luck calling her directly than wading through the layers from the main police number. He ran back to the house.

He found the card quickly enough, but the sight of his name—Alex Court—scribbled on the blotter, with a series of question marks and exclamation points after it, stopped him for a second.

We're real particular about being lied to around here.

He shook his head to clear it of Marita's ominous words. He picked up the detective's card and dialed his cell.

"Garrison."

She sounded odd, a little breathless, but he didn't have time to dwell on it. "Detective Garrison, this is Alex Court. I'm out at Rachel's House, and I just found something I think you should see."

"Oh?"

The bouquet behind Regan's desk caught his eye, and he turned to look at it, shaking his head as he went on. "Everything seems to fit, and if I'm right, your killer may be right here—"

He heard a faint sound behind him. He spun, but something heavy hit him hard between the shoulder blades and he went down. He tried to roll, but a foot came down paralyzingly hard on his left wrist. A hand yanked the cell phone from his numbed hand.

For all the good it did him, he'd been right.

CHAPTER 22

Lynne stared for a split second at her cell phone.

She wondered if she should try to call back. She didn't have Alex's cell number, but she could call Rachel's House. But the uncertainty about what exactly the situation was stopped her.

"Detective Garrison?" A harried-looking county sheriff's deputy approached her. Since the incident had occurred outside the city limits, they had landed the mess. "They're taking him to the hospital now. One of my guys will stay with him until your captain can get there."

"Thanks," she said quickly as she hit the speed dial for dispatch. When they answered, she identified herself and spoke quickly. "Get two units out to Rachel's House. Warn them to approach with caution. We may have a hostage situation, maybe an armed suspect. Find Durwin. I'm on my way."

She raced to her car, cell phone in hand, leaving the deputy staring after her and shaking his head. She keyed in the speed dial for Drew's number.

"Damn it," she swore under her breath as she got

his voice mail again, as she had when she'd first called after her narrow escape. She left a short, sharp message to head toward Rachel's House and call her *now*. She slapped the emergency blue light on the dash and flipped it on, then dialed Drew's pager number as she pulled out of the driveway. She had left the numbers 911, their old emergency message, and hung up before she remembered the last time she'd left him that code. The night she'd lost their baby.

She shoved the memory aside and concentrated on driving. But her mind was still racing. What had Alex found? She knew he was sharp. If he thought he'd found something significant, he probably had.

If she had any remaining doubt, those last few noisy seconds of his phone call would have erased them. Alex Court was in trouble, and he thought it was the killer. Which confused more than it cleared up. But it made one question leap to the fore.

If Nick was here, and Pilson still in custody, who was at Rachel's House?

Regan was surprised to see Alex's truck pulled up behind Mitch's. The front door of the house was standing open. As she reached the porch, the words she heard surprised her even more.

"—thought you understood! You said you did, and I believed you."

Mitch, she thought.

"I meant what I said." That was Alex, and the calmness of his voice made her realize how upset Mitch had sounded. She stopped at the bottom of

the steps, thinking she should wait before intrud-
ing on this, whatever it was.

"You don't understand anything! If you did, you
would never have touched Regan, never have de-
filed her!"

Regan's eyes widened. Marita had once teased
her about Mitch having a crush on her, but she
hadn't taken it seriously.

"Take it easy, Mitch."

"I thought you respected her. When you saved her
from that crazy man, I thought you understood she
was different, that she was pure and holy and good."

My God, Regan thought. *That isn't a crush, it's ob-
session.*

She started up the steps, afraid this was going to
degenerate into a fight. She pulled the screen door
open, then froze when she heard Alex say, from the
direction of her office, "You don't want to do this,
Mitch. You know I called the police."

"They're not here, though, are they? That's because I can't be stopped. No one can stop me. I'm
smarter than all of them. I'll never go to prison. I'm
saving the real victims from their prisons, the prisons those mutants put them in."

Shock smashed through her. Mitch? Dear God,
Mitch was the killer? The ramifications blossomed
in her mind like a firestorm. She tried to tamp it
down, to think. The idea of Mitch Howe as the
Avenger was as absurd as the idea that it was
Marita, or another of the women.

*They won't seem capable of it. They're generally
charming and affable.*

Detective Garrison's caution rang in her head, but it still seemed impossible.

Instinctively, she started to back up and out the door again. But Mitch must have heard her, for he called out her name.

"Regan Keller!" he cried, as if it were a title. And as if he knew it was her. "Come back in here, or I'll kill him, your dirty lover."

"Regan! Get out of—"

She heard a grunt of pain as Alex's words were choked off. She had to believe Mitch would kill him. She couldn't risk Alex's life. Slowly, she stepped back inside.

"Back here," Mitch said. "Now."

"I'm coming," she said, trying to keep her voice steady.

Think, she ordered herself.

Alex said he'd called the police. But had he meant it, or was he bluffing? Mitch hadn't argued with him, so maybe he'd heard him do it. Maybe that was what had set him off.

"Now, Regan! Or I'll take his head off!"

"I'm coming," she said again, feeling herself shaking.

"But I'm not one of them, Mitch," Alex's voice said quickly, as if he were trying to divert Mitch's attention from her. "Won't that ruin your nice neat pattern?"

"It's already ruined," Mitch said, a childish whine in his voice. "That woman who killed her husband, and tried to say it was me. As if I would! And that bitch who lied, and made me . . . made me . . ."

"Kill an innocent man, Mitch? You don't want to do that again."

Regan didn't know what else to do, so as she passed the phone in the outer room she hit the single button that dialed 911, and set the receiver down on the table.

"I have no choice, it has to be done. I have to finish, they all have to die. They're mutants, can't you see? This is pest control. They have to be killed, for all our sakes."

She reached the doorway. Mitch had Alex facedown on the floor and was kneeling on top of him. But more terrifying was what he held.

A razor-sharp curved blade. A machete.

The killer uses something much bigger, probably with a curved blade. . . .

Detective Garrison's voice floated through her dazed mind. She'd seen Mitch use that tool countless times. The handle was wood, a dark color, and it had looked almost new compared to the blade, as if it had been recently painted. To hide something? Blood? She'd never even thought about it being a potential weapon. Not like Mr. Pilson's swords.

It made horrible sense. Mitch had access. He was in her office every day with fresh flowers. How difficult would it have been for him to get into the locked files? He was accepted, they weren't on guard around him. Perhaps he'd used her own key or even managed to get a copy of the key for the file cabinet.

They talked in front of him, or talked with him just outside, all the time. He would know what was happening to the women of Rachel's House almost as soon as it happened.

But he was always so concerned about them and what had been done to them, so protective . . .

So protective.

"Mitch, what are you doing?" Regan said. "Alex hasn't done anything."

"He's ruined everything! Don't you see?"

Mitch seemed to be almost pleading with her to understand. His hand seemed to jerk, and Regan's breath caught as blood began to run down Alex's neck from a long, thin slice.

"It was for you, all for you, because you were so good, so pure, and now he's tainted you and it's all gone wrong."

"You're going to let a little thing like that distract you?"

Alex said it to Mitch, but he was looking at Regan. She didn't miss his intent, but she couldn't think of what to do to distract Mitch enough.

"Shut up," Mitch said to Alex.

In the office, the arrival of the police had served as a diversion, but they couldn't wait for that, not now, not with Mitch waving that lethal blade around. She had to do something, and fast.

"Mitch, please," she said. "I don't want you in any more trouble. The others, no one's sorry to see them go, but Alex didn't hurt anyone."

Except me, she thought.

And in that moment, as a serial killer held Alex with a blade that looked capable of taking his head off, Regan realized how little his deception mattered.

"Just be quiet, I have to think!" Mitch shouted, sounding once more like a wailing child.

A child. . . .

"Would it help if we called your mother? Maybe if you talk to her—"

"Don't you get it?" Mitch was crying, tears spilling down his cheeks. "She's the one who told me to do it! She's the one who told me I had to be a real man. I had to protect you all, because I failed before!"

She'd hit a nerve, she thought. "Failed?"

"My father. *She* had to kill my father, because I was too scared. I have to make up for that, don't you see? I have to make it up to her."

Regan shivered. Mitch's eyes were wild, and she knew she was seeing the insanity that had made him capable of six brutal murders.

"That's very brave of you," Regan began, her tone intentionally patronizing.

"Stop it!" Mitch hissed. "Don't talk to me like a child." He twisted to look at her more directly.

That was all Alex needed. He bucked hard, slamming Mitch back against the front of her desk. Mitch shouted. Alex rolled free. Coming to his feet, he tackled Mitch as he tried to rise. They went down hard.

Regan had to dodge the swipe of the machete as it nearly caught her right leg. She leapt over the sprawling men, looking for anything she could use as a weapon. They were evenly matched in size and fitness, but as tough as Alex was, he was dealing with a madman.

The only thing at hand was the heavy crystal vase that held the bouquet. With a split second of acknowledgment for the irony of it, she threw the flowers to the floor, picked up the vase, and spun around.

Alex didn't need her help. He had Mitch down

and pinned, in much the same position as he himself had been in.

Slowly, she set the vase down on her desk.

When the police arrived, guns drawn and megaphones blaring, it was an anticlimax.

CHAPTER 23

"I'm sorry we didn't get here in time to help," Detective Garrison said. "But it looks like you didn't need us."

Regan smiled, as steadily as she could given how the bandage on Alex's neck and the bloodstains on his shirt unnerved her.

"I feel so stupid," Regan said. "That . . . thing was right under my nose all the time."

"It happens. You see something so often in an everyday capacity, you only think of it in that context." Lynne grimaced. "Besides, talk about feeling stupid. I thought I had our boy all wrapped up at the moment Alex called."

"Really?" Regan asked.

"Yep. He tried to run me off the road up in the hills, so I was sure we were right."

"Not Mr. Pilson?"

"No. Although we're still going to have to confirm some of his story, I'd say he's clean."

"Thank goodness. I would have hated to think he was the one. He's always so nice to us."

"Apparently he's simply lonely. He's always been a solitary type, but it was starting to bother him, when you moved in next door. So he decided to sort of adopt you all."

"Then he's sweeter than we thought," Regan said. "I'll have to be sure Rachel's House welcomes him back in a big way."

"You do that. He was pretty crushed to be suspected, even though we proved him innocent in the end."

"That must be why he stayed away from us, after he knew you suspected him. He was probably embarrassed," Regan said. "Poor man."

Alex asked a question then. "But if this man who ran you off the road isn't the killer, why would he try to kill you?"

"He may well be a killer. Just not a serial killer."

"Your life's been complicated lately, hasn't it?" Alex said.

Lynne smiled. "Indeed. But so has yours. Have you two—"

"Lynnie? Lynnie! Where the hell are you?"

To Regan's surprise, the detective blushed. And then a tall, dark-haired man burst in at a run, slowing only when he saw them gathered in the living room. He nodded hastily at them.

"Are you all right? I went to the station, but you weren't there."

"If you'd check your voice mail like a normal person, you'd have known where I was," Lynne said, and Regan didn't think she was imagining the tension in the detective's voice. "Not to mention your pager."

"I did check my pager! But when I called, I got *your* voice mail. Then I called the station, who told me you'd be coming in with Kelso, that he'd tried to kill you!"

"This went down first. I tried calling from here, but I kept getting your voice mail."

"I was on the phone with records all the way here," he said.

"What—" Lynne suddenly stopped, and looked at Regan and Alex. "I'm sorry. Excuse us for being rude. This," she said, gesturing at the newcomer, "is sheriff's investigator Garrison. He's been on loan for this case. Your case, I mean."

She's feeling pretty edgy right now, about her ex-husband being on loan to work the Avenger case. . . .

Regan glanced at Alex, who looked as if he was remembering those words as well. And if she was any judge, there was a lot of unresolved business between these two. Lately, she felt like an expert on unresolved business.

"Regan Keller, I presume," the man said, and she nodded, shaking the hand he held out.

"Hi," Alex said, and held out a hand. "Alex Court."

The man nodded as he shook it, as if he'd already known.

"He took down our suspect for us," Lynne said. "Did a fine job of it, too."

Alex shrugged. "I had help," he said, nodding at Regan.

"How'd you tumble to it?" Drew asked.

Alex explained about the machete. "Court Corporation did a cursory background check on him,"

Alex added, startling her. She hadn't known that.
"He'd already been working for the previous
owner of this house for over a year, so I guess we
didn't dig deep enough."

"He was well established," Drew said. "Chances
are, you wouldn't have found him out anyway."

"I wonder what set him off?" Alex said.

"Something, obviously. We can't find any record
of anything criminal prior to this."

"I think it had to be Rosa Norman," Regan said.
"He liked Rosa. She loved his garden more than
anyone."

"She was the wife in the first case?" Drew asked.

"Yes. The one who was nailed to her own floor,"
Lynne said.

Drew grimaced. "That would do it for me."

"I still can't believe it." Regan shook her head. "I
feel like a cliché, but it's true, Mitch was so gentle,
and quiet."

"No alcohol or drug problems you knew of?"

Startled, Regan glanced at Alex. She hadn't put
that part together yet. "I . . . there was . . ." she
began, fumbling.

"We found some cocaine, a while back, hidden
outside the house," Alex answered. "We had no
way of knowing whose it was. The hiding place
wasn't used again, nor any other I could find. Probably didn't want to risk it after we had video cameras installed outside."

She hadn't even known he'd been looking. There
was so much she hadn't known.

"That would fit," Drew said. "He probably
needed it to get revved up for a kill. By the way,

Howe's not his real last name. It's Howlett. That's the call I was on, on the fingerprint ID. He must have changed it. Probably because of his father."

His words suddenly reminded Regan. "Has his mother been told? I don't know what this will do to her. They're very close."

"Close? It was all his mother's fault, remember?" Alex said dryly.

"What's this about his mother?" Drew asked, frowning.

"He said she told him to do it," Regan answered, and explained what Mitch had said.

"She didn't tell him to do anything," Drew said.

"That's a relief," Regan said. "I can't believe any mother would really do that."

"We can't say she wouldn't have," Drew said, "but Mitch Howlett's mother died twenty years ago."

Regan gaped at him. "What? But he was always talking about her, taking her flowers from our garden, Mindy even sent her a card on her birthday!"

Drew shook his head. "Part of it was the truth. She did kill her husband, Mitch's father, apparently after years of abuse. But then she killed herself. That's when he was fingerprinted, as a matter of routine."

Stunned, Regan shook her head. "I can't believe it. He talked about her as if she were alive, and he saw her every day."

"Maybe he did," Alex said.

Lynne nodded. "Maybe. Maybe he needed somebody to account for the voice he 'heard' telling him to kill."

"For us. For Rachel's House. To defend us. Like he couldn't defend his mother." Regan shivered.

Alex slipped an arm around her and she leaned against him.

"Don't feel responsible, Regan," Lynne said. "Chances are, if he hadn't fixated on Rachel's House, it would have been something else."

"You know, I almost feel bad for him," Regan said. "Even if he's insane, even if he just used this as his excuse to kill, he only killed those who refused to change. He did what a lot of us have thought about, even wished sometimes we had the guts to do. How can I blame him?"

"A lot of people think about killing, but never do it," Drew said. "Something holds them back, some line within them they don't cross. Mitch doesn't have that line."

"They weren't people to him, they were things. To be exterminated." Lynne seemed to hear her own words, and her mouth twisted. "They're not much more than that to most people, I think."

"Mutants," Regan said. "That's what he called them."

Drew nodded and said again, "That would fit."

"Will he—I mean, with the death penalty . . ." Regan began.

Lynne looked at Drew. "You're the expert. What do you think?" Whatever problems were between them, they clearly didn't involve professional respect, Regan thought.

"Based on my experience, I'd say a good lawyer could get him declared mentally incompetent to stand trial."

"The rest of his life in a mental institution?" Alex asked.

"Better than dead." Drew shrugged. "Some people are genuinely happier out of the real world."

"Court Corporation will see he gets help," Alex said. "Be it lawyer or doctor or both."

"Maybe you could get us a secretary for all this paperwork?" Drew asked, an exaggeratedly hopeful look on his face.

"They already support half the department's worthy causes," Lynne said. "I think we're stuck. So we'd better get started."

"Don't forget the dirt," Drew said.

"Got it."

Lynne had already gathered samples from various parts of Mitch's garden, saying it was for evidence, along with some stained pieces of tarp out of the truck they also impounded. She'd told them they suspected the cloth had been used to mask footprints, but that wasn't for public consumption. Honored by her trust, they'd quickly agreed.

Now Regan watched them go almost regretfully, because she and Alex would be alone and she was nervous. But when she saw them stop at the bottom of the sidewalk, and saw Drew pull Lynne into his arms in an embrace she could sense the fierceness of even from here, Regan forgot her own nerves.

"They may be exes officially, but somebody forgot to untangle them," Alex said. "That was more than just cop to cop when he came in. You don't go that crazy unless you care."

She turned to face him. "No," she said steadily, "you don't. Unless you care a lot."

"They seem like a good match. I hope they—"

Alex broke off suddenly, his eyes narrowing, as if only now had her pointed tone registered. "Regan?"

"I really, really didn't like feeling like a fool, Alex."

He sucked in a breath and closed his eyes. "I know."

"But when I was afraid he was going to kill you, I realized Marita was right. Compared to that, you maybe dying, nothing else mattered much."

His eyes opened. "Regan," he said again, whispering this time. "Does this mean I'm forgiven?"

"It means I'm open to the possibility," Regan said.

"I guess that's a step," Alex said.

"So let's move to the next step," Regan said, looking at him from beneath half-lowered lashes.

"Which is?"

"Convince me."

The convincing, Regan thought, was going along nicely.

She watched Alex walk across his bedroom, unconcernedly naked. And rightfully so, she thought; he was beautiful. Scars and all.

A lovely warmth spread through her as she thought of the last couple of days he'd spent working on that convincing. And the nights. Oh, yes, the nights . . .

He sat on the bed with the morning newspaper in one hand, and two mugs of coffee carefully held by the handles in the other. She liberated one mug as he handed her the paper.

"What's the latest?" he asked as she unfolded it.

They'd found that much of the public felt the

same ambivalence they did. They didn't want to approve of murder, but they were having a hard time feeling outraged because the victims were who they were.

"About the same, all the arguments we've been hearing," she said as she scanned the front-page article.

"Vigilantism, victims deprived of due process, and the other side pointing out that every one of them had been tried and convicted before and it hadn't saved their own victims from more abuse?" Alex asked.

"Yes." Regan grimaced. "You'd think in there somebody would point out that an innocent man also got murdered. No matter what justification, there is nothing that makes it worth that."

That was the bottom line for Regan. Even if for most others it seemed to be that whatever these men had done, their crimes didn't carry the death penalty. And if she couldn't help thinking that their murders had possibly prevented others, committed by them, Regan also knew that could never be proven.

"They still have the lid on about Mitch?"

She nodded. "They're not saying anything else about him or any evidence, nothing that might jeopardize the case."

Lynne had called them to say a search of Mitch's apartment had turned up conclusive evidence, including the "trophies" most serial killers took from their victims, but wouldn't say what they were. She'd just wanted them to know it was certain they had the right man. Regan thought it was good of her to call, and Alex agreed, saying he might just suggest his mother mention Lynne's fine work to her friend the chief.

Regan, thinking that reading the paper in bed over morning coffee felt very domestic, was about to hand Alex the paper when something caught her eye.

"What?" Alex asked.

"This has to be it," she murmured.

"Has to be what?"

"What happened to Lynne that day. Remember, she said some guy tried to run her off the road? It was a cop!"

Alex blinked. "A cop? The guy she said they'd thought was the Avenger?"

Regan nodded, quickly reading the rest of the article, which had received almost as much room and as big a headline as the Avenger story.

"Nicholas Kelso," she read. "He was suspected of being the Avenger because of things Lynne discovered during that investigation."

"But he wasn't, so why would he try to kill her?"

Regan looked up. "Turns out he murdered his fiancée when she broke up with him. And he found out Lynne was asking his friends questions about her."

"So he thought they were going to find him out?"

She nodded. "It quotes Lynne as saying she discovered during the Avenger investigation that he'd been brushing off domestic-violence reports for a long time. That was what started her interest in him."

"So he must have known she would keep digging. She's a good cop," Alex said.

"The real deal, as Marita would say. I hope she and Drew can work things out."

"So you are a closet romantic."

She knew this was the moment. She'd forgiven him for the deception, they'd kissed—and a lot more—and made up repeatedly. She'd asked for time to think about the rest and he'd given it to her, without pressure, without demands. But now it was time.

"Speaking of Marita," she said, and saw by Alex's expression he thought she was changing the subject. "She told me something interesting yesterday. She told me not to blow it."

"Blow . . . what?"

"Us."

His uncertainty turned to a smile. "She did?"

"She said we give them all hope."

"We give me hope, too," he said.

And Regan thought those simple words the most romantic she'd ever heard. An indication, she thought with an inward smile, of how far gone she truly was. And the shiver that went through her simply looking at him was exclamation point at the end of that realization.

"Look," he said, "I know that life in the Court circus can be crazy. But my traveling can change. It's about time anyway, I'm really tired of living out of a duffel bag."

"Never mind that," Regan said, "it's about that scar collection." She'd seen them all now, and pried the story behind most of them out of him, from the helicopter crash landing in British Columbia to the hostage situation in Colombia. "I'd just as soon you didn't add to it."

"That, too," he said, as if it were a given. "No more recklessness."

"Good."

"So . . . will you?"

"What exactly are you asking me?"

"To join the circus?" Alex grinned at her. Then he reached out and took her hands, his expression turning serious. "Remember what you said, that you thought one of the best things about being rich would be to be able to help anyone you wanted to? You could do that. Of course," he added with an echo of that earlier grin, "you'd have to put up with me."

"I would?"

He looked disconcerted, then rueful. "Actually, probably not. Mom's ready to set up a charitable foundation, to do just that kind of thing. She'd love to have you run it. With or without me."

"Hmm," Regan said thoughtfully. "I've been with you. I've been without you. With is better."

She got a smile out of him then. But his voice was solemn as he asked, "Can you do it, Regan? Can you make room in your life for something besides a cause?"

"If that something is you," she said. "I love you."

He reached for her then, pulling her down beside him. For a long, quiet moment he just held her. And then, softly, he said the last words to be said. "I love you, Regan Keller."

And later, as she found the daytime could be as sweet as the night, Regan had the silly thought that she'd joined the circus, and she hadn't even had to run away.